T

A dull throb pulsed from a point above his 1 to touch it, but his arms

Rough fibres bit into his wrists.

Rope.

He was tied to a chair, the bonds twisting his skin, and a tight gag covered his mouth, stifling his cries for help.

A scream tore through the air, high-pitched and terrified. It came from upstairs. Adrenaline surged through Dr Fraser's battered body. He strained against the ties, the chair legs screeching on the parquet floor. The scream stopped. A door slammed.

Footsteps thudded overhead, growing louder as they descended the stairs. Dr Fraser twisted his head. A figure emerged from the shadows, face hidden behind a ski mask.

The figure strode forward, gloved hand reaching into the folds of their dark jacket. Metal glinted under the moonlight spilling through the curtains. A knife? A gun? Dr Fraser's chest heaved, panic kicking hard.

No. A steel funnel and length of hose.

The figure tore off the gag, but before the doctor could cry out for help, fingers seized his jaw in an iron grip and forced his mouth open. The doctor gagged; his captor rammed the hose past his teeth, over his tongue. He thrashed against the chair, but his captor's strength was too strong. The tube scraped the back of his throat. Bile burned in his gullet.

A faint smell reached his nostrils.

Petrol.

Frantic, he redoubled his struggles. The chair rocked dangerously. His muffled screams reverberated in his skull.

The world tilted backwards, and the chair crashed to the floor, his head clipping the corner of a granite hearth. Searing pain exploded behind his eyes. He choked and retched violently, but the figure held his limbs down. The chemical stench filled his senses, suffocating him. He gurgled and spluttered, fighting for a breath, but none came. Shadows crept in at the edges of his blurred vision. His muscles slackened, strength leaching away.

In his last moments, as his life drowned in a chemical hell of agony, the newborn baby's face flashed before his eyes, its mouth slowly curling into a terrifying smile.

Then, at last, the darkness claimed him.

ONE

DCI Duncan Bone knelt closer to the makeshift fire and blew gently at the thin wisp of smoke squeezing out from beneath the damp kindling.

"Come on, Duncan. We're getting eaten alive out here," Alice, his disgruntled wife, said with an anxious sigh. She zipped the hood of her cagoule tighter around her face and swiped at the black haze of midges hovering in front of her eyes.

"Yeah, come on, Dad," Michael weighed in, mumbling through a thick woollen balaclava. He kicked a pebble, and it skittered down the narrow beach into the loch.

"Sorry, guys, I think the wood is damp."

"You don't say." Alice sighed. "We've been out here for half an hour. The midges can't believe their bloody luck."

"They are pretty nasty this year, that's for sure," Bone said, his brow furrowed in concentration as he tried to coax the reluctant fire to life.

"This year? Every bloody year!" Alice replied, her voice laced with exasperation. "Look at the cloud of them over there on the loch, preparing themselves for the second wave."

Bone blew at the teetering tower of tiny twigs, and it collapsed with a pathetic hiss.

"For God's sake," Alice grumbled again, her patience wearing thinner by the minute.

"I'm going to try one more time. I promised you some toasted marshmallows, son, and I will not be defeated." Bone's determination was admirable, if misplaced.

"I'm not bothered, Dad. Can't we just eat them back in the cabin?" Michael rubbed frantically at his midge-assaulted eyes.

Bone ignored him, flicked at the fog of ravenous beasts surrounding his head, and carefully rebuilt the fire, his jaw set with grim resolve.

"Are they not biting you, then?" Alice watched her husband's seemingly futile efforts.

"I think I must have got used to them or something."

"Or they don't like your stink." Michael chuckled, obviously trying to lighten the mood.

"More likely," Bone agreed, a hint of a weary smile playing at the corners of his mouth.

"Are you sure you don't have any of that repellent left?" Alice asked, a note of desperation creeping into her voice.

"The village has run out. Even Gordon has used up his secret supply. They've been that bad."

"Isn't that him over there?" Alice pointed to the tall figure of Gordon Urquhart, the Hotel Manager, at the far end of the beach battling with an overexcited golden Labrador straining at the leash.

"Evening, lads and lassie," Gordon called out between hauls of the leash. The dog yelped at the prospect of meeting, greeting, and licking some strangers.

"Calm down, Connery," Gordon commanded, but the dog ignored him, broke free, and dashed across to Michael. It leapt up and knocked him backwards onto the beach, slurping at his face and yipping with joy.

"For God's sake. So sorry." Gordon ran across and attempted to snatch at the trailing lead, but the dog dived sideways to avoid capture and set upon Alice with more unwanted, over-demonstrative affection.

"He's only seven months and has more energy than an atomic bloody bomb."

The pup dashed over to greet Bone but, spotting him still on all fours by the fire, leapt on his back and thrust.

"Oh, he loves you, Duncan." Alice laughed, enjoying her husband's discomfort.

"Aye. Duncan and table legs are his favourite." Gordon chuckled. "The snip is long overdue, too." He grabbed the dog by the collar and prised him off

Bone's back. The dog whimpered in disappointed frustration.

"What's the snip?" Michael asked.

"Just a wee haircut," Alice cut in before the hotel manager got into the gory details.

Bone stood and straightened his coat. "I never had you down as a dog owner, Gordon." He brushed sand from his knees.

"It's my sister's pup. She's a bloody right one. She buys the thing, then decides to go on a cruise in the Caribbean. And yours truly, as usual, gets lumbered." He yanked at the lead and pulled the pup to his side. The dog cried in frustration. The landlord glanced down at Bone's pathetic pile of hissing twigs. "What the hell is that?" He pulled a face.

"Exactly!" Alice cut in, her complaints vindicated.

"Aw, don't you start as well. It's supposed to be a deterrent for the midges, but the wood's too bloody damp." Bone's defensiveness was palpable.

"You don't say." Gordon smiled. He wafted at the cloud of insects hovering above his head. "Well, you're losing the battle, Duncan."

"That's what I've been saying for over half an hour," Alice added, her arms crossed in frustration.

"You need to give that up, Guy Fawkes, and get over to the hotel. It's fish supper night, and Andy has got some enormous haddock on the go." Gordon's invitation was a welcome reprieve.

"Ya beauty!" Michael piped up excitedly.

"And I'll even throw in a free dessert for the mighty minnow here!" Gordon glanced over at Michael and winked conspiratorially.

"Come on, Duncan. Just leave the bloody thing," Alice prompted, eager to escape the midge-infested beach.

Bone stood, stared at the smoke for a moment, then kicked the twigs across the beach to the shore. "Bugger it. Let's get out of here."

"Sense at last." Alice sighed, relief clearly washing over her.

They followed the manager along the beach, his dog darting between and around his legs until he had to stop and untangle himself.

"Bloody sister!" he cursed, and they carried on.

"How come there are no midges round you, Gordon?" Bone tightened his anorak hood around his face.

"The magic potion!" Gordon replied, a hint of mischief in his voice.

"I thought you'd run out."

"I had, but I made some more up this afternoon."

"Oh, it just gets better and better," Alice said, scratching manically at her scalp.

***

After three enormous courses, two pints of 80 Shilling, and one antacid tablet, Bone flopped down onto the bed, bloated and completely spent. Alice had hit the hay five minutes before and was already fast asleep, her face lost in a sea of messy golden hair, snoring quietly. He lay back, stroking his gut bulging against his t-shirt. His stomach rumbled loudly, but before he could turn onto his side to relieve his indigestion, he passed out.

What seemed like seconds later, he woke with a start. A noise or a movement at the end of the bed had disturbed him. He rubbed his eyes, trying to adjust to the darkness engulfing the room. A shadow shifted sideways. He sat up.

A flicker of light appeared by the door. A tiny yellow flame illuminated the features of a red-haired young boy. The flame moved closer to the boy's face. He smiled broadly, his wide eyes glowing in the luminescence. The flame grew larger and hissed like a sparkler.

The boy glanced sideways, and the flame shot across the room to the drapes on the window. A deep orange ember spread slowly along the fabric. More flames appeared and snaked upwards to the ceiling.

In terror, Bone turned back to the boy in the shadows, but he was gone. He tried to cry out and raise the alarm, but his voice was absent, his body frozen. When the fire reached the top of the curtain, it raced along the ceiling towards Alice, who still lay unconscious by his side.

He tried again to move his arm, reach out and shake her. But still, his limbs would not comply. Blobs of burning paint and plastic dropped from the ceiling onto his head and scorched his scalp and skin. He opened his mouth to scream, but he shook violently, and a voice cut through the roar of the blaze.

"Duncan!"

He opened his eyes. The boy was on top of him, leaning into his face.

"No!" he cried out and tried to wriggle free.

The boy smiled and mouthed the word "fire."

"Duncan," another voice cut in again.

The boy morphed into Alice. His wife was leaning over him.

"Wake up," she said and shook his shoulders again. "Breathe."

Bone fought for a second longer, then took two or three long, deep choking breaths.

"That's it." Alice smiled, her voice soothing.

"What is…?" Bone mumbled, coughing and spluttering, disoriented, the taste of smoke still in his throat.

"Don't speak, just breathe. You're having a dream," she whispered and stroked his forehead.

He twisted round to check the curtains and ceiling, but all was in darkness.

"Calm… shh," Alice persisted, her touch gentle and reassuring.

Bone closed his eyes. His body slumped back down into the mattress.

When she was sure he'd gone back to sleep, she lay on her back next to him, trying to slow her own heart rate. But it was no good. She got up, found her dressing gown, and went in search of some herbal tea, her mind reeling from the night's events.

TWO

In the morning, Michael was up first, so Bone and Alice didn't have a moment on their own to talk about the previous night. The weather had caved in, and the wind and rain rattled the windows and French doors. They all huddled around the kitchen table and ate their breakfast in silence, the howling tempest raging around them. When breakfast was finished, Alice stood.

"Right, you two. I want all this cleared away by the time I get back from the shower."

"Bossy boots," Michael complained.

She disappeared into the bedroom, and Bone piled up the cereal bowls. Moments later, she called for him to come through.

"Just a second," Bone shouted back as he loaded the dishwasher.

"Quickly!" she urged.

Bone set the plates down and hurried through, Michael hot on his heels, wondering what fresh calamity awaited him. He stopped short. Alice stood on top of the bed, holding a waste bin below the ceiling lamp.

"We've got a leak." She shifted the bin this way and that to try and catch the steady flow pouring off the end of the light bulb. "And there's another one over there." She pointed to a puddle by the bedside cabinet.

"Oh, bugger!" Bone exclaimed. "Michael, come with me."

"Have you wet the bed again, Dad?" Michael giggled, holding up the side of their sodden duvet.

"Cheeky sod. Now, come on."

Father and son dashed to the kitchen. Bone fished a bucket and mop from the back of the airing cupboard, snatched up a couple of tea towels, and hurried back to the bedroom. He threw the towels down on the floor and placed the bucket under the drips. Alice clambered down, and together they pushed the bed out of the way. She ran to the bathroom, emptied the bin down the toilet, returned, and placed it on the floor. The water clanged, splattering on the bin's metal base.

"Right, I'll go see what the hell's happened," Bone said. "Check for more leaks. There's another bucket outside."

He marched back to the living room, grabbed his coat, and, tightening the hood around his face, headed out into the wild. The door flew open and smacked against the adjacent cabin wall. He forced it shut and hurried around the side to a storage unit at the rear. Opening the lid, he reached in and removed a folded tarp. Then, from under the cabin, he pulled out a stepladder and manoeuvred it against the side. The gale rattled the aluminium frame, gusts threatening to launch it towards the loch. He put his foot on the first rung to steady it and, shifting it around, slowly climbed until he could see above the guttering.

A few tiles had blown off a section of roof close to the apex, too far for him to reach with the tarp. He'd have to climb farther onto the roof. He was about to attempt it when his phone, buried deep in his coat pocket, vibrated against his hip.

It stopped, then started up again. He recognised DI Walker's familiar habit of calling him twice to alert him that it was her.

"Rhona. Bugger."

Steadying himself with one hand on the ladder, he reached into his pocket and plucked his phone out. The sound of Dizzy Gillespie's trumpet sliced through the growl of the storm. He attempted to press the answer button with his thumb, but his hands were soaking wet, and the handset slipped from his grip. He snatched at it, almost toppling off the ladder. His mobile dropped into a full bucket of rainwater by the side of an overflowing drainpipe. Dizzy's trumpet wail gurgled and stopped. Bone clambered back down and plucked the phone out of the freezing water. He shook the water out and off it, but the screen was completely dead.

"Shite," he muttered, shoving the drowned device back in his pocket.

He emptied the bucket of water and trudged back into the cabin, dripping all over the floor.

"Here's another bucket." He set it down. "There are tiles off the roof, but I can't reach them. I'll have to get Gordon to help me." He wiped the rain from his face. "I think it's easing out there, though."

"Are you serious?" Alice placed the bucket by the waste bin and eyed his soaked form. "You're making a right mess."

"Sorry, love. Couldn't be helped. Can I use your phone? Mine's had a bit of an accident."

"What's wrong with yours?"

"I dropped it in that bucket."

"You bellend!" Alice exclaimed.

"Haha," Michael crowed. "Mum called you a bellend."

"Aye, that she did," Bone agreed ruefully. "And she's not wrong. Phone's knackered."

Alice shook her head. "It's on the kitchen table. But make it quick, this bloody leak's getting worse."

"I will." Bone thought now was not the right time to tell her he needed to call his colleague first. He turned to Michael. "Go and get the towels from the bathroom, mate. Quick as you can."

The boy scampered off, and Bone retreated to the kitchen. He found Alice's phone and called DI Walker back.

"Rhona?"

"Sir?" Walker's voice was tinny, the line crackling. "What number is this? The reception's terrible."

"I'm on Alice's phone. We're in the middle of a bloody hurricane up here. What's going on?"

"Kilwinnoch Fire Brigade called. They've been battling a huge blaze at a house at Horsbrugh Close since two-thirty this morning."

"And?" Bone asked impatiently.

"They've found a body, and it looks like the fire was started deliberately."

"Why are they saying that?"

"Signs of an accelerant, petrol, and also some sort of cryptic message written across the front wall of the property.

Bone frowned. "Whose house is it?"

"Married couple, two doctors. The crews did well to stop it spreading to the neighbouring properties, but the place is gutted."

Bone rubbed a hand over his face. Of all the times for a major incident to hit. "Right. I'm a bit tied up here at the moment, this storm's done a number on the cabin. Can you alert the team and ask Sheila to start pulling background on the property owners. Where are you now?"

"I'm just arriving at the scene."

"Okay, stay there and I'll get to you as soon as I can."

"Will do, sir. I'll keep you updated."

"Thanks, Rhona."

He hung up just as Alice called out from the bedroom, "Duncan! Get off that bloody phone and come help!"

Bone exhaled. *This day's shaping up to be another bloody classic.*

He hurried back to the bedroom, where Alice was now frantically emptying cupboards, the leak having spread. Michael appeared, his arms full of towels.

"Stick those down on the floor, lad," Bone instructed. "Soak up what you can."

As Michael set about his task, Bone turned to Alice.

"Love, I'm sorry, but I'm going to have to head off. There's been a major incident, a suspicious fire. The team needs me."

Alice's face fell. "We need you! Look at the state of this. We can't stay here, not with the place falling down around us."

Bone took her hands. "I know. Could I ask a big favour? Could you ring Gordon at the hotel and see if he can come and patch up the roof?"

"I need to get back, Duncan. Fran, my very kind neighbour, is looking after the animals, and I don't want to take liberties, you know?"

"Yes, so sorry. But it sounds like a pretty serious incident."

"It's always serious, Duncan." Alice sighed. "Okay. Fine. But I will have to leave soon."

But Bone wasn't listening, he was rummaging in his bedside cabinet, pushed over by the window.

"What are you doing?" Alice asked, her agitation with him growing by the second.

"Where's my spare phone, the old one?" He opened a second drawer.

"No idea. I'm a little…"

"Gotcha!" he cried out, and fishing his drenched phone from his pocket, he removed the sim, dried it on his sleeve and inserted it into the old device. He searched the drawer again and found the charger. "Okay, now we're on." He turned back to Alice. "Hopefully, Gordon will sort it and I'll see you at the farm tonight." Bone kissed her cheek, then turned to Michael. "See you tonight, wee squirt."

"Hey, I'm getting bigger."

"I know. You'll soon be towering over me."

"That wouldn't be hard," Alice added.

With a final squeeze of his wife's hand, Bone grabbed his still-damp coat and headed out into the maelstrom, ready to face whatever fresh hell awaited him.

THREE

The howling gales seemed confined to the area around Loch Gillan, so by the time Bone got back to Kilwinnoch, there was barely a breeze, making the morning's chaotic events seem even more surreal. A uniformed police officer waved Bone's car down as he turned the Saab into the cul-de-sac. Bone pulled up and wound down his window.

"DCI Bone." He held up his lanyard.

He stared at the chaos of fire engines, tangles of hoses, and SOCO vehicles parked up on the pavements on either side of the entrance. Plumes of black and grey smoke rose high above a line of trees that blocked a view of the street ahead.

A fire officer standing by one of the engines whistled to the officer and gestured for him to let Bone through. The uniform stood back, and Bone parked up behind one of the forensic Land Rovers. He climbed out. The man approached.

"Chief Fire Officer Gregor Tennant." He adjusted his helmet, which perched at an angle on his head.

"DCI Bone, Kilwinnoch station." Bone looked up at the chief's enormous frame hovering over him.

"Your colleague is already here," the fire chief said, still wrestling with his headgear. "Bloody thing's too small." He removed it and wiped the sweat from his brow. "And as you can see, forensics too, along with fire investigators' search dog and handler."

"Do you have the fire under control?"

"More or less. I'm waiting on word, though it's still a potential bloody death trap, to be honest."

"What do we know so far?"

"Property owned by Doctors Andrew and Katherine Fraser. Fire started around two-thirty a.m. Neighbours called it in. By the time the brigade got here, the place was an inferno. Crew discovered what was left of a body in the living room."

"My colleague said you'd found some kind of message in the front garden?"

"Aye, bloody strange. I'll show you. Follow me, but be very careful when stepping over the hoses. They can behave like epileptic anacondas, whipping about without warning and breaking your bloody ankle."

They negotiated between two fire engines. A couple of officers helped each other out of breathing apparatuses.

"When my crew were finally able to get in, they said the stink of petrol was everywhere. So it looks like arson."

"Only one body?"

"So far, aye. Crews are still searching the upper floors. Watch that!" He gestured to a hose writhing around close to Bone's foot.

Bone leapt sideways to avoid impact. They continued through the trees, and the smouldering remains of the burnt-out house appeared.

The walls were wet and black, windowpanes shattered, and what was left of the roof hung precariously, the damaged rafters still glowing red hot. An engine was parked by the front gate, its ladder extended. A fire officer jumped off the back and approached the chief.

"That final section of the roof space almost out, sir."

"Good work, Kenny," the chief said. He turned back to Bone. "As you can see, it was a particularly ferocious fire. The building has been almost completely destroyed. We had to work very quickly to stop it spreading to the neighbouring houses on either side. That's taken us four hours to get the bastard under control."

"Five, sir," the officer corrected.

"Horrendous, and with all that accelerant in there, a potential death trap for my crew."

"Morning, sir."

Bone spun around. "Morning, Rhona. Nice headgear."

She tapped the fire helmet pulled down over her brow, then handed one to him.

"Really?" Bone said.

"Aye, really," the chief replied.

"Cash?"

"He's just gone inside."

"So, have you been in yet?"

"When I arrived at five, the fire was still raging. They've only just got the thing under control."

"So I heard."

"Did you manage to sort out your roof?" Walker asked.

"Oh, Jesus. Long story. I'll bore you later."

"Something to look forward to." Walker smiled.

"I'll take you in," the chief interrupted. "But be bloody careful, okay?"

He led them through the gate to a narrow strip of lawn with a low-level border wall running along behind. Two forensic officers knelt under a small protective tent, one taking photos, the other unfurling a measuring tape. There was a five-foot-wide message scratched into the rendered surface of the wall, the letters ragged and broken.

Bone cocked his head to read it. "What does it say?"

One of the forensic officers faced him. "'FIRST DO NO HARM.' Looks like it's been etched quickly and forcefully with a sharp, pointed instrument, possibly a screwdriver?"

"What does that mean?" Bone said.

"Something connected to the Hippocratic oath, I think," the second officer added.

"Patient with a grudge?" Walker suggested.

Bone shrugged. "Maybe. Two doctors live here."

"SOCOs are straight through there," Tennant butted in. "I've got to check on the crew working at the rear of the house."

The detectives carefully clambered through the charred remains of the front door, into what was once the living room. The stench of petrol hung thick in the air, mixing with the acrid smell of burned wood and melted plastic. Bone coughed, his eyes watering.

In the centre, amidst the debris, lay a grotesque sight. A charred, blackened corpse, its limbs twisted and contorted. But it was the skull that drew Bone's attention. The lower jaw hung open in a silent scream, and protruding between was a metal object, seemingly untouched by the flames.

"Adult male, from what they can tell." Walker said, holding her hand to her face.

"Andrew Fraser?" Bone murmured.

"Possibly. We'll need dental records to confirm, but…" Walker shrugged.

A figure in black coveralls approached, and Bone recognised the furrowed features of Chief Forensic Officer Frank Cash.

"DCI Bone," Cash said. "Wish I could say it's good to see you."

"Likewise, Frank. News?"

Cash shook his head. "Definitely arson. We found traces of accelerant in multiple locations. Whoever did this wanted to make damn sure the place went up."

Bone pursed his lips. "And the body?"

"Incinerated, unfortunately. We'll need to get it back to the lab for a full examination." He knelt closer to the blackened corpse. "See here?" He gently nudged a fragment of carbon sideways.

"Is that wire?"

"Yup, the proximity to this charred limb here suggests that the victim's hands may have been tied, possibly to a hardwood chair. Some of the wood here has survived the heat."

"What the hell is that?" Bone pointed to a thin strip of melted plastic protruding from the victim's jaws."

Before Cash could answer, a loud crack sounded from above. A firefighter who had attempted to step across a gap in the upper floor tumbled through the burnt rafters. She landed heavily, narrowly missing Bone and Walker, and cried out in pain, clutching her shoulder. A faint murmur of laughter overhead had Walker staring up.

"Man down!" an officer on the floor yelled, rushing to help his colleague. "Get the medics in here, now!"

As the injured woman was carried out, Bone focused on the victim. He was about to take a closer look when the fire chief called from the entrance, "Everyone out now!"

The detectives and Cash made their way out to the relative safety of the front garden.

"So I take it that's all we'll see for now," Bone said.

"It's just not worth it," Tennant said. "My men need time to assess the damage and make it safe."

"And women," Walker added.

"Figure of speech, Detective," Tennant replied, and blew out his cheeks.

"Detective Inspector." Walker scowled. "So some of your team thought it was funny that one of your officers was badly injured just then?"

Bone turned.

"I didn't see that," the chief protested.

"I have to say it was alarming to say the least. Is that something you tolerate as their commanding officer?"

"As I said, Detective Inspector, I didn't hear or see anything, but if I had, then the officers concerned would be in serious shit, believe me."

"Male officers, I believe," Walker qualified.

The chief rolled his eyes. "I thought you lot wouldn't be into using such binary terminology."

"You lot? Are you referring to all detective inspectors or any in particular?" Walker retorted.

"Ach, well, the poor sod isn't going anywhere," Cash said, attempting to deflect the tense stand-off. "As long as your me… er… team don't contaminate the scene any more than they already have."

"My officers, each and every one of them equally"—the chief glanced at Walker—"are putting their lives on the line, SFO Cash. We will endeavour to make the building as safe as we can so that your team can re-enter."

"Yes, but you'd better not send the womenfolk in as clearly they're the butt of some sort of joke."

"Rhona." Bone nudged his colleague discreetly.

"My officers are stressed and tired and, while there is no excuse, they often let off stress and steam with some banter, in this case, probably misplaced. I'm sure you're familiar with banter in your station, or is that considered non-PC now, too?"

"I'll leave you to it. See you later, Duncan, Rhona," Cash said, and with a wry smile, he set off towards one of the Land Rovers.

Walker removed her helmet and thrust it into the chief's hands. "I hope she's okay."

"I'll check on her shortly, and I'll find out what happened back there."

Walker shook her head and marched back to the pool car. Bone handed over his helmet and left the chief wrestling with both.

"What was that about?" he asked, catching up with her.

She shook her head.

"Rhona?" Bone caught her arm.

"Didn't you hear them?"

"I'm not sure what I heard."

"And then that arrogant sod did nothing."

"Maybe it was just a nervous thing, you know, like he said?"

"With respect, does it matter? And then that clown denied he heard it."

"I'm not sure he denied it. He might have just missed it."

"Are you serious?" She stepped back. "Sorry, sir. I mean, with respect. Are you serious? From the get-go, he was 'all my men this, all the men that, men, our men, men, men, blah, blah.'"

"Yes, I can see how that…"

"Annoys the fuck out of me?"

"I was going to say how wrong that is. Rhona, are you okay?"

"Pricks like that really get under my skin."

"Clearly, but it's not like you to lose your rag. That's usually my job."

"I get so…"

"What?"

"Tired of it. Tired of the excuses from misogynistic arseholes, you know? I just think if you're in a position of responsibility and you're ordering your team to risk their lives, you should be more responsible with your behaviour and your language. He's a sexist twat."

"I love how you manage to nail someone's character on a first meeting like that."

"Are you gaslighting me?"

"No, I'm serious. You are brilliant at it. God, Rhona. What is going on?"

"All that turning a blind eye crap, passive complicity. Think they walk on fucking water."

"Like me, you mean?"

"Especially like you." She smiled, finally. "You broke the mould."

"And there's nothing else going on?" Bone pressed.

"Like what?"

"I don't know. You fed up with your job, or is there something at home?"

"Jesus, why does it always have to be something else? It's this sexist dickhead and having to deal with sexist dickheads my entire life." She looked up and took a deep breath. "Apologies again, sir. It's all a bit intense this morning."

"Yes, I can think of better ways to spend my Sunday. If you want, we could stop for a coffee on the way back and talk it out."

"No, I'm okay now. Thank you."

"If you're sure?"

"Yeah, yeah, all good. But maybe later, eh? When things calm down a bit."

"Oh aye, like that's ever going to happen for us," Bone scoffed. "Okay, let's brief the team and sort things out at the station first. But I'm not done with you yet." He waved his finger at her. "See you back at the ranch."

He headed to his Saab and, climbing in, he glanced back at his colleague, who sat behind the wheel of her car, staring straight ahead as though plotting a painful, slow murder.

FOUR

"Morning, all," Bone said as he entered the incident room, Walker following close behind.

He turned. "All fine?" he whispered.

She nodded, and they continued.

DS Baxter stood by the coffee machine, staring morosely at the empty pot. She faced them. "Morning, sir, ma'am. Guess what?"

"Out of coffee again?" Bone smiled wryly. "The universe would feel out of kilter if that wasn't the case. Where's everyone else? Did they not get the callout?"

"Will's in the loo," Baxter replied.

"And Mark?"

"It's Sunday, isn't it? Day of fuckin' rest!" DS Mullens's foghorn voice preceded him through the door as usual, shattering the morning calm.

"Good morning, Mark. Lovely to see you, too," Bone said, voice dry as a desert.

"Sorry, sir. Dinnae see you there." Mullens grimaced.

"So you thought swearing at me was okay, then?" Baxter glared at him.

"Ah, you'll be thanking me in a minute." Mullens rummaged in his rucksack and produced a packet of ground coffee with a flourish. "I stopped at Tesco on the way in, picked up some Colombian Gold, as opposed to Colombian snow." He sniffed.

"Bloody hell, Mark." Bone raised an eyebrow. "What's gotten into you? Such uncharacteristic thoughtfulness."

"The hangover moves in mysterious ways." Mullens shrugged. "Speaking of which..." He grabbed his gut. "I told Andy in the Fells last night that his Guinness was off, but he wasn't having it. Call of the wild, two a.m., and next thing I know I'm practically spray-tanning our new bathroom. Needless to say, the wife was not pleased one bit."

"Mark!" Bone raised his hands in disgust.

Mullens clutched his stomach again, and it rumbled like a passing underground train. "Back in a tick." He hurried out, leaving the door swinging in his wake.

Bone shivered. "Give me strength."

DC Harper chose that moment to appear, copping a nipple tweak from Mullens as they passed in the doorway. Harper let out a high-pitched yelp and clutched his chest.

"One in, one out. It's like the January sales in here," Mullens called over his shoulder, guffawing.

"Have you been on the Fells Guinness as well?" Bone asked in exasperation as Harper scurried to his desk.

"Sorry, sir," Harper replied, cheeks pink. "Got stuck in traffic on the A9. Accident."

"Right, shall we get on? Or do you need to visit the gents' as well, Sheila?" Bone perched on the edge of a desk and surveyed his team.

"I'm good, sir. I'd rather be eaten alive by a pack of famished rats than go in there." She held up the coffee packet. "I'll make a fresh pot."

***

"Sorry for calling you in on a Sunday," Bone finally began, once the coffee was brewing. "Rhona and I have just come back from a suspicious house fire in Horsbrugh Close at a property owned by Dr Andrew and Kathleen Fraser."

"Council tax records also indicate that their twenty-year-old son Josh also lives there."

"Bloody hell, Sheila. You're quick off the mark."

"Simple check, took me a couple of minutes, hence no coffee." She smirked.

"At least one fatality, possibly more," Bone continued. Fire investigators and their sniffer dog are still combing the scene, but the place is burnt to a shell. We did manage a quick peek at the remains of a body in what was once the living room, but it was so badly burned it barely resembled a human being."

"Before we could take a closer look, a fire officer fell through the floor above us, and we were ordered to leave," Walker said.

"Is he okay?" Harper asked.

"*She* was taken to hospital with what appeared to be a fractured collarbone, much to the hilarity of her male colleagues."

"What?" Harper said.

"Another time, Rhona," Bone interrupted and carried on. "The sniffer dog at the scene has detected the presence of petrol. Fire Investigators still to confirm if the fuel was used as an accelerant. But to be honest, the place reeked of it, so unless the doctor was filling up his car in the living room, arson is almost certain." He found his mobile and tried to turn it on. Then remembered it was his old one. "Bugger. Hold on. Two secs." He removed the charger from his rucksack and plugged the phone in. Finally the device sprang to life and he found the photos. "Will, put this up on the monitor, would you?"

"On it." Harper took Bone's phone, the charger cable just long enough to make it to his computer. He looked up. "Wow. This is... old." He turned the handset over in his hand.

"I had a senior moment with the other one earlier." Bone sighed.

A moment later, an image appeared on the large flatscreen on the wall.

"I know the quality's not great, but you can just make out what it says." Bone nodded to the screen.

The team peered at the message scored along the length of the wall: FIRST DO NO HARM.

"One of the forensic officers thought it might be part of the Hippocratic oath."

"It is," Baxter confirmed. "Hold on." She returned to her desk and started tapping. Moments later, she was back.

"Okay, 'First, do no harm' is probably the most famous part of the Hippocratic oath, but it's a modern interpretation or translation of the original ancient Greek word 'deleterious', that is found in the phrase…" She consulted her notes. "'I will follow that system or regimen which, according to my ability and judgment, I consider for the benefit of my patients, and abstain from whatever is deleterious and mischievous.'"

After a moment's pause, Bone said, "Okay, seeing as no one else is going to embarrass themselves. What does deleterious mean?"

"Harmful," Baxter returned immediately.

"Is this some kind of patient revenge, then?" Harper asked.

The door banged open, and Mullens reappeared, adjusting one of the straps of his braces. "What did I miss?"

Bone sighed deeply. "House fire in Horsbrugh Close," he said, knowing Mullens would just keep asking until someone caved and filled him in. "One confirmed fatality, likely more. Probable arson, due to presence of accelerant. I'm being open-minded but one of my working hypotheses is retribution murder."

"That was way quicker than our usual round the houses. I should go out to the loo more often." Mullens chuckled.

"I wonder why," Walker said.

"And that delightful message scrawled into a wall in the front garden." Baxter jerked her chin at the monitor.

Mullens squinted at the words on the screen. "Hippocratic oath."

They all turned in surprise.

"What?"

"Go on then, tell us. How do you know?" Harper asked.

"I'm smarter than I look."

"That's quite a low bar, Mark. Come on, fess up," Bone said.

"It was the sixty-four K question on *Who Wants to be a Millionaire* a couple of days ago."

Bone pinched the bridge of his nose, praying for patience. "Will, you have a question?"

The DC straightened. "Yes, sir. Do we have an ID on the victim? And details on the property owners?"

"Good questions," Bone said. "The fire was intense, so Cash warned dental records would likely be needed for a definitive identification. Dr Andrew Fraser is a consultant at the Royal Infirmary. Dr Kathleen Fraser is a GP at Govan Road Surgery."

"What does the son do?" Harper asked. "I mean is he a student, working?"

"Good question. Don't know."

"Good God. They're not all toast, are they?" Mullens exclaimed, finally waking up.

"Possibly. Fire crews made an initial sweep but found only one body so far. Cash indicated that the victim's hands may have been bound to a chair with steel wire and there was some sort of tube protruding from the jaws of the skull."

"Tubing? Maybe the doc was on one of those peace pipes and set fire to the place," Mullens suggested.

"Do you ever listen? The fire crews said the house reeked of petrol and clear signs of arson."

"Sorry, sir." Mullens adopted his apologetic face, which fell somewhere between constipation and severe pain.

"If Katherine Fraser or the son were not in the property during the fire, has anyone tried to get a hold of them?" Harper asked.

"Yes, I think it would be a good idea to check their whereabouts before we assume the worst."

"What does the worst look like?" Walker asked.

"Dead or dying elsewhere? Abducted? So that's top of our list, and if we draw a blank, then we send out the search teams. But we'll have to act quickly on this. The hyenas will already be circling, I'm sure. A major house fire is hard to keep quiet."

Bone glanced around at his team. "Thoughts on anything else?"

Baxter pushed off the counter to pour the coffee. "Identifying the victim is key, obviously. But building a profile on the Fraser family, searching for any threats or enemies that could point us towards motive."

"Agreed." Bone took the mug Baxter handed him with a nod of thanks. "We'll need financial records, interview family, friends, and colleagues, dig up any complaints or disciplinaries at work, and incidents of any kind."

"I'll get on it," Baxter said, bringing up the actions log and beginning to type.

"What about the neighbours?" Harper suggested. "Someone might have seen or heard something suspicious leading up to the fire."

"Good shout." Bone sipped his coffee. "You and Mullens head over to the church hall, talk to folks who were evacuated. See if any of the Frasers' immediate neighbours are about, too."

"On it," Mullens said, grabbing his coat. "Come on, Boy Wonder."

Harper rolled his eyes and returned to his desk to collect his things. He sat.

"What are you doing, bawheid?" Mullens called over.

"Just checking my messages."

"It's only been what, an hour since you left her? Surely you two lovesick numpties can go a bit longer without having to fawn over each other."

"I'm checking in case anything's come through from Digital. Any CCTV culled from last night." He clacked at his keyboard. "And bingo!" He tapped his desk.

"You got something?"

"Hold on. I'll stick it on the monitor." A moment later, the screen on the wall flickered again and black-and-white footage of a deserted street appeared.

"Is that a speed camera?"

"The email says there's a speed cam at the bottom of the hill on the main road, which is about four streets from Horsbrugh Close."

"Notorious speed trap. The wife, aka David bloody Coulthard, has been caught twice," Mullens said.

"Let me skip and get to a time close to the fire." Harper tapped again. The footage jumped forward until the time stamp read one-thirty a.m.

"Run it from there, Will," Bone said.

Harper pressed play, and the footage started. A minute or two later, barely anything had moved.

"Are you sure this is video?" Bone asked.

Mullens yawed. "I've had more fun clearing out a blocked drain than this."

A shape appeared top right.

"Hold up," Bone said.

A fox crossed to the middle of the road, stopped, looked up at the camera, then carried on. Mullens blew out his cheeks.

Seconds later, in the near distance, at the top of the hill, a vehicle shot across the road.

"What was that?" Bone said.

"Let me slow it down." Harper rewound and replayed the section frame by frame. A van emerged from the left, traversed the road, and disappeared on the other side.

"That's Hagg's Hill crossroads. That van's going some," Mullens said.

"Can you pause it midway?" Bone asked.

"I can. But as it's so far away, with only streetlights to illuminate it, the image is going to be pretty poor." Harper reset and caught the van in its entirety.

Bone approached the monitor and squinted at the grainy image. "Is that a Transit?"

Mullens joined him. "The shape's all wrong for a Transit. That's a Citroën whatsitsface."

"Citroën?" Bone squinted again.

"Hundred percent. I'd bet my left nut on it."

"Can you do anything to improve that, Will?"

Harper was studying his phone.

"Will?"

"Yes, sorry. I'm sure they'll be able to clear out some of the white noise. I'll have a go with my gizmo as well."

"That's great. Okay. So—"

"Sorry, sir," Harper interrupted. "The van is heading on Campsie Lane that leads to Braebank Road, which, according to my phone app, runs right behind Horsbrugh Close."

"So we have a van, travelling at speed, heading towards the crime scene just before the fire was called in," Bone said.

Harper nodded. "That's correct, yes."

"A shoo-in for our psycho?" Mullens said.

"Or overnight delivery?" Walker threw her usual spanner into the mix.

"But we have our first lead, and that's a good start."

"Dispatch!" Mullens bellowed, "Citroën Dispatch. That's the baby."

"Jesus, Mark," Bone said in surprise. He set his mug down and stood. His temples throbbed, a dull ache settling behind his eyes. "Sheila, can you compile a list of all local Citroën Dispatch owners and request some uniforms to make house calls?"

"Also, any reported van thefts?" Baxter added.

"Aye, good call," Bone acknowledged. "I'll ring the super and alert him that this is now a murder inquiry and if there's only one body, he'll need to sign off on a search for the potentially missing wife."

"He'll be over the moon, as usual, I'm sure," Mullens said.

"So we'll need as much as we can glean from both doctors' colleagues, friends, and family. See if they can shed some light on their lives and movements up to the time of the incident. Any kind of thread we can pull, and stick it all up on the board, Sheila? With maybe a few prints from the CCTV."

"Oh, Jesus. Those eyes are following me round the room," Mullens said, shifting this way and that to avoid the figure's demonic gaze frozen on the monitor screen.

"It'll be my boot following your arse round the room if you don't get moving, Mark." Bone tutted. "Rhona, could you check and see if forensics have been allowed back in to the house, and if so, head back there for another snoop around."

"On it."

"And, Rhona, stay clear of the fire chief."

"Spoilsport."

"What did you do to him?" Mullens asked, his curiosity piqued.

"It's what I'd like to do to him that's the problem," Walker snarled.

"I mean it, Rhona."

"Sir."

"And I'll go up to the hospital to speak to Fraser's colleagues."

Harper and Mullens grabbed their things, but at the door, Harper stopped.

"Hold up a sec," he called back into the room. "I know there's never a good time to announce these things, but—"

"Don't tell us. Your balls have finally dropped," Mullens interrupted.

Ignoring him, Harper ploughed on. "Catriona and I have set a date for the wedding."

"What? You're finally getting hitched?" Bone said in surprise.

"We are indeed." Harper beamed and handed out elegant cream-coloured cards with gold embossing.

The front featured two intertwined rings and the names "William & Catriona" in flowing script. Inside, the details of the ceremony and reception were neatly printed, along with a small sketch of Loch Gillan Village Hotel.

Bone read aloud, "'You are cordially invited to the wedding of William and Catriona at the Loch Gillan

Village Hotel—'" He looked up. "In four weeks' time. Wow. That's amazing. But so quick."

"Is it the pitter-patter of tiny feet?" Mullens quizzed.

Harper shook his head. "No, nothing like that. We just felt the time was right and we should just get on with it." He then quipped, "Plus, we really need some new appliances for our kitchen."

"I bet Gordon was chuffed you asked him to host," Bone said.

Harper nodded. "I took Catriona up there on a wee reconnaissance a few weeks ago, and she loved it. She said she's totally envious of you in your cabin, sir."

"So you're not scarred for life after being snowed in for days and days with the er... boss?" Walker nodded at Bone.

"No, I love it up there. I promised Gordon that if we got married, then he'd be our first choice."

"Well, that's just brilliant news, Will. Thank you very much for the invite."

The team all cheered in agreement.

"It's quite short notice. I hope you can all make it."

Mullens butted in again. "What, even me?"

Harper replied, "Aye. I'm afraid so, seeing as you're the best man."

Mullens stepped back in astonishment. "Have you lost your Gameboy mind?"

"For once in my life, I find myself agreeing with Mark," Bone joked.

"You better say yes before I regret asking you."

"Oh, don't worry, there will be plenty of time for that," Bone added.

"Well, that's quite something." Mullens blew out his cheeks. "Thank you, young Skywalker. I'm moved to tears, though these stomach cramps would make anyone's eyes water. Genuinely touched. Four weeks, though. I'd better start working on that libellous best man speech then."

Harper groaned. "Oh Jesus, what have I done?"

"Right then, back to the rotten-to-the-core world that is our day job, I'm afraid," Bone said.

They all filed out, and Bone let them go on ahead. He searched his pockets for his phone, and after a moment to gather his thoughts, he rang Gallacher.

FIVE

A cacophonous wail of hymns greeted Mullens and Harper as they approached the Methodist church. Two uniforms stood by the entrance. Mullens recognised one immediately.

"Morning, Mark," the officer said, then quickly corrected himself. "Sorry. Sir, I mean."

"All right, Boyd. How's the missus?"

"Divorced," PC Boyd said.

"Sorry to hear that."

"Are you joking? It's the best thing that's happened to me since Archie Gemmill's goal in seventy-eight. When we got married, there was no such thing as Tinder."

Harper winced.

"This is Will," Mullens said, poking his thumb at his colleague. "He's on work experience from Kilwinnoch High."

"Very funny." Harper sighed.

"Morning, sir." Boyd shook his head. "How do you put up with him?"

"If I ever figure that out, I'll let everyone know. I'd make it my civic duty."

The singing from inside the church reached a disharmonious crescendo.

"Christ, what's going on in there?" Mullens asked.

"Sunday service," Boyd said. "The evacuees from Horsbrugh Close are using it as temporary digs."

"Bet they're loving the eight a.m. cat chorus." Mullens sighed. "Come on then, choir boy. Once more into the mayhem and all that."

The detectives made their way down the aisle. A short woman with a voice like a foghorn conducted a motley crew of exhausted-looking residents in an enthusiastic rendition of 'Hosanna in the Highest'.

Mullens ushered Harper into the back pew, and they endured an eternity of sermonising on the nature of tragedy and the power of community. After what felt like a reading of the entire Bible later, Mullens's eyelids drooped. His head lolled forward, a gentle snore escaping his lips, until Harper's sharp elbow jabbed him in the ribs.

"Ow! What?" he yelped, the exclamation bouncing off the vaulted ceiling.

The reverend paused, fixing Mullens with a pointed stare. "How reassuring to know my sermons can still bring rest to the weary."

Unusually abashed, Mullens opened his mouth to apologise, but the congregation's titters morphed into full-throated laughter. The reverend continued, unperturbed.

At last, the service ended. As the residents filed out, Mullens and Harper approached the reverend, who was busy collecting dog-eared hymn books.

"DS Mullens and DC Harper." Mullens flashed his ID. "We're investigating the fire."

"Ah, yes. You've just missed my star parishioners. They'll be thrilled you're on the case." The reverend shook their hands, his grip surprisingly firm. "Reverend Colin Dunham. A pleasure, despite the circumstances."

Mullens grunted. Before he could reply, the church door creaked open, framing two elderly women in matching lurid pink dressing gowns. They were identical in every way, from their matching polka-dot slippers to their perfectly coiffed hair. The sisters tottered over, twin expressions of exhaustion etched into their lined faces.

"Ah, Heather, Colleen. Perfect timing," Reverend Dunham said. "These are detectives from the station. They would like a word. They're looking into the fire."

"Has anyone told you if the Frasers are all right?" one woman demanded. "Or if our house is still standing?"

Her sister laid a restraining hand on her arm. "Wheesht, Colleen. Let the detectives speak."

"Don't worry, the fire crews tackled the blaze fairly quickly, and there's no damage to any of the surrounding properties," Mullens said.

"And the Frasers?"

"Could we have your names, please?" Mullens asked, dodging the question.

"Misses Colleen and Heather Finnieston. We live at number six, next door to the doctors. We're terribly worried about them," Heather said.

"Thank you, er… Colleen."

"I'm Heather," the first sister replied.

"Sorry, aye. So left Heather, right Colleen?" Mullens did a double-take.

"What? No!" Heather snapped back. "She's Colleen and I'm Heather. Really, Detective, it's not that difficult."

Harper jumped in before the situation escalated further. "I'm afraid we're still gathering the facts. But I promise, if you help us, we'll have you home as soon as we can." He turned to Mullens. "Perhaps if I talk to the sisters, you could go and chat to the other neighbours?"

Mullens glared at him for a second.

"Sir?" Harper added.

With a smile only Harper would understand, Mullens nodded and left the room, the reverend following behind.

"So, how long you've known the Frasers?" Harper resumed.

"Over ten years, I think," Heather replied.

"It's twelve this June," Colleen corrected. "Lovely couple, lovely neighbours. Can't do enough for us."

"So no problems or disputes, either between them or with neighbours?"

"Not at all. They're just a normal family."

"With a problem son," Colleen interjected.

"Colleen!"

"It's true. He's not been the easiest for them."

"In what way?" Harper pressed.

"Colleen, I don't think you should be bad-mouthing the Frasers like that."

"I'm not bad-mouthing. I'm just giving the detective some background. That's what you call it, isn't it?"

"It's not *Line of Duty*, sis. These are real people whose lives have been devastated."

"Any information at all can be of vital importance," Harper said.

"See?" Colleen nodded.

Heather folded her arms.

"Their son, he's probably twenty now. He's taking a year abroad in Australia after a difficult few years."

Heather sighed again.

"He's always had a tempestuous relationship with his parents, particularly with his father. Since his teens, he's been wild—drugs, alcohol, problems at school. He even dropped out of art college. He would throw parties when his parents were away," Colleen continued. "He's been a bit of a handful. You have to admit that, sis."

Heather reluctantly nodded. "Yes, the parties were quite disruptive."

"Quite?" Colleen chimed in. "The police were called more than once. They got completely out of control. We had young people up to all sorts cavorting on our back lawn, don't you remember?"

"What an eyeful." Heather sucked in her cheeks.

"He's been dealing with psychological issues as well. I spoke to Katherine about it," Colleen added. "She said it was a relief he'd gone to Australia. Hopefully, that will sort his head out, as she put it."

"You mentioned art college. Do you know which one he attended?" Harper asked.

"I think it was the local one. You know, in Lennoxfield? I remember his mum said he didn't have the qualifications to go straight to university and would need some sort of foundation thingy."

"Do the doctors have any relatives who live nearby?" Harper continued.

"Not that I know of. I think their parents are dead. I remember talking to Andrew after his mother's funeral two or three years ago," Heather said.

"What about Katherine's sister in Spain, Heather," Colleen cut in. She turned to Harper. "Actually, I might have her number on my phone. Katherine gave me it one time when they were staying over at hers."

"What do you need that for, Colleen?" Heather rolled her eyes again.

"Just in case there was a problem at the house and we needed to get in touch with them urgently."

"You and your bloody trouble. Honestly."

"Thanks," Harper halted the bickering. "Could I possibly have that?"

Colleen attempted to find the number on her phone but struggled without her glasses.

"I can't seem to find it," she said, squinting at the screen. "Could you help me look, son?"

"Of course," Harper said gently. He took her phone, finding the information and sending it to himself. "Thank you. I know this isn't easy." He handed her phone back and tucked his card into her trembling hand. "If you think of anything else, give me a call."

Colleen looked at him, considering. "There was one other thing."

"Oh, for God's sake, don't bother him with that nonsense of yours."

"What's that?" Harper asked.

"She thinks she saw someone in our back garden last night." Heather shrugged.

"I did. I'm sure of it."

"You are always seeing intruders, Colleen. She has an over-fertile imagination. I can't tell you the number of times she's woken me up and there's not a bloody soul there."

"I'm telling you. A shadow walked past our kitchen door."

"A shadow. Well, I'm sure the whole of Police Scotland will be out hunting down your shadow."

"We have a glass door, Detective." Colleen ignored her sister again. "It's opaque, but you can clearly see shapes and movement, and I definitely saw someone walking or running across the back lawn."

"Oh, they were running now? Last night they were at the window trying to break in."

"I know what I saw. That's all I'm saying."

"Don't worry," Harper said. "We'll check it out. Is it okay to enter your garden and take a look?"

Heather exhaled. "I just worry you'll be wasting your time, young man."

"No, no, it's something we'd probably check anyway, so no bother at all."

"Thanks, Detective." Colleen nodded. "See," she said to her sister, "he believes me. I wish you wouldn't."

"Wouldn't what?"

"Tell me what to do all the time. It's bloody tiring, and I'm getting right sick of it."

Heather's face tightened, and then her eyes filled again.

"Right. I think I've probably kept you long enough," Harper said with a gentle smile. "Thank you again for your help, both of you."

He offered his arms. The sisters took one each and he walked them back through to the prayer room. At the door, they stopped.

"Sorry, Detective," Heather said, her eyes still welling up with tears. "We're just both a bit frayed and exhausted."

"Don't worry about it. You've had a terrible shock. I'd be exactly the same."

"So, you have a controlling sister as well?" Colleen half-joked, proving another withering scowl from her sibling.

"No, just a daft work partner." He smiled.

The ladies giggled. The reverend approached and took over, and Harper made his escape.

Back at the car, he collapsed into the passenger seat. Mullens arrived a few minutes later.

"How did it go?" he asked, climbing in.

"Sibling rivalry that would put the Gallacher brothers to shame, but we now have a sister in Spain, a son in Australia, and a possible intruder in the Finniestons' back garden."

"Holy fucking macaroni. That's quite a haul you got there."

"What about you?"

"Nada. Just a bunch of shocked toffs out of their comfort zone, complaining about being kicked out of their houses."

"A bit harsh. You realise you're an inverted snob?"

"If the cap fits, comrade. But I won't be doffing it anytime soon for those privileged bawbags."

"Anyhow… did they give you anything on the Frasers at all?"

"Oh aye, the docs are the life and soul apparently, but they all seemed more concerned about their homes than their neighbours. So you see, my summation was accurate after all, bawbags, they are." He glanced over. "And did I miss the memo when you got promoted to detective inspector?"

"What? Oh aye, sorry about that. I just thought you were winding the sisters up. Not that they needed any encouragement. They could do that fine by themselves."

"It's all right, young Skywalker. Showing initiative. But if you ever get promoted above me, I reserve the right to still kick your bony arse from time to time."

"Fair enough." Harper sighed.

A knock at Mullens's window took them by surprise. An elderly man nodded and tapped the glass again.

Mullens opened the door, and the man shuffled back, almost toppling over the kerb.

"Whoa, watch yersel!" Mullens caught his arm.

"Sorry, Detective. I'm very tired. It's been a long night."

"It has indeed. How can I help you?"

"I just wanted to let you know that I... er... It's a bit embarrassing."

"What?"

"I live three doors down from the Frasers. I have a camera set up in our loft room trained on the back gardens and woods behind. I am a bit of a twitcher. Well, more than a bit, if I'm honest. You see, there are two owl nests in the woods behind our properties, and they come into the gardens to catch mice and other rodents. I didn't say anything before as I worry the neighbours might find my camera a little invasive of their privacy, but I only film when we retire to bed."

Harper leaned over. "Is it a night-vision camera?"

"Yes, recommended by the Ornithological Society. It starts recording when it senses movement. I have it on a timer to activate between ten-thirty p.m. and five a.m."

"Is the Frasers' back garden visible?" Mullens asked.

"Partially, yes. That's why I thought it might be helpful. I know we aren't allowed back home yet, but you have my permission to take it and check the SD card." He rummaged in his coat pocket and produced his house keys.

"That is extremely helpful, Mr…?"

"Joseph Harker, number seven Horsbrugh Close." He handed Mullens the keys.

"We'll get these back to you right away."

"No trouble. It's such a terrible thing, and if anyone was behind it, then they need bloody locking up." He turned to leave.

"Would you like a hand?" Mullens asked.

"Not at all." He waved a dismissive arm and carried on.

"Well then. Brownie points for us, eh?" Mullens said, and slumped back down in the driver's seat.

"Two leads within an hour. What's going on?"

"Don't mention it, or you'll jinx the bastarding thing."

Harper stretched and yawned. "Right, I fancy a coffee after all that."

"Jesus, not another of your vegan vanilla soy latte-less lattes?"

Harper licked his lips. "They are tasty. You should try one."

"I'd rather have colonic irrigation through my eyeballs. Right, let's go. You can fill me in on these leads of yours on the way to Sodom and Gomorrah—sorry, I mean that house of horrors you call a café."

Harper fished his phone out of his pocket. "I'll ring Rhona and see if she's gone back. And then Sheila. Maybe let her deal with Katherine Fraser's sister?

"Coward."

"Yup."

"I like how you didn't ask me to call her."

"Oh, I wonder why not." Harper chuckled.

"Hey, I'll have you know I can be sensitive when I need to be," Mullens protested.

"As sensitive as a brick through a plate-glass window, maybe," Will mumbled. "After the coffee, we can pick up the night cam and then can we head up to Lennoxfield Art College?"

"God, are you doing your 'O' grades already?"

"How did my life come to this?"

"To love and to hold forever and ever, darling." Mullens blew his colleague a kiss, and the pool car roared to life.

SIX

Bone pulled into the car park of Kilwinnoch Golf Club, eyeing the clubhouse with a mixture of bemusement and disdain. The recently completed new members' building was a dog's dinner of competing styles, as though the architect had blindly thrown darts at a board that featured every awful design trend from the 1970s.

A phone call to Gallacher's wife earlier had confirmed Bone's suspicions—his boss was here, indulging in his favourite pastime.

Bone shook his head as he climbed out of the Saab. For the life of him, he couldn't comprehend the appeal of golf, a sentiment that bordered on treasonable for a Scotsman. But then, he'd always preferred the challenge of unravelling a complex murder case to the tedium of chasing a tiny white ball across an expanse of sterilised, over-manicured grass.

Squaring his shoulders, Bone marched towards the clubhouse entrance, his worn brogues sinking slightly into the too-perfect turf. He could only imagine the reception he'd get from the starched collars and pressed slacks crowd, with his rumpled suit and perpetual five o'clock shadow.

After a brief tête-à-tête with a frosty receptionist on the front desk, Bone found Gallacher on the seventeenth tee, lining up his shot with the intense focus of a surgeon wielding a scalpel. He waited until he'd swung—a vicious slice that sent the ball careening into the trees—before calling out.

"I hope there wasn't money on that, sir."

Gallacher spun around, his ruddy face darkening further when he saw Bone. "What the hell are you doing here, Duncan? I thought we agreed, barring a nuclear holocaust, Sundays were sacrosanct."

Bone held up his hands in apology. "Normally, I'd agree. But we've got a bit of a situation. Your wife told me I might find you here."

"Grass."

"She told me she's just been given the all-clear. That's the best news."

Bone clapped his boss on the shoulder, a swell of emotion rising in his throat. He'd watched the Gallaghers battle with cancer and seen the toll it had taken on them both. Now, the strain of the ordeal had visibly evaporated from his boss's face. But as Bone filled Gallacher in on the events of the last few hours, his boss's frown returned full force.

"Christ almighty," he muttered, running a hand through his over-Brylcreemed hair. "And there was me thinking I'd be spending my Sunday in blissful ignorance, slicing balls into the rough."

"You and me both, sir. But it gets worse. We're trying to track down Dr Katherine Fraser's whereabouts, along with the son. But I have a very bad feeling about the wife, and I think it's highly likely we'll need to initiate a full-scale search for her, sooner than later."

Gallacher's brows fell further. "That's going to set the panic merchants spinning, not to mention the friendly hack pack." He puffed out his cheeks, visibly weighing the options. After a long moment, he nodded. "Aye, you're right. I'll line up whatever resources you need—uniforms, dogs, the lot. If she's out there, we need to find her."

Relief washed through Bone. He'd half expected Gallacher to put up more of a fight and moan about resources, as usual.

"Thank you, sir. I'll keep you updated on any developments."

"See that you do. And Duncan?"

"Sir?"

"Try to keep the temperature down as much as you can on this, will you? The Frasers are well-respected. Pillars of the community and all that. It's only a matter of time before this blows up into a right shitstorm."

Bone cracked a smile at his boss's catchphrase.

"I'll do my best. But as we know, once the press gets their fangs in, they're like Dracula's virgin brides gorging on Van Helsing's nephew."

"You started watching the Hammer reruns on Netflix as well, I see." Gallacher sniffed and turned back to his ball and lined up his club.

Bone's phone pinged.

"Sorry, sir. That wasn't deliberate." Bone checked the message. He looked up. "It's from McKinnon."

"What, *Chronicle* pond life McKinnon?"

"The very one."

"What does he want? As if I couldn't guess."

"He wants to see me, at his house."

"His house? Get him. So you have to go running after him now, is that it?"

"Absolutely. But it's a bit odd as he's usually hanging about the station steps like a bad smell. Why invite me to his home? He's sent me his address. Maybe I should hold my nose and call in on him later. Find out what the dung beetle wants. But I'm in no hurry to see his ugly roach face."

"He might want to finally thank you for saving his life."

Bone laughed. "Aye, right."

Gallacher turned to his shot, paused, and glanced back at Bone.

"Right. Fuck off then, and let me finish my round in peace. Some of us have earned our day of rest."

Bone gave him a mock salute. "Enjoy, sir."

"I'm playing golf, man. Joy doesn't come into it." Gallacher puffed.

At the edge of the golf course, Bone stopped to catch a glimpse of Gallacher's shot. A huge clump of grass flew high into the air. The ball skittered across the fairway and into the nearest bunker. Bone chuckled and carried on to his car.

SEVEN

Walker ducked under the police tape cordon and stopped at the Finniestons' front gate. She held her nose, the cloying stench of wet ash and burnt plastic still lingering in the air, an unpleasant reminder of the inferno that had consumed the neighbouring house not even twenty-four hours before. She glanced back at the young constable trailing behind her.

"PC Callahan, was it?"

The baby-faced officer nodded, looking slightly awestruck to be accompanying a DI. Walker suppressed a smile. She remembered that feeling all too well.

"Right then, Callahan. Let's see what we can find."

They went through the side gate and continued along a narrow path with overhanging trees to the rear of the property. The back garden was immaculate, the lawn well-manicured and bordered by tidy flowerbeds bursting with early summer colour. A far cry from the charred ruin next door. She scanned the perimeter, searching for anything out of place, any signs of disturbance.

She turned to the PC. "Okay, you go round that way and I'll meet you at that back gate at the rear perimeter wall. But be careful where you tread. We don't want to contaminate the scene, and the last thing you want is to be up on an arson charge."

"Ma'am." The PC set off slowly, purposefully placing one foot in front of the other.

Walker chuckled quietly and continued around the edge of the lawn. As she approached the back fence, her steps slowed. The gate was ajar, the lock dangling uselessly from the latch. But when she knelt to examine it more closely, she couldn't see any signs of forced entry.

Walker pushed through the gate and stepped into the lane behind. It was narrow, just wide enough for a bin lorry to pass through, lined with wheelie bins on either side. She moved farther along, and the lane narrowed even more until it was no longer wide enough for a car. The dirt track ahead led into thick woods.

She carried on into the woods, stalking the track. The going was tough, with low-hanging branches snagging at her clothes and roots threatening to trip her at every step. She had to duck and weave, pushing aside leafy obstacles, pressing on.

A little farther in, Walker came upon a slight clearing. Her eyes widened, and she took in the scene before her. Two empty twenty-litre petrol cans lay discarded on the ground. Tyre tracks cut deep into the mud and broken branches littered the area, where it appeared a vehicle had forced its way through from the other side.

She crouched to examine the tyre tracks more closely, noting the distinct tread pattern. Standing, she followed the trail of crushed vegetation and snapped branches until she came to another lane that wound its way up towards the hills.

A whistle pierced the air. Walker turned back. She retraced her steps through the woods, negotiating the treacherous terrain once more until she emerged back into the Finniestons' garden. She found PC Callahan crouched by a flower bed near the house, his focus on the ground. She hurried over.

"What have you got?"

Callahan pointed. Pressed into the damp earth was a single, perfectly formed shoe print. The tread pattern was crisp and clear, the outline unmistakable.

"Well spotted, Constable." She clapped Callahan on the shoulder, the PC flushing at the praise. "Don't touch it. We'll need a decent cast of that."

"I'll guard it with my life," the young constable said earnestly.

"I wouldn't go that far, just keep an eye on it until SOCO get here." Walker paused, then added, "In fact, go tell SOC to get round here and start combing the garden and woods. There are petrol cans and tyre marks in there."

"Jeez." The uniform's eyes widened. "On it, ma'am," and he set off at a brisk pace but still with an eye on the path.

Walker turned to leave, but something caught her eye. On a windowpane near the back door, she spotted a handprint, smudged but distinct against the glass. She stepped closer for a better look. The print was faint, the oils from the skin already fading, but it was definitely there. A left hand splayed wide on the pane.

She stepped back, her mind racing with the implications of all they'd found. While there was plenty of evidence to corroborate the neighbour's story of an intruder, something about it troubled her, a detail that didn't quite fit. With a shrug, she headed back out the front.

EIGHT

As Mullens and Harper drove towards Lennoxfield Art College, Mullens's mobile buzzed insistently, rattling against the dashboard of the pool car. He glanced at the screen, frowning at the unfamiliar number. Probably another cold caller trying to flog life insurance or double glazing. He let it ring out, focusing on navigating the lunchtime traffic snarled up on the high street.

Beside him, DC Harper was downloading Mr Harker's SD card onto his laptop, his brow furrowed in concentration; he attempted to hit the right keys despite Mullens's erratic driving. The phone started up again, vibrating like an angry wasp.

Harper glanced up, his irritation finally getting the better of him. "Are you going to answer that or what?"

"It's just some lackey from Lagos or somewhere trying to sell me fucking loft insulation, a concept I'm sure he's—"

"Just answer it. It's driving me nuts," Harper interrupted before Mullens's insults descended any further.

Mullens swerved to the side of the road and the car screeched to a halt. Harper's laptop tumbled onto the floor.

"Jesus!" Harper cursed.

Mullens snatched up the handset and jabbed the answer button.

"Before you ask, my whole hoose is double glazed, so is the garage, and so is the bloody dug's kennel."

"Hello, is this Mark Mullens?" a woman asked, sounding confused. "George Mullens's son?"

Mullens straightened in his seat. "Aye, that's me. Who's this?"

"This is Sunnyside Care Home. I'm afraid there's been a bit of an incident with your father."

"It's not the home's number. You know I'm a police officer."

"Allegedly," Harper chipped in.

"Aye, sorry. The landline's down here this morning for some reason, so I'm on my own mobile. I'm Siobhan Edwards, in the office. We've met a couple of times."

"Okay. You say an incident? What's he done now?"

"He's... Well, he's not quite himself. We think it's best if you come down right away."

"What, now?"

"Yes, please."

"He's not been flashing his tackle at the cleaners again, has he?"

"Best if you come down."

Mullens's grip tightened on the phone. "I'm on my way."

He hung up, already swinging the car into a U-turn that had Harper yelping and grabbing his seat belt.

"What's going on?"

"It's my dad. Something's happened at the care home."

Harper's eyes widened. "Christ. Is he all right?"

"They wouldn't say, which worries me."

"Maybe he's just kicked off again. You know, like that time he barricaded himself in the TV room and wouldn't let anyone change the channel from *Bargain Hunt*."

Mullens snorted despite himself. "Aye, or when he convinced himself the care staff were Russian spies and tried to report them to MI5."

"Oh, what about when he 'escaped' via the kitchens and led the local police on a low-speed mobility scooter chase down the high street?"

"While starkers from the waist down." Mullens shook his head, marvelling at his father's capacity for causing chaos.

But beneath the humour, worry gnawed at his gut. As mental as his father could be, the care home knew how to handle his episodes. For them to call him in without explanation, it had to be serious.

"Just what I need," Mullens said.

"Okay, stop the car."

"What?"

"Stop!"

Mullens hit the brakes.

"You go on, I'll sort this here."

"It's still a couple of miles."

"I'll live."

"How will you get back?"

"Don't worry about me. Just go." Harper jumped out.

Mullens nodded his thanks and accelerated back up the street.

***

Lennoxfield Art College looked very different from when Harper used to visit his mate back when he was at uni. A couple of arts grants had transformed the main building from a dilapidated fifties eyesore to a gleaming glass-and-steel architectural success story.

Harper climbed the majestic wide steps gracing the front and went into the large atrium reception area adorned with enormous murals and eclectic student artwork. He walked up to the front desk.

"Phil Cowan, Head of Graphic Design. I called earlier. I believe he's running community classes today?"

A bored-looking security guard, barely glancing up from his *Daily Record*, sighed. "Who are you?"

"DC Harper from Kilwinnoch station. I called…"

The guard sat back. "Police?"

"That's right."

"Oh, sorry, sir. I thought you were a student."

"I'll take that as a compliment, I think." Harper grinned and pushed his glasses up the bridge of his nose. "Mr Cowan?"

"Aye, that's right. He's in studio three, top floor. Just follow the corridor to the end and take the stairs to level four."

"Thanks." Harper attempted to go through, but the barrier froze and he almost toppled over it.

"You'll need one of these." The security guard sniggered and handed him a visitor's card.

With an embarrassed nod, Harper carried on.

Studio three was crammed full of men and women of all ages working away at easels. It took Harper a moment to spot the life model—a naked elderly man lying prostrate on a chaise longue, his withered, wrinkled legs open, one bent, the other hanging over the side in an off-putting seductive pose.

Harper winced.

The tutor at the front of the class, spotted him and approached.

"Can I help you?" the man whispered.

"I'm Detective Constable Harper from Kilwinnoch Police Station, and I'm looking for some information on one of your former students, but I can see you're busy."

"No, no, it's okay. The challenges of the human form will keep this lot occupied for hours."

"Are you Phil Cowan?" Harper asked.

"Yes," Cowan replied, looking a little bemused. "If you come through this way, there's a coffee area at the back of the studio."

They weaved through the easels. Harper glanced at a couple on the way past, and the students' attempts were very impressive. The old man winked at them as they passed.

Harper tried to avoid making eye contact with the model's substantial tackle, but he tripped over a stool and just managed to save himself from tumbling onto him. The stool skittered across the wooden floor with a clatter, and a wave of laughter rippled through the art room.

"Sorry." Harper gestured to the group. Flushed-faced, he hurried through.

"Would you like a coffee, Detective? It is detective, isn't it?"

"Yes. I mean, no. I mean, yes, I'm a detective, and no, I'm… I don't want coffee. It's fine," Harper replied, still rattled.

"I get a funny feeling you're out of your comfort zone." Cowan smiled.

"I'm more of a numbers kinda guy."

"Really?" Cowan replied playfully. "I never would have guessed. Okay, take a seat. I'll just grab a coffee, if you don't mind?"

Harper nodded and scanned the tiny space. A cluster of comfortable sofa chairs stood over by the window. He picked one and sat, sinking so low his knees almost came up to meet his chin.

"Yes, they are very soft." The tutor came over with his coffee cup. "I'm not sure why the college bought them. It sends students to sleep and, quite frankly, that's the last thing they bloody need." He settled in a firmer chair.

"Very impressive that you are in on a Sunday," Harper said.

"I love my community classes. I tell you, that wonderful bunch out there have more enthusiasm for art than an entire student year group. It's what keeps me going, if I'm honest." He took a sip of his coffee. "So, who is it you're looking for?"

"One of your former students, Josh Fraser. We believe he studied graphic art but dropped out, uh, over a year ago perhaps."

Cowan thought for a moment, then glanced up in surprise. "Josh Fraser. Of course I remember him. I was his personal tutor. Why do you want to speak to him. I hope he's not in trouble."

"There was a house fire at his parents' house and we're trying to get a hold of him."

"God. I heard the sirens last night and wondered what that was? Was anyone hurt? Is Josh okay?"

"We think he might be in Australia on a year out," Harper continued, ignoring the tutor's questions. "Do you know if that's the case?"

"It was actually closer to two years ago that he quit college. I'm afraid I don't know his whereabouts now, sorry."

"Can you tell me a little more about him?"

"He was a very talented student with bags of potential. Some of his art I'd even describe as exceptional. But he was troubled."

"In what way?"

"Oh, he had so many personal issues. He seemed to be at permanent war with his parents."

"Why?"

"I could never work that out. I spoke to both doctors a number of times. My impression of them was that they were caring, kind, worried parents and as perplexed as everyone else was about their son's behaviour and mental state. Though, probably late-teen self-destruction. He was into all that Goth stuff, you know. It was as though he'd read the handbook on self-destructive artist stereotypes."

"Did he have issues with drugs?"

"Oh yes, and drink. As I say, textbook. I had to send him home a few times when he turned up pissed or off his face on something. But it was his relationship with his father that seemed to upset him the most. He hated the guy. But anytime I tried to get to the bottom of it, he just shut down. I think he had issues with being from a middle-class, well-heeled background. He thought his dad was a 'bourgeois prick', as he described him often. He worked for the NHS."

"That's right."

"But all the son could see was privilege. He had some sixth-form harebrained conspiracy theories as well, which didn't help. So he dropped out. To be honest, if he hadn't left, we would've had to terminate his studies. He was just so disruptive and was affecting other students' performance and behaviour."

"Did he have any friends that we might be able to talk to?"

"Not that I know of. He wound people up big time. And if he did hang out with anyone they were probably as off the rails as him." He thought for a moment. "He was in a band though for a while. He was a more than decent drummer as well. Another of his talents."

"Did he play locally?"

"Yes, I went to see them. Sort of a Goth-metal mashup. Uh…" He looked off to the right, thinking. "What were they called?" He tapped his forehead. "B-Moth. That's it. I think they had quite a big following."

"So they're still gigging?"

"Yeah, I think so. I often see their name on posters around the college. But it sounds like he left them, too." He stopped again. "Actually, you could pop down to the student café on the ground floor. There's a bunch of posters on the noticeboard down there. You might find B-Moth's gigs listed somewhere in amongst all that mess."

"You mentioned conspiracy theories?"

"Oh, you know the sort of thing, secret business societies running the world, brainwashing media, all that anti-capitalist malarky."

"Was he anti-science?"

"Oh yeah. That's another biggie on the conspiracy nutters' list of evils."

"And medicine?"

"I would think so, yes."

"So, another possible reason why he might hate his parents?"

"Indeed." The tutor glanced at the door.

"Sorry, I won't keep you much longer. Was he ever violent?"

"Violent? God, no. He was soft as anything, despite all that anger and bluster. You don't think he had anything to do with this fire, do you?"

"Suicidal?" Harper pressed on.

"He was angry. Depressed, maybe. And I'm sure his drink-and-drug habit compounded that. But he never expressed any suicidal thoughts or feelings. Not to me anyway. As you can imagine, we deal with quite a few vulnerable and challenging young people here. So I'm well versed in spotting people who look like they're on the brink, you know? And if I am worried, I refer them to our in-house counselling service. They're trained professionals, so they're better placed to deal with things that are serious. I did suggest he speak to them a couple of times, but he consistently refused." He sighed. "Just such a terrible waste, really. Incredible talent."

"Do you think they'd mind me asking a few questions?"

"The counselling team?"

Harper nodded.

"I'm not sure they'd be into that, to be honest. They have confidentiality agreements with those who they help. I think they might be worried about breach of trust issues."

"Thanks, Mr Cowan. You've been very helpful."

"Well, if you do catch up with him, send him my regards." He glanced at the door. Right, I best get back before Mr Murphy starts misbehaving with the students again."

"The life model. What does he do?"

"You really don't want to know." Cowan laughed. "Let's just say I never thought the human body could do something so bizarre as that."

Harper winced again. He tried to get out of his chair.

"You want a hand?" The tutor smiled.

"Another ten minutes in this and I'd say definitely, yes." Harper struggled to his feet and pushed down his suit trousers.

"You can go that way." The tutor pointed to the door at the rear of the kitchen. "Unless, of course, you'd like to witness the impossible contortion."

"I'll pass. Here's my card. If you think of anything else, however small, please give me a ring. That's my direct line."

Cowan took the card, and with a nod, returned to the studio. A roar of laughter bellowed out the door, and he shut it behind him.

Harper went back down to the atrium. The guard was gone from the front desk, but he spotted the café in a glass extension opposite. It was abuzz with music and chattering students. The noticeboard stretched the length of the side wall. It was plastered with flyers, for sale signs, and posters of various sizes and descriptions. A student approached and pinned a card on the board.

"Can you see a poster with the band B-Moth on it?" Harper asked.

The student looked him up and down. "You like B-Moth?" she asked in disbelief.

"Yeah," Harper lied, unconvincingly.

"Right." The student helped him search. A few moments later, she tapped the board. "Here. They're playing at the Student Hub tomorrow night. Battle of the Bands."

"Where's that?"

"In here. They clear the tables and set up a stage over there. It's actually quite a good venue. I've seen a few bands in here. Are you a student?" she asked with an expression of incredulity.

"I'm an A and R spotter," Harper replied, unsure of why he was lying or what he was talking about.

"Isn't a spotter usually for football?"

"Aye, we do that, too. Our record company is a very… er… broad church."

"Right, well, I'm sure the bands will all be very excited to know that there's a football spotter in the building."

"And music," Harper qualified lamely.

"Aye, right." She exhaled and returned to her table.

Harper glanced around the café and furtively unpinned the poster, slipped it into his suit pocket, and headed back to his car. "That all went well, then," he mumbled, shaking his head.

NINE

At the hospital, Bone knocked on Dr Fraser's office door. A short, grey-haired woman in a neat trouser suit answered. She was about to say something but stumbled sideways against the doorframe. Bone caught her before she fell.

"Oh dear, let's get you seated."

"I'm just beside myself with worry. When I saw the fire on the news this morning and then he didn't come in for his first appointment—" She took two or three short breaths.

"I'm DCI Duncan Bone from Kilwinnoch station."

"Oh, dear God. Is he… Is he okay?"

Bone guided her to a chair by the window then sat himself. "What's your name, ma'am?"

"Mrs Ormond, Carol. I'm Dr Fraser's secretary."

"Does Dr Fraser usually come in on Sundays?"

"Yes, as long as I've worked for him. He's been one of the few consultants who willingly does."

"And you work weekends, too, then?"

"As long as he needs me, I'll be in."

"How long have you worked for him?"

"A long time. Such a lovely…" She bit her lower lip.

"So what time were you expecting him this morning?"

Mrs Ormond's hands shook again. "My God, he must have been in there. And what about Katherine, his wife? Are they both safe? Please tell me."

"We're just in the initial stages of our enquiries, Mrs Ormond. You mentioned a first appointment?"

"Yes, at nine-fifteen. He didn't show up, and I had to send the patient home. That's very unusual for him. Actually, unheard of. I can't remember the last time he missed an appointment. That's why I'm beside myself."

"So, he's definitely not taking a last-minute holiday, or perhaps there's been a family emergency or something?"

"Well, I know that their son is abroad on his gap year or whatever they call it these days."

"Where is he?"

"The last I heard, he was somewhere in Australia working on a mango farm or some such."

"Dr Fraser is a paediatric consultant, is that right?"

"Yes. Pre- and post-natal. He's considered one of the best in the country."

"Did Dr Fraser raise any concerns about home security or personal safety? Anything like that in the last few days or weeks?"

"Do you think someone might have broken in and started the fire deliberately, then?"

"As I said, this is all just initial enquiries. We have to ask these sorts of questions."

She took a deep breath. "He is a…" she started, her eyes welling with tears.

Bone reached into his jacket pocket, found a packet of tissues, and handed it over.

She took one and patted her eyes. "Sorry, Inspector. I'm just so worried. Dr Fraser is a wonderful doctor, and I consider him a professional friend."

"I understand this is distressing for you. Would it be possible to speak to some of his colleagues and perhaps the head of the maternity unit, his boss?"

"Of course, yes. But many are off today. Professor Baird, Dr Fraser's senior, is on paternity leave at the moment."

"Do you have a contact number for Professor Baird, and Dr Fraser's colleagues, fellow consultants, registrars, nurses, that sort of thing?"

"Of course, yes. He's Professor Patrick Baird, by the way, and his full title is Medical Director. Dr Fraser is head of paediatrics."

"If you could send those over to me, that would be most helpful." He fished one of his cards out of his pocket and handed it to her. "You can use my email address on the back of the card. How long has Professor Baird been off on paternity leave?"

"About four months. But he's actually been off on sick leave for longer, possibly getting on for almost seven months now."

"Why is that?"

"No one is sure exactly, but there is a common consensus that he was off with stress. It's been horrendous the last few years. It's like an epidemic; so many are off or have left the profession altogether. It's not just the medical professionals, it's administrators and ancillary staff, too. We are literally on our knees. I'm sorry, it's probably the same for you, too, isn't it?"

"Not far off. What about Katherine Fraser? Are you acquainted?"

"I've met her at a few functions and events, things like that. She's a lovely lady. She's also my next-door neighbour's GP. He has nothing but praise for her."

"Her practice is in the Burngreen, is that right?"

"Yes."

"Dr Fraser never expressed any concerns about his health, his mental well-being, or anything like that?"

"He complained about being overworked, not very much, though, unlike some other members of staff. But he has a very resilient personality. I can't remember if he has ever been off sick. He rarely complained about his workload. If anything, I suppose he just cares too much about his patients, if that's possible. That would probably be his only flaw, if you would call it that. If he was suffering from some sort of mental distress, he kept it well hidden from me. But I doubt it. I doubt it very much."

"Okay, Mrs Ormond, that's all for now."

She grabbed his arm before he could stand. "Please, Inspector, you have to let me know as soon as you hear from him."

"I will, Mrs Ormond. I promise. But please try not to worry. Would you like me to make you a cup of tea or perhaps one of your colleagues could come and talk to you?"

"No, no. You need to get on." She looked at him, eyes pleading. "Just find him, Inspector. Please."

Bone gave her a tight smile and left, her words echoing in his ears.

TEN

Mullens sped towards Sunnyside. His mind raced with possibilities, each more dire than the last. Had his father fallen, broken a hip? Wandered off and got lost? Set fire to his room? Murdered a delivery van driver? The possibilities were endless.

He drew into the car park, barely remembering to pull the handbrake before leaping out. He charged through the front doors, nearly bowling over a startled receptionist.

"Oh, Mr Mullens. Thank goodness you're here," the receptionist said, regaining her composure. "Your father is in a right old state."

"What's going on?"

"Best if the doctor speaks with you."

"The doctor? Is he all right?"

She nodded towards the stairs. "Third floor. The doctor will meet you up there."

Mullens marched through reception and took the stairs three at a time. At the top, he stopped dead, gasping for breath. A cluster of nurses stood outside a closed bathroom door, talking in low, urgent tones. And in the middle, her white coat stark against pastel scrubs was a tall, serious-looking doctor who clutched a clipboard as though her life depended on it.

She looked up as Mullens approached, her expression grave. "Mark Mullens?"

Mullens nodded curtly. "What's happened? Where's my father?"

"He's locked himself in the loo. We're hoping you can persuade him to open the door."

"Is that all?" Mullens took a deep sigh of relief. "Bloody hell. I thought for a minute—"

"No, I'm afraid it's a bit more than that. He's locked himself in because he's turned yellow overnight," the doctor cut him off. "We think it's his liver. We need to run some tests, but the jaundice, it's not a good sign."

Mullens swallowed hard, trying to process the information. "Yellow? What the hell is that? He was fine a couple of days ago. Confused and offensive as usual, yeah, but physically…"

"These things can come on quickly, especially in the elderly." The doctor laid a hand on his arm. "We're going to do everything we can. But first, we need to get the old devil out of there." She smiled. "Before he says anything else to offend the nation."

"Oh no. What? Wait, don't tell me. I can guess."

The doctor nodded apologetically. "He's from a different time."

"Aye, Jurassic Park." Mullens sighed. "Right, let's do this."

Outside the shower room, he could hear George sobbing, mumbling incoherently.

"Da? It's Mark. Open the door, eh?"

"Piss off!" George yelled from the other side.

"Da, come on. That's enough now."

"Ah'm no' coomin' oot. Yer aw tryin' tae do me in."

"No one's trying to do you in, Da." He glanced at the medics. "Though, by Christ, we would all love to," he murmured.

One of the nurses choked back a laugh.

"Come on, Da."

The lock finally clicked, and Mullens was in. He closed the door behind him. George was slumped on an adjacent bench, completely naked, his skin the colour of a nicotine-stained wall.

"Oh, Dad…" Mullens knelt beside him and averted his eyes from his father's withered nethers. "What's all this, then?"

"They've turned me into a banana, son!" George wailed. "A fuckin' banana!"

"You are many things, Da, but you are no banana. You're ill, that's all."

"But look at me! If I'm no' a banana, then I'm a fuckin'…"

"Da, No!" Mullens stopped him before he broke another law.

"I told you they were putting some sort of ha-ha pills in ma food, but they were fuckin' banana pills. I want to go home."

"Da, this is your home now. Where's your dressing gown?" Mullens searched the shower cubicle and found his robe lying on the floor. "There, put this on. Nobody wants to see that wee banana." He wrapped the robe around his dad's shoulders.

"Where's yer mother? I bet she's havin' a right old laugh at her bananaman." He stopped, and a smile crept across his face. "Mind you, she always did fancy a wee bit of fruit in the bedroom. Did I ever tell you about the time we—"

"Christ, Dad. Don't make my ears bleed!" Mullens cut him off, shuddering.

George cackled, then his face fell again. "She'll be worried sick about me, son. A right one for the worrying, so she is."

Mullens swallowed hard. "She's doin' the crossword. You know how she gets if we disturb her." He had been using the same lie now for a few weeks and hoped George would buy it again.

"Oh God, aye, the menopausal Godzilla."

Mullens sighed. "Mum knows you're in good hands here, Dad. The docs will sort you out, aye?"

"I suppose. But you'll tell her I'm okay? Don't want her fretting."

"Course, Dad. I'll let her know. Now let's get you up, eh?" He helped his dad to his feet and guided his hand into the sleeve of his gown.

"Where are we going?"

"Back to bed."

"Aye, and you shouldn't be up this late. You've school tomorrow. I hope you've done your homework, my boy."

"You know me, Da." Mullens winked.

"Aye, pay yer mates to do it for you, you sneaky wee shite."

"Exacto." Mullens took his dad's arm and slowly led him out and back into the care of the medical staff.

***

In the doctor's office, Mullens braced himself for the worst.

"We suspect a bile duct blockage," the doctor said. "Could be gallstones, could be a tumour. We'll need to operate to be sure."

Mullens nodded, not quite taking it in. "You mean a cyst?"

"Possibly, but we won't know until we have a closer look," the doctor said. "But to be honest, I think you have to be prepared for worst-case scenarios. George is eighty-six. The odds on something simple are short, I'm afraid. But let's just see and then we'll take it from there. One step at a time."

Mullens nodded in agreement, but his mind was in overdrive.

Back in George's room, Mullens sat on the edge of the bed. His father, almost invisible under the blankets, was now half asleep. A nurse hovered by his bedside.

"We gave him a wee sedative, as he was still quite distraught," the nurse whispered.

"Is he asleep?"

"Naw he's no', so no bad-mouthing me just yet," George muttered.

"I'll come back in a wee while, George, see how you're doing," the nurse said.

"Who's she?" George glared at her.

The nurse gently patted his hand and left.

Mullens pulled over a chair. "The doc says you need an operation, Da. But you'll be right as rain after, aye?"

"A whit?"

"A wee operation?"

"They're going to cut me open?"

"Aye."

"Fuckin' gangsters. Will I have scars?" He ran his hand across his face.

"Aye, Da, you can kiss goodbye that *Vogue* photoshoot next week. Of course, you won't, ya eejit."

"Hey, less of the lip, young man." He took a deep breath and suddenly looked distracted again. "Where's your mother?"

Mullens's face tightened. "It's her girlie night tonight." He tried his second get-out-of-jail lie and glanced up, hoping his dad would take it.

"Aww, dear God. I forgot. The witches of Eastwick. Are they doonstairs?"

Mullens exhaled. "Aye, so best if we keep out their road, eh?"

"Oh God, aye. They'll be doon there noo, stirring their big pot of poison."

"Vodka and tonics more like. Don't worry, Da. I'll keep them at bay if they come looking for you."

"That's good." George took Mullens's hand and squeezed it weakly. "You might be a total horse's arse, but you're my total horse's arse."

"Thanks, I think," Mullens said.

"You know your mother and I are very…" George's eyes closed, and moments later he was snoring gently.

"Proud of you," Mullens said. "Me, too, Da. Me, too, ya daft old bastard."

As Mullens left the care home, jaw clenched and fists balled, one thought pounded through his head: whatever was causing his da's illness, it had picked the wrong man and wrong family to fuck with.

ELEVEN

Bone squinted at his phone, the Google Maps app insisting he'd reached his destination. But unless Professor Patrick Baird lived on a cut-through overgrown with half-dead rhododendrons, the useless thing was having a giggle at his expense, as usual.

"Bloody technology," Bone grumbled. He reversed the Saab back onto the nearby lane, parked up in a cloud of oil fumes, and set off up the path, reluctantly relying on his rebellious map. Through the bushes, he came to a playing field, and he spotted the back of an imposing red-stone mansion at the far side—Baird's palatial pad, he presumed.

He continued across a waterlogged football pitch, his brogues squelching and slipping in the mud. When he reached a chest-high wall, he searched for a way around, but it seemed to extend forever in either direction, with no sign of a back gate. He checked his phone again, and his screen screamed back, "You have arrived at your destination."

Bugger.

After a rather undignified scramble over the wall, Bone found himself in an immaculately landscaped garden with pristine lawns, artfully trimmed topiary, and a pond big enough to accommodate Moby Dick.

He glanced down at his sodden feet and mud-spattered suit trousers and felt a little underdressed for such a carefully manicured environment. He trudged up to the rear kitchen door and knocked. No answer. He peered through the window, only to spot a figure hunched over on the floor, grappling with something or someone out of view.

Fearing the worst, Bone hammered on the glass. "Police! Open up!"

The figure sat back, startled, arms aloft, hands smeared with a suspicious brown substance. The figure jumped to their feet, and moments later the door flew open. The tall, stooping frame of Professor Baird emerged, a naked baby wriggling and grumbling in his arms.

"What the bloody hell are you playing at?" the flush-faced Medical Director demanded, his cut-glass Edinburgh accent slicing through the air.

Bone cringed, both at the posh tones and the pungent aroma wafting from the man's hands. "Sorry, Professor. DCI Bone, Kilwinnoch Rural Crime Unit."

Baird rolled his eyes. "Well, congratulations, Inspector. You've just interrupted a nappy change." He glowered. The baby grabbed the professor's glasses and threw them with force onto the tiled floor.

Bone quickly picked them up. "Sorry, I think one of the lenses might be cracked." He handed them back.

Baird sighed. "Third bloody pair." He put them back on, but they sat at a crooked angle on his face.

The baby giggled and tried to snatch them again.

"Leave, Matilda," the director ordered, as though attempting to control an errant puppy. "Well, are you coming in, then?"

"Thanks." Bone stopped. "Sorry about the muddy feet."

"That's the least of my worries at the moment." Baird shrugged and marched inside.

Bone followed him into a once-luxurious kitchen, now strewn with dirty dishes, open cupboards, and an explosion of baby paraphernalia. In the adjacent living room, Baird laid the wriggling baby down in the centre of a play mat, a halo of toys and burp rags surrounding her like a tiny, slightly soiled Stonehenge.

"I apologise for the mess," Baird said, kneeling to finish dealing with the poonami. "I'm on paternity leave, and it's been a bit hectic."

Bone nodded, memories of early fatherhood flooding back. "Aye, I remember those days. Teeny wee tornados of chaos."

Baird disposed of the toxic nappy and put the baby on a cloth play carpet. She kicked enthusiastically at the mobiles dangling from a polka-dotted cloth arch. "So, I take it this is about Andrew. I saw in the news there had been a fire at his house. Is everyone okay?"

Bone cleared his throat, trying not to gag on the lingering stench of digested formula. "We're in the initial stages of our enquiries."

"But he's not hurt, is he?"

"I'm afraid I can't comment at the moment."

"Oh, come on, Inspector. Clearly, if a detective chief inspector is involved, something pretty catastrophic must have happened."

"We are trying to establish the Frasers' movements before the fire."

"You are stonewalling me?"

"Yes, I'm afraid I am," Bone acknowledged. "When is the last time you saw either of them?"

"In case you haven't noticed, I'm on paternity leave. I've not been at work for over a… well… a while."

"So you've not had any contact with either of the doctors since then?"

"Not at all. I've been somewhat busy. My wife had a difficult pregnancy and birth, and she has ongoing problems, so it's been all hands to the pump, or my poo-covered hands, mainly."

"And the last time you saw Andrew Fraser. In what capacity was that?"

"Capacity?" Baird frowned. "We both attended a meeting regarding proposals for a new research centre at the hospital."

"How was Dr Fraser at the meeting?"

"His usual vociferous self."

"In what way?"

"He holds strong views on how the NHS should be run and where limited resources should be spent."

"So he was against the research centre?"

"Not against it, but his priorities are usually very different from that of hospital management."

"How long have you worked with Dr Fraser?"

"I've known him for nearly eight years, since he first joined the hospital as a registrar. He quickly rose through the ranks to become head of paediatrics."

"And has your relationship always been robust?"

"We've had our moments over the years, yes."

"So, you found him difficult to manage?"

"You're putting words in my mouth." Baird's brow furrowed. "We had our disagreements, yes—funding, staffing, the usual NHS bureaucratic nonsense—but they were professional discussions about complex issues and developments that needed a great deal of thought and care. Debate and disagreement came along with that. It's all normal practice."

"Did these disagreements ever bleed over into your personal lives?"

The professor stiffened. "Just what are you insinuating?"

"I'm not insinuating anything, sir. I'm just trying to gather all the facts."

Baird's face fell. "Our conversation is beginning to seriously worry me. Andrew Fraser is an exceptional clinician, surgeon, and a valued colleague. I have nothing but respect for the man. But my concerns for his wellbeing are mounting. Please, Inspector, reassure me that Andrew survived the fire."

"We have concerns for them both. We are investigating the possibility that they were not at home when the fire occurred. Dr Fraser didn't show for his appointments this morning. Is there any possibility that the two doctors could have gone off on a last-minute holiday or conference trip?"

"Not that I know of. I don't think Andrew has missed a day's work in his life."

"That's what his secretary said. She also mentioned that you were off sick prior to taking your paternity leave."

"Yes, what of it?"

"I don't wish to pry, but could you tell me why?"

"Not that it's any of your business, but I had to take some stress-related time out. I had been overworking somewhat, and then, when my wife became very ill in the latter stages of the pregnancy, it was all rather challenging. So I decided that I needed to step back, take stock, to have enough mental and physical strength to support my wife."

"Sorry to hear that." Sensing Baird's obvious discomfort, Bone changed the subject. "And you've had no contact with Dr Katherine Fraser?"

"We've only ever met at functions and Christmas parties. That sort of thing."

"You wouldn't happen to have a contact number for her, would you?"

"Why would I have that?" the director snapped back. "I barely know the woman."

"Okay, as I said, we are exploring every avenue to try and locate them both."

"This is all very sinister." Baird shook his head. "Andrew does not behave unpredictably or irrationally. He wouldn't just swan off somewhere without informing his secretary or colleagues."

"How would you describe the Frasers' relationship?"

"Married, happily, from what I've seen."

"So, no tensions between them?"

"If there were any, I would probably be the last person Andrew would confide in. As I said, our relationship was strictly professional, and that goes for his wife, too."

The baby started crying. Her toe was stuck in one of the swinging teddies.

"How did you manage that?" Baird asked, and gently prised her foot out of its temporary stranglehold. The baby continued to cry. "She's had enough. She needs her mum."

"I won't keep you much longer, sir. Did he ever mention any threats or abuse from patients or their families?"

Baird clicked his teeth. "Abuse of NHS staff is at epidemic levels, but Dr Fraser is the consummate professional. He saved countless lives, both mothers and babies. He is widely respected within the hospital and the broader medical community. People love him, you know?"

The professor's voice caught, and he blinked rapidly. Bone offered a sympathetic nod, allowing the man a moment to collect himself.

"I'm sorry. It's all rather shocking and intense."

Bone cleared his throat, preparing for the pushback. "Just one more query. Where were you last night, around two-thirty a.m.?"

Baird bolted to his feet. "I was right here, trying to soothe a colicky newborn, while my wife wrestled with pain and post-natal problems upstairs in bed. Where the baby should be now."

"Thanks for your time. I'll leave you to it. And I hope your wife has a speedy recovery."

The baby's wails escalated.

"I'll show myself out."

Baird grunted, picked up his distressed daughter, and rocked her in his arms, but the screams continued. Bone beat a hasty retreat out the front and back to his Saab, the reek of infant excrement clinging to his suit. He climbed into his car and called Baxter.

"Sheila, can you run some checks on Professor Patrick Baird, Medical Director at Stirling Royal? He's Dr Fraser's boss."

"What am I looking for?"

"Anything that indicates a troubled relationship with his staff, and the doctor in particular. Apparently, they didn't get on. Something not quite right about him."

"Okay, got it, though you do say that about most people."

"An unhealthy mistrust of humanity. One of the many wonderful perks of the job."

He hung up and with a nervous sigh, he slowly turned the ignition key. The engine coughed to life and rocked back and forth as though trying to catch its breath.

"That's my girl." He tapped the dashboard and gently persuaded first gear to engage.

TWELVE

Walker stared at the phone, her finger hovering over the call button. She'd delivered her fair share of bad news over the years, but it never got any easier. Especially when the recipient was in another country, miles away from the support of family and friends. She took a deep breath and dialled the number. The line clicked and went silent. She was about to hang up when it started ringing.

"¿Sí?" a woman's voice answered, the Spanish lilt unmistakable.

"Eliza Collins?"

"Eh… yes. Who is this?"

"I'm Detective Inspector Rhona Walker from Kilwinnoch Police Station in Scotland."

There was a pause, a sharp intake of breath. "What?"

"Detective Inspector Walker from…"

"I heard you, but is this… Is it something to do with my sister? Is she okay? My sister, Katherine Fraser?"

Walker closed her eyes. "That's why I'm calling, Mrs Collins. I'm afraid there's been a fire at your sister's house."

"Is she… is she all right? I mean, are they all right?"

"I'm afraid it's very serious. Fire crews are at the scene now."

"Oh my God! Is she all right?" Mrs Collins repeated, her voice rising in pitch, the panic setting in.

Walker gripped the phone tighter. "We are waiting for news from our forensic team, but I'm afraid it's likely that your brother-in-law, Dr Andrew Fraser, may have been caught in the fire."

"Is… is he hurt? And what about my sister? You haven't mentioned my sister."

"There was one male casualty at the property, but we haven't as yet formally identified who that is."

"But what about my sister? Where is she?" Mrs Collins snapped back.

"We haven't managed to locate your sister yet, Mrs Collins. There was no sign of her at the property."

The line went silent again, save for the sound of ragged breathing. Walker waited, giving the woman a moment to process the devastating news.

"Hello? Mrs Collins? Are you still there?"

"I just… I can't take this in. What happened?" Mrs Collins rasped, her voice cracking.

"I'm so sorry, Mrs Collins."

"I was on the phone to Katherine only a couple of nights ago. Where is she? What's she doing? What's going on?"

"We hoped you might be able to help us with that," Walker said gently. "Has she mentioned anything about coming out to see you, or anywhere she might be that we could look for her? Any friends? Relatives you have in the town or…?"

"She has lots of friends. She's a GP. I can certainly give you a few names if that would help find her."

"That would be very good. Thank you. And what about relatives in the area? We've been informed their son, Josh, is in Australia. Do you know if that's correct?"

"My God, Andrew is dead?" The penny finally dropped.

"As I said, we haven't formally identified the casualty. Do you and your sister have relatives in Scotland or the UK?" Walker steered Mrs Collins away from the brink again.

"Our parents passed away, so… and we don't have any aunts or uncles or grandparents, anything like that. It's just the two of us."

"And the son?"

"Yes, he's off finding himself on the other side of the world."

Walker made notes on her iPad. "So, your sister didn't mention anything unusual or strange going on at the house when she called you? Any possible break-ins in the street or the neighbourhood, perhaps?

Maybe a problem at work or a difficult patient, something of that nature?"

"No, nothing. So, this was a break-in? Did someone do this deliberately?"

"I'm sorry, I have to ask you this, Mrs Collins. Was your sister getting on okay with her husband? No marital issues, anything like that?"

"You think he did this?"

"We are just exploring all avenues."

"Of course not. That's just insane. They loved each other very…" Her voice broke, a sob escaping. "I just can't believe it. Andrew. My God!"

The line clicked and went dead.

"Mrs Collins?"

Walker pressed the phone to her ear, but the line wailed. She rang back, but there was no answer. She tried again.

"¿Hola, Señora?" a new voice answered, the Spanish accent thicker, older.

"Yes. Is Mrs Collins there?"

"Sorry, she… she is very sad."

"Who are you?"

"I am her friend from next door."

Walker could hear Mrs Collins sobbing in the background.

"Can you make sure she's okay?"

"What? Sorry? My English is not good."

"Can you look after her? Care for her. She's probably in shock."

"Shock. Sí. So terrible. I will tell her she can telephone anytime."

Mrs Collins's heart-wrenching wails strengthened. Walker exhaled.

"I have to… I will go now," the neighbour said.

"Yes. Thank you."

Walker hung up, her hand shaking slightly. She closed her notebook with a snap and swore repeatedly until her anger subsided at the devastation whoever did this was causing.

THIRTEEN

At the station, Sergeant Brody stopped Bone in the corridor. "Ah, you're here, sir. CFO Cash wants to see you."

"Please don't tell me I have to go back to that horror story again."

"No, he's here. They've moved the victim back."

"Bloody hell, that was quick."

"He said they had to work fast as the whole house is so unstable, the body and any valuable evidence could have been buried under tons of burnt-out rubble."

"Not to mention our officers."

"Indeed."

Bone sighed. "And here was me thinking I could call it a day."

"Chance would be a fine thing," Brody scoffed.

"Is anyone in upstairs?"

"All gone home, I think."

"Good. They're going to need all their wits about them tomorrow." Bone started for the basement stairs.

"Hold on, sir. I saw the CFO earlier in the canteen. I think he's still there. And a warning: he looks like he might be having another of his episodes," Brody whispered with a wry smile.

***

Bone found Cash alone in the deserted staff café slumped over his coffee, staring at the tabletop as though it held the secrets of the universe.

"Afternoon, Frank," Bone said, approaching. "Or should that be evening?"

Cash looked up. "Duncan." He attempted a smile that didn't quite reach his eyes. "Always a pleasure, never a chore."

Bone slid into the seat opposite. "I don't normally find you in here. Didn't think you actually ate or drank. Well, maybe blood."

"Very droll." Cash's frown deepened; he clearly wasn't in the mood for their usual banter.

"Everything all right?"

Cash shrugged. "Just some kitchen-sink dramas. Nothing to bother you with."

"Go on. As well you know, I'm the king of kitchen-sink dramas."

"My wife has left me," Cash said flatly.

"What?"

"Gone. Split. Vamoosed." He gestured, making a soaring plane with his hand. "She described me as… hold up, let me just recollect her exact words… 'The most morose, negative, depressing person I've ever met,' and she wished she'd dumped me on our first date when she had the chance."

Bone tried to suppress a smirk. "To be fair, she may have a point."

"Cheers for that." Cash scowled.

"Is that why you're here so late, drowning your sorrows in canteen coffee?"

Cash sighed heavily. "She kicked me out."

"So *she* left *you*, but *you* had to leave?"

"Exactly. I've been sleeping here at the station."

Bone's eyebrows shot up. "Where? Not in the morgue, surely."

"Give me some credit. I've got a camp bed in the storeroom off my office." Cash shook his head. "I'm the king of fucked-up relationships, Duncan. No idea why Alice took you back after the hell you put her through."

"You and me both, pal. It took a hell of a lot of work to get to where we are now. Have you tried talking to your wife? Really listening to her?"

"Bit late for that now, she's changed the locks," Cash muttered.

"It's never too late. You need to sit down, shut that mouth of yours, and let her speak. Really hear her out. Then apologise, sincerely. She'll know if you're just paying lip service."

Cash snorted derisively. "What, you're suggesting marriage guidance? The futility of trying to find meaning and connection in an indifferent universe destined for entropy and oblivion?"

Bone chuckled. "With that attitude, it's a wonder she didn't leave you sooner. I'm serious, though. Counselling helped me and Alice enormously."

"I think I'd rather go another round with our crispy friend in the body bag," Cash said. He drained his mug and stood. "Anyway, you needed an update on the fire victim?"

Bone held up a hand. "Hang on, Frank. You can't just land this and then walk."

"I appreciate your concern, Duncan, but I shouldn't have bothered you with it. We have work to do."

"The work can wait a minute. You're no good to anyone, least of all yourself, like this."

Cash sighed heavily, sinking back into his chair. "What do you want me to say? That I'm a miserable bastard who's torpedoed the best thing that ever happened to me? Mea culpa, mea maxima culpa."

"Admitting it is the first step," Bone said gently. "But you can't just wallow in self-pity. You need to take action, make changes. Show her you're willing to put in the work."

"I wouldn't even know where to start," Cash mumbled.

"That's what counselling does. It gives you the start, a neutral space to shout at one another. Trust me, she'll probably need to do that more than you.

Make the appointment, even if she won't go with you at first. Show you're serious about fixing things."

Cash was quiet for a long moment. "I suppose I could look into it," he said finally. "No promises, mind."

Bone smiled. "There you go. You can't just let… How many years have you been married?"

"Twenty-two next month."

"Jesus Christ. I mean it. This is too important for you to sit there moping. Get on with it."

"You're a bully, you know that, don't you?"

"Yes, and I'll be on your case until I know you've at least tried your damnedest to turn this around."

Cash nodded.

"Good. Sensible move. And remember, if you need to talk, or another kick up the arse, give me a bell. God knows you've listened to me moan about my marital woes often enough. Call it karma if it makes you feel better."

"Now that you put it like that," Cash said, the corner of his mouth threatening a smile. "Thanks, Duncan." He stood again. "Come on then, let's go and taste the smell of more human failure."

Bone rolled his eyes and followed Cash out.

In the examination room, they approached a table draped with a grey plastic sheet. The acrid stench of charred flesh mixed with petrol fumes assaulted Bone's nostrils, and he fought the urge to gag.

"I told you it was rather pungent," Cash said, snapping on a pair of gloves.

Bone nodded, not trusting himself to speak.

Cash wheeled over an overhead lamp and turned to Bone, his eyes wide.

"Ready?"

"As I'll ever be," Bone mumbled through his hand.

Cash peeled back the sheet, revealing a grotesque tangle of blackened limbs, a charred ribcage, and a skull stripped of skin, frozen in a silent scream. Bone exhaled slowly, trying to steady himself.

"The fire was incredibly intense," Cash explained. "Most of the body has been consumed. And then there's this, hidden under the body" He reached down and pulled a tray out from under the examination table and placed it on an adjacent worktop.

"Aye, that. What the hell is it?"

"A steel funnel, presumably to help pour petrol down the victim's throat into the stomach. We found remnants of melted tubing inside the victim's chest cavity. You can see what remains of it hanging down here." He picked up a spatula and flicked gently at the melted blob hanging from the victim's lower jaw. The concentration of damage to the abdomen suggests the presence of significant amounts of accelerant. Unleaded petrol, to be precise."

"Good God!" Bone clutched at his mouth.

"I ran some tests. It's the type of rubber used in fire extinguishers, but the ferocity of the inferno even managed to melt that."

"No wonder there's nothing left."

Cash nodded. "But it's a bit amateur when you think about it. Petrol needs a spark, oxygen to ignite.

Filling a stomach with it is more likely to cause drowning or toxic poisoning than spontaneous combustion. Once the fire takes hold, though, the fuel will leak out and add to the inferno."

"So, this was more a statement than an effective method of murder?"

"Possibly. A bit naïve, but no less brutal for it." Cash went to a storage unit, removing a tray. "A couple more things. We retrieved these around the remains, most likely wrists and ankles." He held up a bag containing coils of wire. "As I suspected, galvanised steel. Used to restrain the victim, tied to that hardwood chair."

"So definitely not suicide, then."

"The tube rather ruled that out, don't you think?"

"Nasty, evil bastard."

"The descent of man continues unabated." Cash sighed. He opened a second bag and fished out a ring. He held it under a magnifying lamp. "Platinum wedding band. Look at the inscription."

Bone squinted at the image. "'To my beloved Andrew, always mine.'"

"I think we can safely say the good doctor is dead." Cash sighed.

"But where's his wife?"

"Certainly not in the fire. We've been through the house, and there's no sign of a second body." Cash produced a final evidence bag containing a soot-blackened box. "Found this near the body. A cash deposit box, with a combination lock."

Bone examined it. "Any chance of getting it open?"

"I took the liberty of contacting the manufacturer, and they provided a universal code. Thought I'd wait for your go-ahead, though."

"Its proximity to the body makes it vital evidence. Open it up."

Cash carefully dialled in the code. The lock clicked, and he raised the lid. The cash tray was empty, but beneath it lay a single square of card. Using tweezers, Cash lifted it out, turning it over to reveal a faded photograph of a baby in an incubator.

"Premature newborn," Cash said. "Very poorly, by the looks of it."

Bone stared at the image, mind whirring. "Why would Fraser keep this locked up? He must have delivered hundreds of babies."

"Guilty secret, maybe? A dalliance resulting in a child? Or one he lost through negligence?"

Bone shook his head. "Can you date the photo?"

"I'll send it over to Digital. See what they can do." Cash returned the items to their bags. "I'll get copies sent over to Harper. See if our resident techno-wizard can uncover anything else."

"Good. And Frank… anytime, okay?"

Cash met his gaze, nodding. "In for a penny, eh?"

"Promise me you won't say that to her, ever," Bone said and shut the door behind him.

Out in the corridor, he stopped to take in a few lungfuls of air to try and clear the stench still lingering in his nostrils. He spotted Harper at the far end, firing coins into a drinks machine.

He crept up behind him. "Detective Constable Harper!"

Harper spun around, losing half a cup of vomit-coloured chicken soup. "God, sir. I just about…"

"Drank that? You can thank me after for saving your life. What are you still doing here?"

"When Mark and I visited the Methodist church this morning to interview the neighbours, a Mr Harker gave us the SD card of a night-vision camera he's got aimed out the back window of his house."

"What?"

"Nothing sinister, quite the opposite, in fact, but lucky for us. He thought there was a possibility his camera might've recorded something last night."

"Don't tell me, you've abandoned your beautiful fiancée and a warm, welcoming bed to go through hours of footage."

"That's the sum of it, sadly, yes."

"Found anything?"

"Ah, well." He stopped. "Come and see for yourself."

Harper glanced down at the dregs of powdery goo in the bottom of his polystyrene cup and deposited it in the bin. They took the stairs back to the incident room.

At Harper's desk, the young detective woke up the screen. "I rattled through the file on the SD card. These night-vision cameras are activated by movement. The timestamp top right tells you where we are in the course of the night."

He clicked the file, and a black-and-white view out of Harker's attic window appeared.

"You can see, the lens is fairly wide and captures Harker's rear garden at number seven, the Finnieston sisters' at five, and the edge of the Frasers'."

"Bit of an oddball thing to do, isn't it?" Bone pulled a face.

"Harker is a twitcher, and he was trying to capture barn owls hunting in his garden. The night light is invisible to birds, so it doesn't scare them, but the camera picks them up clear as day. If I move it a little farther, you'll see it wasn't a barn owl he caught on camera, though."

Bone moved closer to the screen.

"So this is one-fifty a.m., approximately forty minutes before the nine-nine-nine call came in."

The wooden gate of number seven swung open, and a shadowy figure emerged, paused, and went through a gap in the fence onto the Frasers' property.

"Did they look up there for a second?"

"Yes. Let me try again." Harper scrolled back, and the figure appeared at the gate. "Just about… there!" He hit the pause button, capturing the figure glancing up towards the camera.

"Is that some kind of mask covering the face?"

Harper tapped his keyboard, and the figure enlarged. He shifted the centre of the frame and magnified it, but the image over-pixelated. He reduced it slightly.

"I reckon that's a black ski mask with only their eyes peeking through."

"That's sinister." Bone recoiled.

"The night light bounces on the back of the retina. But yes, not a pleasant look at all."

"So what time is that?"

"The figure disappears through the Frasers' gate at exactly one forty-eight a.m."

"That's got to be our killer, hasn't it?"

"Too early for a postman, and a very weird route for the milkman to take," Harper said. "I've already sent this, along with the speed cam footage, over to Digital. Hopefully, they'll get back with some better imaging tomorrow."

"Could you send that out to the rest of the team, and once that comes back, possibly enhanced, wing a copy over to the super? He'll want to see this. I think he might be up for releasing this to the public to speed up the investigation. Let me broach that subject first, though."

"Of course."

Bone nodded. "Great work, Will."

"Thanks, sir, but this is the sort of stuff I love, so I'm in my element, really."

"You do realise that's possibly the saddest thing I've ever heard. Get your conscientious arse out of here this instant and stop showing up all of us useless old farts."

"Sir." Harper shut down his computer and grabbed his things.

"Seriously, though, Will. Next round of promotions, I'll be putting your name forward."

"No way?"

"Hold on, no, I'm joking. You're shite," Bone deadpanned. "Of course. You are so much more than a constable now. And to be honest, you'll be needing the extra cash for after that wedding when the midnight emergency nappy runs kick in."

"Babies? I don't think so. Not yet anyway."

"Oh aye, we'll see." Bone smiled.

"Thank you, sir. Wow. I wasn't expecting…" Harper paused. "You know what that means, though, don't you?"

"What?"

"I don't have to take any more shit from Mark."

"Are you kidding? We all have to take shit from him. That is something that never ends, regardless of rank."

"Night, sir," Harper said, and left.

With a final glance at the incident board, Bone turned off the lights and followed him out.

As he drove back to Alice's, he suddenly remembered McKinnon's message that morning.

"Ah, bugger."

He checked his watch and pondered whether it was too late to call in on him. But then, spotting an approaching lay-by, he swung the Saab in, and did a quick turnaround.

FOURTEEN

A few miles out of Kilwinnoch, Bone came to a row of dilapidated quarrymen's cottages that looked like they'd seen better days. He double-checked the address and squinted up at the tiny, decrepit flat above a boarded-up shop. The incessant roar of traffic along the main road was almost deafening, a constant assault on the senses.

"Christ, McKinnon," Bone muttered, and climbed the narrow, rickety stairs to the upper floor, each step groaning under his weight. "This better be important."

He rapped his knuckles against the peeling door, paint flakes drifting to the floor with the impact. For a long moment, there was no response. Just as Bone was about to knock again, the scrape of a lock turning sounded. The door creaked open, revealing a face that was almost unrecognisable.

Colin McKinnon, usually so polished and put together with his expensive suits and slick hair, seemed like a man on the brink of collapse. His eyes were bloodshot, his cheeks hollow and covered in patchy stubble. His once-crisp shirt hung off his frame, stained and creased.

Bone's initial irritation softened as he took in McKinnon's haggard appearance. "Christ almighty. You look like shit."

A flicker of the old McKinnon surfaced in those dull eyes. "Ever the charmer, DCI Bone. Come in. I have something to show you."

Bone followed him into the flat, ignoring the mess and stench of neglect. "You said that in your text. What's all this about, and why the invite to your house?"

McKinnon led him to a cluttered desk, where a laptop screen glowed dimly.

"I received an email earlier today," McKinnon said, his voice shaking slightly.

Bone leaned in, squinting at the screen. The message was short and chilling:

> *Public Enquiry Now for Kelly Dobson, and Katherine Fraser walks free unharmed.*

"What's this?"

"It's from the *Chronicle's* public email, where people can send us stories or tips. New emails are auto-sent to me."

"What about the sender's address?" Bone asked, his mind racing.

McKinnon shook his head. "It just says unknown."

"Any idea who this Kelly Dobson is?"

"No clue."

Bone eyed him sceptically. This uncharacteristic act of altruism from the usually cut-throat journalist set off alarm bells in his head.

"What are you planning to do with this?"

"I'm not planning on anything, but knowing the *Chronicle*, someone else might be following up on it."

"Come on, McKinnon. What's this really about?"

"Jesus Christ. It's about me handing this over to you as I saw Katherine Fraser's name there and thought it might be important," McKinnon snapped back. "It could be some sick hoax, though. That mailbox is inundated with crap like this all the time."

"Well, we'll need access to the *Chronicle's* mailbox and server."

"I'm not sure that'll do you any good. They have all sorts of sophisticated firewalls and encryption to ensure privacy, and if it's from a VPN, which is likely as it's from an anonymous source, I'd say your chances of tracing it are less than zero."

"We need to try."

"And then, of course, you have our beloved editor-in-chief who will not be too keen on letting the local constabulary rummage around in the newspaper's files and folders."

Bone slammed his fist on the desk. McKinnon jumped.

"That's withholding vital evidence! There's a woman's life in real danger here!"

McKinnon held up his hands. "I know. That's why I asked you to come over. Wish I hadn't bothered now."

"I'm not buying this. Why the sudden change of personality, McKinnon? What's your angle here?"

McKinnon exploded. "Fuck you, Bone. Not everything is a conspiracy. Maybe I'm just trying to do the right thing for once in my miserable life."

Bone let out a cynical laugh. "The right thing? That's rich, coming from a bottom-feeder like you. How many lives have you ruined with your trash reporting? How many times have you twisted the truth to suit your own agenda?"

McKinnon glared at him for a moment, his eyes filled with fury. But then his face cracked. He crumpled down into the chair, his head in his hands, and he sobbed. Bone stood there, shocked and embarrassed by the sudden display of emotion from his nemesis.

"What's happened to you, McKinnon?" Bone asked, his voice softening.

McKinnon looked up, his eyes red and puffy. "Nothing. This was a mistake. Just fuck off."

"It's clearly not nothing. Come on."

McKinnon took a few deep breaths. "Since the reservoir… Since that psycho bitch tried to drown me… I haven't been the same. The nightmares, the flashbacks, the constant feeling of dread… I'm losing my mind, Bone."

Bone moved to sit next to him, understanding dawning. "That's PTSD, Colin. And it will destroy you unless you face those demons head-on."

McKinnon shook his head. "I can't. I'm fucking terrified. I have these… these dark thoughts."

Bone leaned forward. "Go on. It's okay."

McKinnon swallowed hard. "About… about harming myself. Ending it all. I never wanted any of this. I can't live like this anymore."

Bone's eyes widened. "Jesus, McKinnon. That's bloody awful, but I know what you're going through. And believe me, it'll only get worse unless you face it and deal with it. You need to find a way to stop being scared of it."

McKinnon let out a shaky laugh. "Easier said than done."

Bone shrugged. "That's the joy of the bastarding thing. But it's necessary. You need professional help; counselling, therapy, medication… whatever it takes."

McKinnon scoffed. "And what, pour my heart out to some stranger? Let them pick apart my brain? No thanks."

Bone sighed. "I get it. I felt the same for a long time. Why should I let someone in here, when I don't even want to be in here?" He tapped the scar on his temple.

"But trust me, it helps. I've been going to this PTSD support group. It's full of people like us, people who have seen and experienced things that no one should have to. It makes a difference, talking to people who understand. I was scared out of my mind when I first went. Thought I might, I don't know, just totally lose it, or resent everyone else who was there because they were just like me. And I was like that a few times. But slowly, I could feel the fog starting to lift and the intensity of the fear, the anger, subside. They saved me, Colin. And they will save you, too, if you let them."

McKinnon was quiet for a long moment. "I don't know."

"Just think about it. And in the meantime, don't do anything stupid, all right? Even though it would fill my heart with unbridled joy if you did."

McKinnon glanced up, and Bone smiled.

"And if you feel like you might, call me. I really mean it, Colin."

McKinnon nodded, wiping at his eyes. "I never thought I'd see the day where DCI Duncan Headbanger Bone would be my personal therapist."

Bone chuckled. "Yeah, well, I never thought I'd see the day where I'd risk my own life to pull your sorry arse out of a sinking car. And let's not forget the mouth-to-mouth. You owe me big time, McKinnon."

McKinnon managed a weak smile. "I suppose I do. Thanks, Bone. For… for everything."

Bone stood. "God, I think this bromance might be worse than us tearing strips off each other." He made his way to the door. "Remember, I've been there and it will get better."

With that, he stepped out into the grimy stairwell, the door closing behind him with a resounding click. He exhaled, the memories of those darkest of times flooding back in rapid quick-fire images. In the Saab, he quickly pinged McKinnon's email to Gallacher and the team with a brief explanation. Then took the coward's way out and messaged Alice to tell her he had to head back to the cabin to deal with more problems with the roof. He needed to be surrounded by cold water to try and halt the runaway express train still careering through his skull.

FIFTEEN

On his way up to Loch Gillan, Gallacher rang him back, so by the time he got there, his brain was well and truly fried. But as he drove into the village, the fading light of dusk still lingering in the sky, the burden of the investigation slowly slipped from his shoulders. The serenity of the mountains beyond offered a momentary escape from the dark depths of the investigation. Pulling up alongside his cabin, he noticed the front door was wide open. He climbed out.

"Hello?" He approached the entrance, the door swinging back and forth in the breeze. He was about to step inside when a figure leapt from the cabin roof and landed directly in front of him. Instinctively, Bone threw a punch to defend himself, but the figure swerved, and his fist sailed past, failing to connect.

"Whoa, Duncan!" The man staggered back before Bone threw another.

"Junior?" Bone said in surprise. "What the hell are you doing?"

Junior, the village 'character', stood before him, his arms raised in defence. "What the fuck do you think? Gordon sent me over to fix your arsing roof. That's some thanks right there."

"Jesus, sorry, mate. You startled me. You shouldn't just jump down right in front of a police officer like that. You're asking for it."

"Oh, so no thanks whatsoever, and I deserve a kicking now as well?" Junior huffed.

"Well, thanks very much. It was chaos this morning."

"Lucky for you, the rain cleared. Three or four of the bastarding tiles have blown off. And of course, from the most fucking awkward part of yer roof. Christ knows where they are now. You were heading for a flooding."

"Let me know how much I…" He spotted Junior's attire. "What's with the lederhosen?"

"All my clothes are in the wash, and this was all I could find in the back of my cupboard."

Bone raised an eyebrow. "Daft question possibly, but why lederhosen?"

Junior shrugged, a bewildered expression on his face. "No idea, mate."

Shaking his head, Bone offered Junior a drink, but he clambered back onto the roof like a nimble spider and resumed his repairs. Moments later, his head popped over the guttering.

"I've remembered. I won a fell run in Munich a few years back. The trooosers were the second prize, but the runner-up dinnae want them."

"Can't imagine why not. Height of fashion in Kilwinnoch now."

"You takin' the piss?"

"No, no. You're a trendsetter, Junior."

"Fuckin' wanker."

Bone sniggered. "So what was the first prize, then?"

"As much beer as I could drink. The only reason I entered."

"Emptied the country of its entire supply, no doubt," Bone said.

"I gave it my best shot." Junior smiled, and disappeared again.

Inside the cabin, Bone rubbed at his throbbing temples, the migraine intensifying with each hammer strike from above.

Desperate for relief, Bone quickly changed into his swim gear and headed down the path to the beach. The cold waters of the loch beckoned, promising a temporary escape from his pain. The water was calm, a sheet of glass stretching out to the horizon line and the distant, faint lights of Balhuish village.

He dropped his towel and waded in, the icy waters shocking his system as he swam out across the bay. With each powerful stroke, the tension and anguish slowly melted away, replaced by a sense of clarity and focus.

He swam until his muscles ached and his lungs burned, pushing himself to the brink of exhaustion. Finally, he rolled onto his back, floating peacefully. He gazed up at the sun's final flourish painting the sky in a breathtaking array of deep oranges and pinks.

But his meditative moment was short-lived; a sharp whistle pierced the tranquil air. Bone turned in the water to see Junior waving from the shore.

"Your phone!" he shouted.

With a resigned sigh, Bone swam back to shore. He waded out of the water, but Junior was nowhere to be seen. He scanned the beach.

The red-haired boy appeared at the far side. The same child who had been haunting his dreams for weeks. The boy raised his arms and beckoned Bone. Bone resisted. But flames engulfed the boy's hands and quickly spread up his arms. The boy smiled and beckoned again.

Panic surged through Bone's chest. "No!"

He sprinted across the pebbles, his feet slipping and sliding, his heart hammering against his ribs. He neared the spot and lunged, desperately trying to grab the boy. But when his hands made contact, the fiery figure transformed, and Bone rammed straight into Junior.

The impact knocked them both to the ground, sand and stones flying in all directions. They lay still for a moment, tangled. Bone's brain was still locked in confusion.

Junior's loud guffaw broke the silence. "Fuck sake, Duncan. You are sending some seriously mixed messages here. First, you want to kick the fuck out of me, and now you're trying to get ma lederhosen aff. Make up your fuckin' mind, mate."

They disentangled, and Bone stumbled to his feet. "I'm so sorry… I thought… Never mind." He shook his head, trying to clear the disturbing vision from his mind.

"I was just trying to tell you, yer phone rang three times. Thought it might be important."

"Thanks," Bone said sheepishly. "Well?"

"Well, what?" Junior shrugged.

"My phone?"

"Oh, I dinnae want to touch it, you know, thought maybe the polis would think I'd stolen it."

"How would they know it wasn't me?"

"Oh, don't give me that. You guys can trace anything, can't you?" Junior asked nervously and glanced upwards, as though scanning for a spy drone.

"Who do you think we are, Mission Impossible? We're so strapped for cash, I'm still waiting on a stapler I requested eight months ago."

"Ach, okay. It's up in the cabin." Junior sighed, his relief tangible.

Shivering and disorientated, his head still pounding, Bone returned to the cabin and checked his calls. Three from Alice. He hesitated a moment and then rang.

"Everything okay?" he asked when she answered.

"Yes, why?"

"You rang me three times?"

"Not me."

"Well, it's your number."

"That's weird."

"Pocket dialled?"

"No, my phone's by the TV…" She paused. "Hold on," Alice said, and a second later, the handset clacked.

"Hi, Dad," Michael picked up.

"Ah, it was you who called me?"

"Yup. I just wanted to say that I'm on level five of *Kill Zone 3*."

"Five? How the hell did you do that?"

"I'm a bloody genius."

Alice reprimanded Michael in the background.

"Oops, I swore," Michael whispered.

"Well, I'll be right on your tail when…"

"You okay, Dad?"

"I've just been for a swim and I need a hot shower."

"Are you coming home tomorrow?"

"Absolutely, and now you're on level five, well, the gauntlet is down, my friend, and you will pay the bloody price."

Michael giggled. "Dad said it as well!" he called back to his mum.

The handset clacked again, and Alice returned.

"Sorry about that. You okay?"

"Aye, just a bit cold. Nice to speak to him."

"He misses you, Duncan. We both do."

"I know. I'll sort things out here and I'll be back tomorrow night."

"Promise?"

"One hundred percent. I've run out of toilet paper, so…"

"You don't sound so great."

"No, I'm just freezing my nuts off."

"Charming. Okay, I'll let you go. See you tomorrow," Alice said with a hint of a warning.

"Missing you both, too."

"Finally!" Alice sighed and hung up.

After a long shower, Bone poured himself a whisky and collapsed into a chair, seeking solace in the soulful voice of Billie Holiday soaring gently from his old Dansette record player. He closed his eyes, willing the haunting image of the boy to fade from his mind.

Suddenly, the boy's face appeared before him, whispering a chilling, "Boom!"

Bone lurched back, toppling from the chair, spilling his whisky and crashing into the Dansette. The record needle screeched across the turntable.

"Fuck!"

He scrambled to his feet and went through to the bedroom. Tucked away in the farthest corner of a cluttered cupboard, hidden behind a jumble of boxes and old case files, was a locked cabinet. Bone fished the key out of his pocket and opened it, revealing a single, bulging file.

With a heavy sigh, he retrieved the file, carried it back to the living room, and placed it down on the table. He poured himself a large whisky, the amber liquid sloshing against the glass before righting, and he settled in his chair again. The label on the file stared back at him.

The Peekaboo Murders.

With a heavy sigh, he took another swig of whisky and opened it up.

As he flipped the first page, he flinched, memories of the attack flooding back with visceral clarity; the searing heat of the explosion, the shrapnel tearing into his flesh, the agonizing pain that had engulfed his entire existence.

He absently rubbed the scar on his temple, the physical remnants of the devastation Peekaboo had wrought on his life and his family. He shook his head and focused on the file, sifting through the papers until a small, black-and-white borderless photograph fluttered to the desk.

He picked it up, his brow furrowing. It was a grainy family portrait of Peekaboo and his parents lined up in a ramshackle room. Strange objects hung on the walls. Skinned animals and birds of various shapes and sizes dangled by their necks from low rafters.

Bone studied the boy who would become a killer, but there was no resemblance. His apparition was not Peekaboo. He held the photo closer to the lamp and noticed that the left edge was slightly crooked. He ran his finger along it. It felt rough compared with the others. It was as though a section had been carefully torn off. In the bottom corner, there was what looked like a shoe and a trouser leg. Someone else was present in the picture.

"Who is that?" He racked his brain, thinking through the Meiklejohns' dysfunctional psychotic family tree, but couldn't remember any other relatives or siblings.

"Ah, damn you to hell, Meiklejohn!" He flicked the photo back between the pages and slammed the file shut. "Enough!"

His migraine was worsening by the second. He stumbled into the bathroom and popped a couple of co-codamol, his last line of defence. Quickly undressing, he switched off the bedroom light, collapsed on top of the bed, and with a deep, long sigh, he closed his eyes and was out cold in seconds, snoring so loudly the vibrations rattled the glass by his bed.

SIXTEEN

The ambulance pulled up outside Flat 14B, wheels crunching on debris strewn across the pot-holed car park of the crumbling Northfield Estate, Kilwinnoch's low-rent, low-life cesspit.

Paramedic Rob McNeil, a veteran on the frontline of emergency services, wearily climbed out of the cab. Another hoax call, the third one this shift, and the umpteenth one this month.

He stared up at the dim glow of light flickering behind the torn bedsheet in the flat's filthy window and scowled. Just another smackhead getting their late-night kicks.

"Maybe we should go up and give the wee shite a talking to," his colleague, Dave Souter, said, joining him at the bottom of the urine-reeking concrete stairwell.

"And catch something? Nah, no' worth it." McNeil checked his watch—two forty eight a.m. "Let's get back and grab a coffee. We're done in ten."

Starting up the engine, Souter flicked on the radio, filling the cab with a blast of techno. McNeil switched it off.

"Fancy some tunes, no?" Souter asked.

"Are you bloody serious?" McNeil scowled. He glanced over at his colleague. "Sorry, buddy. It's just been one fuck of a day."

"Isn't it always one fuck of a day?"

"Is it just me, or is this job just getting pretty bloody intolerable?" McNeil exhaled.

"No, that's just you. Come on, let's go home." Souter started up the ambulance and accelerated out of the estate.

Usually, the short distance back to base took five minutes max, but tonight, roadworks on the Glasgow Road forced a detour down an unlit backroad. The ambulance cruised through the darkness, high beams carving a tunnel through the night.

McNeil leaned back, eyes fixed on the road ahead, willing his mind to stay awake. A second roadworks forced them to a stop again.

"Bloody hell. As if it's no' late enough," McNeil complained. He peered through the window into the darkness, and the familiar outline of a derelict barn appeared. A van that had been tailgating them for some distance revved its engine and tore round them, running the red light and disappearing into the night.

"Fuck's sake, idiot." Souter shook a fist at the windscreen.

A few minutes later, the red light still refused to change.

Souter tapped the steering wheel. "Oh, I can't be bothered with this. If that's gas works shit, then there's probably half a dozen of these bloody things ahead. I'm going to turn back and try going round the top of the town."

MacNeil sighed. "Listen, mate, I'm probably less than a couple of miles from my house. Seems bloody stupid going all the way back to the station when I'm nearly home. I'm just going to walk it from here."

Souter frowned. "You sure? It's a dark stretch, and it's late. And there are twats like that numpty careering about."

McNeil waved off his concern. "I know it like the back of my hand. And I need to clear my head before I tackle domestics. No worries." He grinned. "And if I do get clobbered by a car, I'll attend to myself, coz I'll be dead before a bloody ambulance arrives, what with all these cuts."

Souter snorted. "Ain't that the truth? All right then, mate. But watch yourself, okay? I'll sign you out. See you tomorrow."

"Cheers, and not if I see you first, arsehole."

With a wide grin, McNeil grabbed his bag and hopped out of the rig, giving his colleague a playful middle finger as the ambulance pulled away.

He set off down the unlit lane, hands jammed in his pockets, breathing in the cold night air. It had been a brutal day, one harrowing call after another. He needed this walk, this solitude, to decompress. He negotiated the roadworks and took a right.

Halfway home, a flashing light in the distance caught his eye. He peered into the darkness. The van that had passed earlier was nose-first in a ditch, hazards pulsing, the back doors gaping open.

Shit. An accident.

His paramedic instincts kicked into gear.

He sprinted over, adrenaline surging.

"Hello? Ambulance service!" He dashed around to the driver's door and peered inside. Empty. The keys dangled from the ignition, engine still running.

What the hell?

He did a quick sweep of the area, senses on high alert.

"Is anyone there? Are you hurt?"

Nothing but the whisper of the wind in the trees answered him.

Pulse quickening, he circled back to the open rear doors. A pungent chemical smell hit him, sharp and sickly sweet. Petrol. A red jerry can lay on its side, contents glugging onto the tarmac.

A cold shiver ran down his spine. Something wasn't right. He reached for his radio hooked on his jacket but then realised he'd left it on the dash of the ambulance.

The crunch of footsteps sounded behind him. He spun around.

A figure lunged from the shadows, arm raised, ski mask obscuring their face.

Before Rob could react, something struck him hard on the side of the head. His world went black.

He came to slowly, the rumble of the engine and the sway of the van penetrating his foggy mind. A searing pain shot back and forth inside his skull. He was lying on cold metal, wrists and ankles bound tight, a gag stuffed in his mouth. Total darkness pressed in on him.

The air was thick with the stench of petrol, cloying and suffocating. He struggled weakly against his bindings, trying to yell for help, but the gag muffled his cries. Blood trickled into his eyes from the gash on his forehead.

Minutes passed. He drifted in and out of consciousness, a concussion making it hard to keep his thoughts straight. The sickly smell of petrol saturated the space around him.

Eventually, the van stopped. Silence.

He tried to cry out but choked instead, the gag cutting into the corners of his mouth. Suddenly, smoke filled his nostrils, acrid and smothering. Fumes seared his throat and lungs.

He desperately scraped at the hot, unyielding metal beneath him. But his fight for life seemed futile. This couldn't be happening. Not like this. Not to him.

As the smoke thickened and the heat intensified, a surge of adrenaline coursed through McNeil's battered body. With a desperate burst of strength, he kicked out wildly at the van's rear doors.

Once, twice, three times. Each impact sending shockwaves of pain through his bound legs. On the fourth kick, he felt something give. The door creaked, then flew open with a metallic groan.

Cool night air rushed in, momentarily clearing his head. Rob rolled out onto the hard ground, his bound limbs making the fall awkward and painful. Intense heat surged at his back as he desperately crawled away from the inferno, his cheek scraping against rough asphalt.

A deafening boom shattered the night. The van exploded. The force of the blast threw him forward, and a searing pain lanced across his back. He tried to push himself farther away, his vision swimming. The world around him blurred and distorted, trees and shadows melting into a surreal landscape.

McNeil's body convulsed uncontrollably, his muscles seizing as if gripped by an invisible force. Consciousness slipped away, and his last, fleeting thought was of the bitter irony — after all those false alarms, he now found himself in desperate need of the very help he'd so often provided to others.

Then, everything went black.

SEVENTEEN

Bone's phone woke him with an unwelcome start. "Jesus Christ!" He fumbled under the pile of garments abandoned by his bedside and snatched it up.

"DCI Bone?" a voice asked.

"Who's this?"

"It's Fire Chief Gregor Tennant. Sorry to call so late… or early, I suppose."

"What's this about, Chief?"

"One of the crew mentioned that a metal funnel was recovered from the scene."

"And?" Bone said, still irritated at being woken.

"That set alarm bells ringing."

"Why's that?" He stifled a yawn.

"Nine years ago, when I worked at Selkirk Fire Station, there were a series of arson attacks. Three fires in six months, and all with a very similar MO."

Bone sat up, suddenly alert. "Go on."

"The arsonist was some animal rights extremist. Scott Scanlon. Early thirties, bit of a loner. He targeted people he saw as 'animal torturers'—doctors, researchers, pharmaceutical companies. Anyone involved in animal testing."

"What's similar about the MO?"

"Paraphernalia that was recovered at the scene of the fires included a funnel and hose contraption and gallons of petrol accelerant."

Bone's voice tightened. "Did he kill anyone?"

"No, the investigators thought he might have bottled it, but his intention was clear, and it looks as though he's finally insane enough to do it. Scanlon is a sick bastard. When the detectives grilled him, he ranted about cleansing the world of evil. As I said, a total headbanger."

Bone frowned. "Why has it taken you so long to tell me this?"

"I didn't know about the funnel until last night when I spoke to one of the crew. I tried to dismiss my worries, knowing the arsonist was still serving his stretch in prison. But something didn't sit right. So, just to put my mind at rest, I called a former colleague in Jedburgh. We'd attended the fires together."

"And?"

"He told me Scanlon had been released early. Good behaviour, if you can believe it. Out, after serving just eight years of a ten-year sentence for multiple arson attacks and attempted murder. Absolutely shocking. The security guard I pulled from one of his fires was lucky to survive."

Bone cursed under his breath. "So, is Scanlon still a resident of Jedburgh?"

"I've no idea, and my colleague had no clue either. You should speak to the governor at Selkirk Prison. They'll have his records, psychological assessments, release plans, the lot. Might give you an idea of where he's headed or what he's planning."

"Right. Thanks for the tip, Chief. This could be a major lead."

"Just staying up half the night, doing my job as usual," Tennant joked. "Hope you catch the bastard. And if it is him…"

"Yeah?"

"Make sure justice is served. Properly. Men like that don't change. They just get better at hiding."

Bone hung up and called Walker. It was going to be another long day.

EIGHTEEN

Arriving at the incident room, Bone was surprised to find Baxter busy at her desk. He checked his watch.

"Jesus, Sheila. I'm supposed to be the insomniac here. It's not even seven o'clock."

"I'm a good sleeper, sir. Well, I was until I ended up married to a middle-aged old fart whose snoring could compete with North Sea oil field test drilling. And then I'm just lying there going slowly insane, and before I know it, I'm back here staring at case reports and that surprised look on that face of yours, sir." She stopped for a breath. "But I have filled the percolator, so there is that."

Bone poured a coffee and pulled a chair over. "Aside from the test drilling, are you two okay?"

"Oh aye, rattling along. In more ways than one. He's always at me to retire and up sticks to some back of beyond gîte in Brittany or somewhere like that. But I know my face might not say it most of the time, but I actually love what I'm doing. But for God's sake, don't tell Mark that."

"Well, for want of a better expression, we'd be totally fucked without you, Sheila. We'd have been shut down, mothballed, bulldozed out of the way for admin space years ago."

Baxter smiled. "No, don't worry. He can bugger off to his gîte. I'm happy here. And I might even get some bloody sleep, if I'm lucky. Though now that we've added a hostage situation to the case, I don't think that'll be happening anytime soon."

"Speak of the devil. Anything on the arsonist?" Bone nodded to her monitor.

"Well, yes, very interesting stuff, as it happens. But just in case you haven't seen it yet, the initial Fire Investigator's report came through."

"And?"

"Fire started in the living room, in close proximity to the victim. Confirmed use of petrol as an accelerant. Fire quickly spread throughout the property, assisted by the presence of more accelerant.

"Okay. So now we have it confirmed. So what about this pyromaniac?"

"Mr Scott Scanlon, a forty-two-year-old male, registered address Nineteen Causeway Road, Jedburgh, was convicted of multiple arson attacks over a period of six months, eight years ago.

"He had previous convictions for two similar offences when he was a teenager, but his sentence was reduced as he pleaded guilty and was psychologically assessed as having a pyro fixation. Basically, he's a fire-starting nutcase. There were no fatalities, thankfully. But his third attack resulted in a security guard being badly burnt in the fire."

"Anything tangible connecting him to our fires here?" Bone asked.

"I was getting to that. He was a member of a couple of animal activist groups known to the Counter Terrorism unit for extreme behaviour and plotting to attack medical establishments, companies, properties, and individuals connected in any way, shape, or form to animal testing.

"Intelligence linked him to a specific organisation that they were monitoring, SAT or Stop Animal Torture. But his notes also contain a wide range of weird and wonderful conspiracy theories that he raved on about during his cross-examination. His targets included the scientific head of a pharmaceutical lab; a drug storage unit, that's where the security guard was burnt; and the home of a retired professor of medicine who had been a vocal supporter of animal rights testing."

"Fraser fits the MO," Bone said.

"At the storage unit, fire investigators and forensic teams discovered three empty fifty-litre drums of petrol. All of the properties had been doused with the fuel, using it as an accelerant to start the fires. So yes, the attacks are similar. When he was finally caught and questioned, that's when he started spouting diatribe about avenging the death of all of the murdered animals.

"There's an even more significant connection, though, with Kilwinnoch itself, or Lennoxfield, to be more precise. His brother, Craig Scanlan, resides at Lennoxfield Residential Care Unit."

"An old folks' home?"

"A palliative care unit for the terminally ill."

"Good God!" Bone exclaimed. "There's our link. We need to find this guy ASAP. Have officers checked in on his brother to see if he's been in contact?"

"I only spotted this family link half an hour ago, but I can certainly organise."

"What about this SAT? Are they still active?"

"Ah yes, that's the fly in the ointment."

"There's usually at least one."

"I just received an email from Counter Terrorism, who confirmed that the group is no longer active."

"You did all of that this morning?"

"Yes, I was surprised someone at Counter Terrorism answered the phone."

"Maybe they sleep with a walrus as well?"

Baxter chuckled and continued, "Following Scanlon's attacks and his affiliation going public, two of the leaders were subsequently arrested and convicted of multiple break-ins, criminal damage, threatening behaviour, you name it. So that was the end of SAT. But they did say there's nothing stopping individuals from taking matters into their own hands, and that despite Scanlon's reprogramming, as they called it, while in prison, he may still be capable of more attacks."

"And this Kelly Dobson person mentioned in McKinnon's email?"

"I checked to see if there was any mention of a Kelly Dobson in Scanlon's records, maybe a fellow-arrested animal rights campaigner, but I couldn't find any link, so far."

Their conversation was interrupted when the door swung open and Walker entered.

Bone turned. "Bloody hell. Not you as well! Now don't be thinking you'll all be getting any overtime out of the tight sphincters at head office if that's what you're after." Bone smiled.

"Morning, all," Walker said. "I got your message last night. Do you think the arsonist Scanlon character is behind the cryptic email sent to McKinnon?"

"A no-brainer when you look at his profile. But the email is odd and very specific. Not some fanatical animal rights war cry, as we would expect from his radicalised past."

"Have you requested a trace?"

"It's on the *Chronicle* server, so by the time we get a warrant, or should I say, *if* we get a warrant, and Digital tries to crack into their security, our firestarter could have killed half a dozen more people. And I think the killer knows that."

"So, what's got into McKinnon then, all this human kindness all of a sudden?"

"That's what I was wondering, too," Baxter agreed.

"Long and sorry story." Bone rolled his eyes.

Walker approached her desk and unzipped her anorak.

"I wouldn't bother taking that off," Bone said, stopping her. "We need to get over to Lennoxfield Residential Care Unit as soon as possible."

"What's going on?"

"I'll fill you in on the way."

"I'll update the incident board, sir," Baxter said.

Bone glanced over at the myriad of lines, arrows, headers, and photos.

"Good God! The minute I'm off duty, you get up to all sorts, don't you, Sheila?" He went over for a quick peek. He scratched his head. "This case is only hours old, and look at this tangled, bloody web." He tapped the board. "Anything on Fraser's boss, this Baird character?"

"Senior manager at the hospital for twelve years. Deals with a lot of sharp-end stuff related to funding, shortages, and so on. As a result, he's quite a public figure. The hospital seems to send him out every time there's a crisis."

"That's every other day, then?" Walker quipped.

"But no skeletons as far as I can see… yet, no pun intended."

"Okay. Make sure the sleeping beauties are up to speed with this when they get in, Sheila."

"Sir," Baxter said, adding another header to the mind map.

"Right. Let's go."

Walker dashed over to the percolator, poured a shot into a mug, and downed it in one.

"Okay, I'm refuelled." She followed him out.

***

In the foyer, Desk Sergeant Brody knelt by an elderly, flushed-faced woman sitting at the side. She breathed heavily between sips from a cup of water.

"Ah, DCI Bone," Brody called over and gave Bone a quick, furtive wink. "This lady would like to speak to you." He turned back to her. "You have some information regarding the fires, is that correct?"

"Yes," the woman panted. "I couldn't wait any longer." She peered out the front door. "But I'm beginning to regret coming down. That shower out there almost knocked me off my bloody feet. Then some rude young woman practically chased me up the steps."

"I'm so sorry about that," Bone said, and he sat next to her. "Yes, the press are a bloody nuisance. Just take your time and let yourself recover. I'm DCI Bone, and this is my colleague, DI Walker." He looked back at Brody. "Can you go and sort that lot out down there? Just let them know that if they don't behave themselves, then we'll move them to the end of the street. Or better still, we'll lock them all up and throw away the bloody key." He smiled at the woman. "What's your name, ma'am?"

"I'm Mrs Conroy, Helen. I live opposite the Frasers' house." She exhaled. "What a terrible state of affairs." She sniffed.

"Okay, so you told our desk sergeant that you had some information?" Bone continued.

"Yes. I know who started the fire."

Bone glanced up at Walker.

"What?"

"But I'm…"

"Just take your time. It's okay." He put his hand on her arm.

"I'm just a little afraid to point fingers, but I know exactly who it was, and to be honest, I'm not surprised one bit."

"Right. I think we should talk about this in private. Are you okay to stand?"

She handed Bone her water, and he took her arm and helped her up.

"Is it possible to speak to your colleague here? DI Walker, is it?"

"Of course. No problem at all," Bone said.

"Call me Rhona," Walker said, swapping places with Bone, nudging him playfully out of the way. She walked the distraught woman slowly through the security barrier.

"I'll follow up on the other thing," Bone said.

Walker nodded and continued through.

***

Sergeant Brody was halfway down the steps hollering at a sea of agitated, animated journalists, camera lenses, and voice recorders crowding the gate.

Bone walked out onto the steps of Kilwinnoch Police Station, joining Sergeant Brody, who was struggling to keep the press clear of the entrance.

"If you lot don't move back, I'll order the riot squad to come and disperse you with water cannons and pepper spray!" Brody shouted, his face turning a shade of red that clashed horribly with his uniform.

As soon as the press spotted Bone, the frenzy intensified. They pushed and shoved, hurling questions about the fire. Was it an accident or deliberate? Any suspects?

Bone scanned the sea of faces for McKinnon, but the weasel was nowhere to be seen.

With a bellowing "Oi!", Bone quieted the rabble. "This investigation is in its early stages," he said, his voice stern. "Detective Superintendent Gallacher briefed you yesterday. We have no more to add at this stage. We ask that you respect the privacy of those affected. When we have more information, we will update you."

"Can you confirm if there are any suspects?" a reporter shouted from the back.

Bone sighed, pinching the bridge of his nose. "As I said, it's early days. We're following several lines of enquiry, but we can't comment on specifics at this time."

Another journalist piped up, "What about the cause of the fire? Accident or arson?"

"That's what we're working to determine," Bone said, his patience wearing thin. "Now, I must ask you all to clear the entrance and return to the street. You're obstructing access to the station, and we have work to do."

The reporters shouted more questions, their voices blending into a cacophony of noise. Bone raised his hands, his exasperation evident.

"Move back to the street and keep the entrance clear, or I'll have you all removed. Do I make myself clear?"

A grumble of discontent rippled through the crowd, but they finally dispersed, slowly backing away from the gate.

Bone turned to go back inside, but a young woman in a beanie hat and a long hippie skirt shouldered her way through the front of the pack, and through the gate, her eyes gleaming with a mix of curiosity and something more unsettling. She thrust a recorder towards Bone's face.

"DCI Bone, how does it feel to be investigating another fire, especially after your own traumatic, life-changing experience?"

"Where do you think you're going?" Bone asked, incredulous. "Did you not hear what I just said?"

The woman stepped back across the threshold, arms raised in faux submission.

"That's it. Off you go." Bone waved her away like an irritating midge. He carried on up the steps.

But she continued to follow.

"I mean," the journalist resumed her cross-examination, "it must be triggering for you, right? All those memories, those emotions..." She let the words hang, a smile flirting with the corners of her mouth.

Bone's blood pressure rose, his fingers itching to snatch that bloody recorder and introduce it to the nearest bin.

"So, you're saying this isn't pushing any buttons for you, stirring up any old traumas?" the journalist persisted.

Bone took a step forward, using every inch of his imposing frame. "The only button being pushed is the one marked 'Patience', and you're testing it to its bloody breaking point."

Brody moved back into his peripheral vision, ready to intervene. But Bone held up a hand, stopping the sergeant in his tracks. He had this under control. For now.

"Are you?" the journalist continued.

"Am I what?"

"At breaking point, again? I heard that happens to you a lot."

"Right, that's enough. Who the hell are you? What rag sent you down here to waste my fucking time?"

"Carrie Simpson, Social Affairs Reporter, *Kilwinnoch Chronicle*."

"I should have guessed. So, you're McKinnon's replacement?"

"He's off with stress. I'm covering for him."

"Do you make a habit of telling all and sundry confidential medical information about your colleague? Oh yes, I forgot that you have no soul."

"After what happened at the loch, when he nearly drowned," she continued, as though she hadn't heard a word he'd said.

"How long do I have to suffer your presence, then?" Bone asked.

"I'm contracted for six months." She looked him up and down. "Hell of a thing you did, saving McKinnon's life. Did that trigger your PTSD as well?"

"Get your hippie arse back down those stairs or I'll have you arrested for public nuisance."

She held up her hands again in mock surrender, then retreated out of the gate.

Bone about-turned and marched back into the station. He needed a few minutes to calm down before he did something he'd possibly regret.

NINETEEN

Once he'd negotiated his Saab through the throng of journalists by the gate, and resisted ploughing straight into them, Bone drove over to the end-of-life unit on the leafy outskirts of Lennoxfield.

He rang the buzzer, and a nurse opened the front door.

"Detective Chief Inspector Bone, Kilwinnoch Police Station, here to see Mr Craig Scanlon." He held up his lanyard.

"Come in, Inspector. I'll fetch the manager for you." The nurse ushered him inside.

Bone followed her through a tidy, brightly lit foyer, the lingering scent of disinfectant hanging in the air. She stopped just beyond the reception desk and knocked on an adjacent door before poking her head in.

"Inspector Bone from..." The nurse looked around. "Oh, she's not here." Checking her watch, she smiled. "Ah, coffee time. This way, sir."

They continued down the corridor, passing an open double door. Bone peered in, spotting a few residents propped up in wheelchairs by a set of bi-fold doors that stretched the width of the room, offering a view of the well-tended garden. Two frail, elderly men sat side by side, strapped into oxygen masks, their breaths rasping in the quiet.

At the end of the hall, they descended a staircase to the basement, emerging into a snug, windowless kitchen.

"Here she is." The nurse nodded to a middle-aged woman in a technicolour floral dress.

"I knew you'd be in here," the nurse teased as they approached the manager, who was just about to pop an entire mini muffin into her mouth.

She turned, eyes wide with surprise.

"Caught me." She grinned and lowered the muffin discreetly. "And who's this?"

"Detective Chief Inspector Bone from Kilwinnoch Police Station," the nurse said, introducing him.

"Come to arrest me, have you?" the manager joked, her eyes twinkling.

Bone smiled politely. "Actually, I'm here about one of your patients, Craig Scanlon."

The manager's expression sobered. "Ah, yes, sorry. It's been a tough morning, and it's only just started. Can I get you a coffee, Chief Inspector?"

"No, thanks. I'm fine."

"Or a muffin? They're homemade," she tempted. "My go-to when things get tough, which, as you can see, is more frequent than I'd like." She giggled.

Bone shook his head. "I'll have to pass, but thanks."

"Your loss," the manager said with a wink.

As they sat at a nearby table, the nurse excused herself, leaving the pair of them to talk.

"Craig was admitted just over three months ago," the manager began. "Leukaemia, stage three. Nasty bugger, that one. Pardon my French, but cancer doesn't deserve polite words."

Bone nodded sympathetically. "It got my dad in the end."

"I'm so sorry for your loss, Inspector."

"No, it's fine. It was a good few years ago now, and it was self-inflicted mostly. He was a two-pack-a-day man, with an overenthusiastic liking for whisky."

"Ah yes, the cancer sticks, or as we call them here, nails in the coffin. But whatever the background, lifestyle, or cause of a patient's illness, we do our best to make sure our residents here are loved and can live out their last days with dignity and as pain-free as possible."

"The reason for my visit," Bone said, steering the conversation back on track, "is that we've learned Mr Scanlon's brother, Scott Scanlon, failed to turn up for his parole meeting in Selkirk."

The manager's brows shot up. "Parole?"

"He served eight years for multiple arson offenses and attempted murder."

A corner of the manager's muffin fell from her fingers on to the floor. "Good Lord. I had no idea." She shook her head. "Craig isn't here."

"What?"

"Scott came to collect his brother a few days ago when Craig decided to discharge himself. Against the strongest of medical advice, I might add."

Bone leaned forward. "What day was that, exactly?"

"Let me think… Monday, I believe. He'd called us a couple of days prior, then came to support his brother's wishes that he be cared for at home. Scott assured us that he'd be looking after Craig." She sighed. "We were all shocked, concerned even. Craig is gravely ill, and his decision came out of the blue. Before that, he seemed calm, content, and happy. We warned his brother about the level of care required. Feeding, cleaning, medication, the works, but they were determined to go."

"And then they left for Scott Scanlon's house?"

"Yes. We sent a nurse and auxiliary along with some of the essential equipment and medicines Craig would need and to help them set up correctly, but there were complications."

"How so?"

"He's here today, one of the nurses, if you'd like to hear it firsthand."

"Yes, please. And I'll need that address."

"Of course, aye." She stopped. "Oh God, Craig's brother doesn't have anything to do with that terrible fire the other night, does he? I saw the news footage. My God. Those poor doctors."

"We just need to speak to them both."

"Right… er…" She swept a stray lock of hair away from her eyes and exhaled. "I'll fetch you that address, then."

The manager reluctantly dropped the rest of her muffin in the bin and led Bone back upstairs. Halfway along the corridor, she stopped next to a carer who knelt by an elderly woman in a wheelchair. "Oh, Martin, this is DCI Bone from Kilwinnoch Police Station. He has some questions about Craig Scanlon."

Martin, a young man with kind eyes, looked surprised but readily agreed. "Of course. What would you like to know?"

They walked a little farther along the corridor, out of the residents' earshot.

As Bone repeated his inquiries, Martin's face fell.

"It's true. I went with them to the house. But when we got there, the brother refused to let us in. Wouldn't say why. I tried to reason with him, but he was difficult. To be honest, the whole thing has been bothering me."

"Thank you, Martin. This has been really helpful," Bone said, and turned back to the manager. "If I could get that address, I'll let you get on."

"This way, Inspector." She took Bone to her office, and after a moment or two on her computer, she scribbled on a Post-it.

"That's where we dropped them," she said.

Bone studied the address. "Thanks."

"I hope everything is okay. Craig is a kind soul. I hate to think of him suffering in any way."

With a grateful nod, Bone rushed back to the Saab and called Harper.

The number rang out.

"Come on, Will. Pick up." He tried again.

The line clacked.

"Will!"

"Good morning, sir."

"Listen. Have you left for work yet?"

"Yes, on my way now. Why, am I late or something?"

"You need to turn round and go back to St Mungo's Terrace."

"Where?"

"St Mungo's Terrace, Corstorphine."

"That's the next street from my house. What's going on?"

"Just turn around, and I'll explain while you drive back. Do you still have the night-cam footage on your phone?

"Yes."

"Okay. Send that over to Rhona. I'll wait."

"On it now. Give me a sec to get off the motorway."

Bone put his phone on speaker and reversed out of the car park.

TWENTY

Walker ushered Mrs Conroy into the counselling room, her hand hovering protectively at her elbow.

"Let's get you settled here, Mrs Conroy," Walker said, her voice gentle. She eased the old woman slowly onto one of the worn armchairs. "Now, I think you need a cuppa with a wee bit of sugar to help steady your nerves. How does that sound?"

Mrs Conroy nodded, sinking farther into the overstuffed armchair. "Aye, that would be lovely. Two sugars, if you don't mind."

Walker busied herself with the kettle, keeping one eye on the trembling woman. The horror of the fire, the loss of her neighbours, the media circus—it was a lot for anyone to handle, let alone a respectable pensioner such as yourself."

She placed the steaming mug in Mrs Conroy's hands, watching as the elderly woman took a tentative sip. A bit of colour seeped back into her cheeks.

"Thanks, dear. That's a lovely cup of tea."

Walker sat opposite her and leaned forward. "Once again, please accept my sincerest apologies for the way you were treated outside the station. Those journalists had no right to harass you like that, and I'm deeply sorry you had to endure it."

Mrs Conroy took another sip of tea, then set the mug aside. "It's not your fault. I just… I feel so guilty."

Walker frowned. "Guilty? Why on earth would you feel guilty?"

The old woman took an anxious, shallow breath, her hands twisting in her lap. "I should have come forward sooner. I've been worrying myself sick over it, but I… I was scared."

"Scared of what, Mrs Conroy?"

She hesitated, her gaze darting around the room as if searching for hidden dangers. When she spoke, her voice was barely above a whisper. "Of him. Councillor Blackwell. He's a powerful man. A man of position. I didn't know what he might do if he found out I'd seen him that night."

Walker's eyes widened, but she kept her tone gentle. "I understand. It takes a lot of courage to speak up against someone in authority. But let me reassure you that we'll treat the information you give us as confidentially as we can. You are safe here."

"Yes, you're right. He shouldn't be allowed to get away with it. And I shouldn't be afraid of a pathetic bully like him."

"That's right. Good on you." Walker smiled. "So, can you tell me more about what you saw that night?"

Mrs Conroy gathered her thoughts. "It was just after half two in the morning. I remember the time because that's when I always get up to let Rebus out for his business."

"Rebus?"

"My fourteen-year-old, incontinent cat. He's been at death's door for years, thyroid, bladder, bowel problems. You name it. You should see my vet bills. My brother says he'd hit him with a hammer for me, but that's my bloody brother for you."

Walker listened patiently, allowing Mrs Conroy to relax a little more.

"So, then what happened?" she pressed finally, before the cat saga continued any further.

"I was standing at the front door, waiting for the old boy to finish his routine, and I saw the councillor coming out of the side garden of number six. The house next to the one that…" She swallowed hard. "He was moving quickly, like he was in a hurry. Kept looking over his shoulder, too, as if he was afraid of being seen."

"Where did he go?"

"Down to the end of the road, then he cut up the side lane."

"Did you see him again?"

"No." She bit her lower lip. "It just didn't feel right, you know? What was he doing coming out of the Finniestons' property at that time of night?"

"And you're certain it was Councillor Blackwell? It must have been pretty dark."

Mrs Conroy's expression hardened. "I'd know that over-inflated balloon of a face anywhere. Had a run-in with him at a community meeting a few months back about the cuts to the bus service. He was all for it, never mind that it's a lifeline for folk like me."

"And the Finnieston sisters were at this meeting, too?"

"Oh, aye. We were all furious. They detest him as much as I do. The cuts would mean catching three buses to Scotfresh in town. Utter bloody nightmare. He's selfish, that one. Out for himself and his developer pals, not us regular people."

Just then, Walker's phone pinged. She glanced at the screen, her eyebrows raising slightly. "Excuse me for a moment. I need to check this message."

She stepped out of the room, closing the door softly behind her. Opening the text, she scanned Harper's message and tapped the video file attachment. Her eyes narrowed as she watched the footage. After a moment, she nodded to herself and returned to the room.

"Mrs Conroy," she said, her voice measured, "I've just received some potentially important evidence. My colleague has just sent me a video taken near the scene on the night of the fire, around the time you saw that man crossing the road."

Mrs Conroy sat up. "A video? Of the man I saw?"

Walker nodded. "Possibly. I'd like you to take a look, if you're feeling up to it. See if you recognize the person in the footage."

Mrs Conroy set her tea down, her hands trembling slightly. "Yes, of course. If it will help with the investigation, I'll do whatever I can."

Walker smiled reassuringly. "Thank you. Your cooperation means a great deal. Now, let me just pull up the video on my iPad. The screen is a bit larger, so it might be easier for you to see the details."

She retrieved her iPad from her bag and navigated to the video file. She handed the device to Mrs Conroy and added, "Take your time. If you need me to pause or replay any part of the footage, just let me know."

Mrs Conroy nodded, her gaze fixed on the screen. The video began to play. She squinted at the display, studying the figure in the footage.

"That's him," she said, pointing at the iPad.

Walker leaned in. "Are you sure it's the councillor?"

Mrs Conroy squinted again, uncertainty creeping into her voice. "Without my glasses, I couldn't be one hundred percent sure. And what's that he's wearing?"

Walker examined the footage. "It looks like a black coat, possibly a parka?"

The woman frowned. "That's odd. When I saw the councillor, he was in a grey suit. But maybe he took the coat off. It's been quite mild of late. I've had to change the duvet to a lower tog on my bed." She paused, then asked, "Can you play it one more time?"

Walker obliged, and Mrs Conroy watched intently. After a moment, she looked up at Walker, doubt creasing her face. "It was definitely him in the street that I saw, but this person here... I'm not sure."

Walker nodded. "Thank you, Mrs Conroy. That's incredibly helpful."

The old woman's eyes welled up. "I just keep thinking, if I'd called it in, maybe those poor souls wouldn't have..." Her voice cracked, and she pressed a hand to her mouth.

Walker reached out and patted her hand gently. "Now, none of that. You've done a brave thing coming forward. I know it wasn't easy for you."

Mrs Conroy gave Walker a watery smile. "You're a kind soul, dear."

"The only person responsible for this tragedy is the one who started the fire. And with your help, we're going to make sure they face justice. That's more than enough for now."

Walker stood, helping Mrs Conroy out of the armchair. "I'll ask the sergeant to accompany you out the back to save you another encounter with the hyenas at the gate."

"Thank you for being so kind, Detective Inspector. You're a good yin."

She walked her to the door and back to the foyer. "Please escort Mrs Conroy out via the rear entrance and make sure those damned reporters don't get within shouting distance."

The sergeant nodded, offering his arm to the elderly woman. They disappeared down the corridor, and Walker allowed herself a moment to absorb the gravity of what she'd just heard and how this escalating nightmare would play out if the councillor turned out to be the arsonist. She returned to the incident room, her mind a box of live electrical wires.

TWENTY-ONE

Harper slowed the car and double-checked the house number on the pebble-dashed bungalow that was squeezed between two new-builds that ominously surrounded their diminutive neighbour.

He exhaled at the ugliness of the characterless, fake zinc-clad monstrosities. The prospects for his own inherited relic of a house didn't bode well, though on the bright side, house prices had soared in Corstorphine, so why stand in the way of progress?

He chuckled at his own hypocrisy and pulled over to survey the scene. The front garden was a tangle of weeds, bins, and recycling containers strewn haphazardly across the narrow path.

He climbed out, picked his way through the chaos, and rapped on the door.

No answer.

He tried again, peering through the grimy bay window that looked about to crumble away from the main wall. The front room was shrouded in darkness, but he could make out a single bed rammed against the far wall, medical detritus piled high upon it. An oxygen tank lay on its side, tubes and masks spilling onto the floor.

Another knock, more silence. Harper moved to the side gate, testing the handle.

"Can I help you?"

A middle-aged man in a boiler suit stood on the path behind him, a hammer clutched in his fist.

"Easy," Harper said, raising his hands. "Police."

The man squinted. "William? Is that you?"

Harper blinked. "Mr Burroughs?"

"It is indeed. Sorry about that. I thought someone was breaking in. I live just over there." He pointed to another identical bungalow on the opposite side of the road.

"I didn't know you lived here," Harper said.

"When my wife passed, I found our house too big, with too many memories. And I couldn't manage the stairs."

"So sorry for your loss." Harper nodded at the hammer. "Mind putting that down?"

"Sorry, force of habit." Mr Burroughs lowered the tool. "And likewise, your mother. I guess it comes to us all in the end." He sighed, and his smile returned. "She was absolutely ruthless at the bridge club. Took no prisoners, your mum."

"I haven't seen you for years. You know I live in my mum's house now?

"Greenbank Gardens?"

"The very one."

"That's ridiculous. I should have stayed in touch with your mum. But when I left the club a few years ago to look after Maureen, we lost touch. It was a tough few years."

"So sorry. How are you keeping now?"

"Ach, you know, doddering along. Don't get old, son. That's all I can say. So you're a police officer now?"

"Detective Constable."

"Well I never. A detective constable. Last time I saw you, you were waiting on your exam results for your Highers."

"Ooft." Harper rolled his eyes. "Let me guess. Long hair and *Star Wars* t-shirt?"

"Aye." The old man chuckled. "I had you pegged for Google or Micro-whatsit."

"Change of plan."

"Fancied yourself as a bit of a Taggart, then?"

"Who?"

"Ah yes, too young. Lucky you! You here on police business, then?"

"I am, yes. Any ideas where the owner is?" Harper nodded back to the bungalow.

"Craig? Is there a problem?"

"I just need to speak to him. Do you know Mr Scanlon?"

"Only to say hello to. He kept to himself and then disappeared when the cancer hit. Heard he was in palliative care. Terribly sad. He'd been ill for months. The place has gone to wrack and ruin. The bulldozers will be in next, I suspect."

"He was a resident over at the palliative care unit in Lennoxfield. But he discharged himself last Monday. His brother was meant to be looking after him here."

Mr Burroughs frowned. "Not seen a soul. No lights, no cars, not a peep for a while."

"You didn't see the ambulance? The care staff?"

"I go to the train yard most days." Mr Burroughs gestured to his overalls. "Steam trains are a passion. You can take the engineer out of the army—"

"We need to speak to them both rather urgently," Harper politely interrupted.

"What's this about? No, sorry. You probably can't tell me anything. I watch a lot of true crime documentaries. I know how these things work."

"That's right. But if you see either of them back here, could you either ring me directly or call nine-nine-nine and report it?"

"Nine-nine-nine? It must be serious."

Harper handed Mr Burroughs his card.

"I will indeed. I know I shouldn't say this, but it's all very intriguing and exciting. I can see why you chose this line of work. A policeman. I still can't get over it. Your mother would have been very proud."

"It's really good to see you after all these years, Mr Burroughs."

"Good to see you, too. And keep in touch, neighbour." Mr Burroughs smiled with a hint of sadness in his eyes.

As Mr Burroughs turned to go, Harper called out, "Hold on. I've got something for you."

He ran over to the car, rummaged in the glove compartment, and returned with a wedding invite. Mr Burroughs squinted at it, patting his pockets.

"Glasses," he muttered. "Must've left them at the yard."

"I'm getting married."

"You are not? Who's the lucky lady?"

"Catriona. We met at work."

"Another police officer?"

"No, a handwriting expert."

"That's wonderful news."

"Third of July, Loch Gillan Hotel."

"Oh. That's a bit of a trek."

"I can sort a room, on us."

"Nonsense. Gives me an excuse to get the old Saab out."

Harper did a double-take. "Saab?"

"Sixty-four. Rebuilt it myself."

A slow grin spread across Harper's face. "You won't believe this, but my boss has a ninety-six V4. Obsessed with it."

Mr Burrough's eyes lit up. "I'd love to meet him. Sounds like we're friends already. We could talk pistons."

"Starting to regret this invite now." Harper laughed. "I'll check in with you nearer the time. No pressure if you can't make it."

"Wouldn't miss it for the world. Though you're still too young for all that marital nonsense." Mr Burroughs winked and set off home.

With a glance at the empty bungalow, Harper jumped back in the car, but before he could report the Scanlons' absence, his phone sparked to life.

"Hi, Will. The boss wants us all in for updates," Baxter said.

"On my way. No sign of anyone at Craig Scanlon's property. Looks like the brother has taken him somewhere. We might need to initiate a search."

"Another one?"

"Yup."

"Right. I'll pass that on."

"I'm on my way in." Harper looked back at the bungalow and set off for the station.

TWENTY-TWO

Bone stood at the front of the incident room, frowning, as he surveyed his team.

Mullens slouched in his chair, his usual swagger replaced by a sullen expression. He blew out his cheeks.

"What's up with your face, Mark?" Bone asked, eyebrow raised.

"Nothing, sir. Just a bit knackered, that's all," Mullens replied, avoiding eye contact.

Bone let it slide, for now. "Where's Will?"

"Here, sir." Harper arrived, flush-faced and out of breath. "Traffic was horrendous out of Edinburgh."

"Last time I saw a face that colour was when my Uncle Gary came back from Torremolinos," Mullens said.

"Right, let's get started," Bone interrupted. "I had a call from Fire Chief Tennant last night."

"Mr Feminist himself," Walker snarled.

"He informed me that nine years ago, when he was a young firefighter, he worked down at Selkirk Fire Station."

"The borders?" Harper asked.

"The last time I looked, Selkirk's still there, yes," Bone replied sarcastically. "During his time, there were a series of arson attacks that led to the arrest and conviction of a Scott Scanlon. Believing that there were similarities between the Borders attacks and the Frasers' fire, he contacted a former colleague who told him Mr Scanlon was released a month ago, on good behaviour."

"Hold on. Why has Tennant not come forward with this before?" Walker asked.

"One of his men told him about the funnel and hose, which triggered a memory of the Scanlon case. But here's the key part. Scanlon failed to show for his parole meeting last Thursday."

"Oh fuck," Mullens said.

"Can you fill the team in on what you've unearthed about this character so far, Sheila?"

Baxter unbuttoned her tweed jacket and consulted her notes. "Scott Scanlon, forty-two, responsible for an arson campaign that went on for over six months in and around the Selkirk and Jedburgh areas between March and September, 2014. He targeted doctors, clinicians, and pharmaceutical bosses involved in animal testing. Got ten years, reduced to eight for good behaviour."

"Local police must have been thrilled when they finally nailed the bastard," Mullens said.

Baxter nodded. "It was the near-death of a security guard that finally led the investigating team to him. Apparently, when he spotted the guard, he legged it out through the front of the building and CCTV cameras picked him up removing his ski mask. Prison records show impeccable behaviour during his term, with details of attendance at many counselling and deprogramming sessions."

"Deprogramming?" Walker asked.

"Yes, he was an animal rights activist, had associations with extreme groups, and believed wild conspiracy theories."

"Fuck's sake. Flat Earth heid the baw," Mullens grumped. "I mean, if the world was flat, cats would have shoved everything off the end by now."

Walker chuckled.

"Could all that good behaviour have just been an act to reduce his sentence?" Harper suggested.

Baxter shook her head. "The parole board didn't think so."

Mullens threw up his hands. "Oh, and they never get anything wrong, do they?"

Bone shot him a stern look. "Mark, what the hell is the matter with you?"

Mullens muttered something.

"What was that?"

"Nothing."

"Why are you being so bloody disruptive? If you carry on with this, I'm going to ask you to step out. We have urgent work to do here."

Harper chimed in to calm things down. "Scanlon's brother, Craig, lived in Corstorphine, but following a terminal cancer diagnosis was in a palliative care unit in Lennoxfield."

"But he discharged himself last Monday with Scanlon's help," Bone added.

Harper nodded. "And now both brothers are missing. There was no sign of them at Craig Scanlon's property."

"So, Scott Scanlon's our number one person of interest?" Baxter asked.

"Absolutely," Bone confirmed.

Baxter went over to the incident board and shifted Scanlon's mugshot from the side to the top.

Bone turned back to the team. "Any more updates from the scene?"

Walker checked her notes. "Forensics are combing the area of woods behind the Frasers' house. I found two discarded petrol cans, with tyre treads leading from a path out onto a lane."

"Again, that matches the MO from the Scanlon arson case. Where does that lane go?"

"Out onto Brae Road."

"Straight into the hills, then," Harper said.

"That's right," Walker said. "The path in the woods is narrow and not designed for vehicles, so there's a lot of damage to tree branches, the height of which suggests a van, similar to the Transit picked up on the speed camera."

"Citroën Dispatch," Mullens qualified.

"The driver would have had to force a van through."

"Any houses on the other side?"

"Unfortunately not. Horsbrugh Close backs onto the Campsies, and the next building is a farm about three miles up Brae Road, so the perfect getaway."

"Perfect for lugging heavy petrol cans," Mullens said.

"And kidnapping someone," Harper added.

"And speaking of that, did you all get my message regarding the *Chronicle* email?" Bone asked.

The team nodded.

"Who's this Kelly Dobson, then?" Mullens asked.

"The million-dollar question," Baxter replied. "But unfortunately, with no connecting threads, it's like firing a pistol at the moon, hoping to hit it."

"What we do have is a potentially confirmed hostage situation," Bone said. "I spoke to Gallacher last night, and he's going to request assistance from other forces to swell our search coverage."

"That's good. Door-to-door is underway, but we're thin on the ground and could definitely do with more support," Walker said. "I spoke to her sister, Eliza Collins, in Spain. She's totally distraught but had nothing in particular to share that might help our investigation. She said the Frasers' relationship was sound and Katherine was happy."

"Are we talking a national search?" Harper asked.

"If the killer took her in a van, they could be anywhere by now, but Gallacher is on it. And uncharacteristically for him, he even suggested a public appeal and releasing some of the footage, see if it sparks any more memories." Bone faced Harper. "Has Cash sent through some photos yet?"

"Let me check." Harper went to his desk and tapped at his keyboard. "Yes, eight images in total."

The monitor flashed and the first image appeared, of the remnants of the hose protruding from the victim's gaping charred jawbone. The team recoiled in horror. "Cash identified this as the remains of a length of hose, most of which was inside the victim's abdominal cavity. It would appear the killer fed this tube down the gullet and poured petrol down into his stomach."

"Evil fuck!" Mullens growled. "Tapeworm from hell."

"Move on, Will," Bone urged.

A second image flashed up, of the steel funnel.

"This was also found under the body, after forensics moved the remains."

"To assist the flow of fuel presumably?" Walker said.

"Indeed. Tennant told me it was the discovery of this funnel that triggered him connecting the fire to Scanlon's arson campaign in the borders."

Walker pulled a face. "So not the cryptic message scored into the wall then?"

"Strangely, that wasn't part of Scanlon's original MO, and probably also explains why Tennant didn't immediately join the dots. But along with an actual murder, this may worryingly indicate a major escalation."

Bone turned back to the monitor. "Are there any of a money box and a baby photo?"

"There's more?" Mullens interrupted.

Harper clicked forward, and the money box appeared.

"This was also recovered within a few feet of the corpse. A thirty by twenty-centimetre steel combination lock cash box. Will, the next one?"

Harper tapped his computer, and the baby's face appeared.

"This was the only object found inside, an old Polaroid style black-and-white photo of a premature baby. You can see the feeding tube removed and resting alongside. Cash reckons this was taken in post-natal intensive care and the baby might be deceased."

"Poor wee soul," Walker muttered.

"Begs the question, why was a single photo of a dead baby locked in a money box?" Bone continued.

"And why was it found by Fraser's body? Was he looking at it when he was attacked?" Harper cut in.

"Baxter, I need you to dig into this. Find out who the baby is and why Fraser had the photo locked away. And while you're at it, do a deep dive into Dr Fraser's professional and personal life."

"Mark and I also unearthed more information on their son, Josh," Harper said.

"Go on," Bone urged.

"He dropped out of art college two years ago. Tutor says he's a troubled lad, into drugs. We're looking into a Goth-metal band he used to play drums with called B-Moth."

"Worth interviewing his bandmates?"

"Yes, we thought of that," Harper confirmed. "When I checked online, all the band members have changed their names to characters from what I think might be Edgar Allan Poe stories. The singer goes by Roderick Usher, the bassist is Montresor, and the guitarist is Fortunato. But they are playing in a battle of the bands competition tonight at the student union, so Mark and I are going on a date."

"Are we?" Mullens asked, surprised. "I think I'd rather have rats gnaw on my gonads than spend an evening with moth-infested bat people."

"Good work, Will," Bone interrupted. "Enjoy your date, Mark." He frowned at his colleague.

Mullens exhaled.

"I had a chat with Fraser's boss, the director of medical care. Seems they had a pretty volatile relationship," Bone said.

Baxter consulted her notes. "I ran a search on him, sir, as requested. He's ambitious, ruthless when it comes to hospital budgets, but otherwise clean as a whistle."

"Aye, and with a sick wife and a new baby at home, I doubt he's running around setting fires," Bone agreed.

Walker smirked. "You think, sir? Many's a sleepless night I've had to resist."

Bone pressed on. "Lastly, there's the neighbour. She claims she saw a Councillor Blackwell crossing the street around the time of the fire."

"She had a bit of a wobble when I showed her the night-cam footage," Walker said. "I'm not sure how reliable a witness she is."

Sergeant Brody, who had been standing quietly at the back of the room, cleared his throat. "Sir, there's been a development."

The team turned to face him.

"Missing Persons just got a call. A paramedic, Rob McNeil, never made it home from his shift. His wife's frantic. Normally, they'd wait forty-eight hours, but given that he's medical personnel, they thought there might be a connection to the Fraser case."

The room fell silent, a palpable sense of unease settling over the team.

Brody continued, "His colleague said he dropped McNeil on the high lane about two a.m. There were multiple roadworks, and Rob was near his home and decided to walk it. Thought it would be quicker."

"Clearly not," Mullens said.

Brody shook his head. "His colleague is worried because it was so dark, and from experience he knows there are plenty of drunk drivers who use that road to avoid patrol cars. But McNeil insisted."

Bone sighed. "Oh, Jesus. Not another hit-and-run. I'm not sure I could cope with that." He took a moment to compose himself, then addressed the team. "Right. Here's what we're going to do. Baxter, I want you to look into Councillor Blackwell. See if there's any dirt we can dig up."

Baxter nodded. "Consider it done, sir."

"Harper, check in with Digital. See how they're getting on with enhancing the footage collected so far and see if any more has turned up. Mark, I want you to keep tabs on the various searches. Any developments, I want to know immediately."

"Aye, sir," Mullens replied, his earlier sullenness replaced by a glimmer of his usual cheek.

"Meanwhile, I'll update the super," Bone said, "and let him know a local dignitary is now in the frame."

Walker grimaced. "Oh, he's going to love that."

Bone turned to her. "Walker, wait for me. We'll deal with the councillor together."

She nodded. "Yes, sir."

He addressed Sergeant Brody. "And keep me informed about the paramedic. Let's hope and pray he's just flipped out and gone to blow his savings at the casino or an all-night bar or something."

As Bone left the incident room, Harper caught up with him in the corridor.

"Sir, a word about Mullens?" Harper said quietly.

Bone nodded, and they stepped to the side.

"He just found out his dad might have liver cancer. He went to see him, and the doctor was very concerned. I don't think he's dealing with it very well."

Bone's expression softened. "Christ. That explains a lot. Keep an eye on him, Will. Make sure he doesn't lamp anyone and get himself suspended."

Harper nodded. "Will do, sir."

Bone patted him on the shoulder and headed off to update the super.

TWENTY-THREE

Walker settled as best she could into the lumpy passenger seat of Bone's pride and joy.

As Bone coaxed the engine to life with a series of alarming coughs and splutters, Walker swivelled to him, a question on her lips.

"So, how did the meeting with the super go?" she asked, bracing herself as the car lurched out of the station car park, past a group of journalists huddled together, clutching takeaway coffees and breakfast rolls.

Bone shrugged, his eyes fixed on the road ahead. "For the second time in two days, he agreed to everything without so much as a paddle, creek, or shitstorm. Seems to be a lot mellower since his wife's health scare."

Walker raised an eyebrow. "Really? That's not like him."

Bone sighed, tapping his fingers on the steering wheel.

"What?" she said.

"This is between us, okay?"

"Oh shit. Is his wife sick again?"

"No. He told me that head office wants him out. They're offering him an early retirement package."

"Seriously?" Walker's eyes widened.

"Might explain why he's so relaxed. Doesn't give a shit anymore because he's planning on moving to a golf resort on the Costas."

Walker chuckled, shaking her head. Then she frowned. "Hold on. If he goes, then we lose our champion with the top knobs."

"Correct. And he's fended off the hatchets and accountants who've wanted to shut us down for years."

"It's a bloody disaster. Do you think he'll take it?"

"I think he might. After his wife got sick, his priorities changed. I get the impression he just can't be arsed with any of it anymore. Life's too short, literally."

"God. Who would they get to replace him? Would you take it if they offered?"

Bone laughed loudly, almost steering off the road. "You're joking, right?"

"You are qualified, overqualified."

"I'm a fucking pariah in Edinburgh. I can't think of one person who has any respect for me at head office.

They think I'm a washed-up nutjob who shouldn't be on active duty and probably not even in the force."

"Yeah, I know. But aside from that. Would you take it? In theory?" She grinned.

"Having to traipse up to lick the top brass's arses every week and sit stagnating behind a desk the rest of the time? Are you serious? I'd last five minutes before I either killed someone or was banged up at Carstairs Psychiatric Hospital."

"Speaking of which. If you're up for that chat we talked about, I'm all ears."

"It's been an odd few months, but I won't bore you with it. The short answer is, I'm now dealing with it. I'm going to the next group session this week, and I'll corner my counsellor while I'm there, too. Vigilance. Always. Thanks for reminding me that I was behaving erratically again."

"That's good to hear. We wouldn't want you killing anyone, or at least, the wrong people. And how's Alice dealing with it?"

Walker's question caught Bone slightly off guard. "Supportive, as always."

She looked at him sceptically. "I hear a but."

"I feel guilty every time this shit returns, however small. I don't want to put her through any of it ever again."

"You need to talk to her. Be absolutely straight about it. Don't be messing her around again. Vigilance. Always."

"Always bloody right." He smiled and crunched the gearstick into fourth, but the Saab complained and he returned it to third.

Walker groaned. "This car."

"Is so pretty. That's what you were going to say to Bertha, weren't you?"

"If it means we get to the councillor's house without having to walk there, then yes. Pretty Bertha." Walker stroked the dashboard but crossed the fingers on her other hand.

A couple of miles into the journey, she suddenly noticed the unusual silence in the car. "Hold up. Why aren't you playing your shitty music on the eight-track player?"

Bone grinned, reaching for the ancient stereo. "Oh, thanks for reminding me."

He jabbed at a button, and the car filled with the tinny, crackling strains of Herb Alpert and the Tijuana Brass.

Walker groaned, sinking lower in her seat. "Oh, Christ. I had to ask, didn't I? Whose cat is being strangled now?"

"Picked this up in a charity shop for fifty pence."

"You were robbed."

Bone just smiled, tapping his hands on the wheel and making gentle trumpet sounds with his lips as they trundled through the streets of Kilwinnoch, enjoying a moment's respite before they faced the nightmare that lay ahead.

When they finally arrived, Bone turned off the engine. "See? Compliments go a long way with my girl."

"Or a short way, but any farther and you're in deep doo-doo," Walker added, and climbed out.

They approached the councillor's red sandstone villa, and Bone rang the bell. After a moment, the door swung open to reveal a dour-faced man in his sixties, clad in a plaid dressing gown and carpet slippers.

Bone flashed his warrant card.

"Angus Blackwell?" Bone asked.

"Yes, that's right," the councillor replied, appearing a little flustered.

"DCI Bone and DI Walker, Kilwinnoch Rural Crime Unit. Can we come in?"

"I take it this is in relation to that horrendous fire?" the councillor asked. "Though, I thought that sort of task would be below your pay grades."

"Probably best if we talk inside," Bone said.

"Of course, yes. Come in."

Blackwell ushered them into an austere hallway adorned with faded landscapes and a grandfather clock that looked like it hadn't ticked since the Boer War. A stack of accounting journals teetered precariously on a side table.

The living room was equally dreary, with doilies on every surface and a collection of faded photographs depicting a younger, trimmer Blackwell glad-handing various local dignitaries. A well-worn calculator and a few dog-eared spreadsheets lay scattered on the coffee table.

Bone and Walker settled on a dusty velvet sofa that wheezed under their weight, and they leaned awkwardly towards each other.

"Such a tragedy." Blackwell lowered himself into a worn armchair. "Poor Dr Fraser. And his wife! Do you have any news on their condition?"

Bone shook his head. "The investigation is still in its early stages, Councillor. I'm afraid I can't share any details at this time."

Blackwell nodded, his jowls quivering. "Of course, of course. It's just, the provost is a personal friend of Katherine Fraser. She's absolutely beside herself with worry."

"How long have they been friends?" Bone enquired.

"Oh, a good few years now. They met through formal events some time ago."

"And you, Councillor? Are you friends with Katherine Fraser?"

Blackwell recoiled at the suggestion. "Me? Heavens, no. I barely know either of them. As far as they're concerned, as head of council budget, I'm an axe-wielding penny-pincher." He glanced up guiltily. "I mean, I've never actually wielded an axe in my life. A calculator is more my style." He chuckled nervously, then fell silent.

"I spoke to Dr Fraser's boss, Professor Baird, the regional medical director," Bone said. "He mentioned that rows in meetings often escalated between him and Dr Fraser over hospital budgets. I heard they didn't get on."

Blackwell shifted uncomfortably. "Well, yes, I suppose there were some disagreements."

"So you were in attendance at these meetings?"

"Yes. The rather complex entanglements of NHS and local authority fiscal regulations."

"Did Dr Fraser have disagreements with you as well?

Blackwell hesitated. "Professional disagreements, nothing more, Inspector."

Bone leaned forward and switched topic. "When were you first aware of the fire?"

"When I heard the fire engines. They woke me up."

"So you were in bed at two-thirty Sunday morning?" Walker asked.

"Yes, getting my beauty sleep." He wiped away a bead of sweat trickling down his forehead.

"That's odd." Bone removed his notebook and flicked forward. "We have a witness who placed you…" He turned to Walker.

She pretended to consult her notes. "Outside the Fraser residence around two a.m."

Blackwell's bushy eyebrows shot up. "What? That's preposterous! I was here, tucked up. I'd had a late night going over spreadsheets, so I was exhausted."

"Spreadsheets on a Saturday night?" Bone asked.

"What can I say? I love accountancy."

"The witness was quite sure it was you," Walker continued. "They said you came out of the Frasers' next-door neighbour's garden, crossed the street, and disappeared down a side lane to the next road. Your road."

"Let me guess, it was those two old spinsters from down the road, wasn't it? The Finniestons?"

Bone kept his face neutral and continued to eyeball him.

Blackwell huffed. "Well, whoever it was, they're lying. Those Finnieston women have had it in for me ever since I supported the council's decision to cut funding for public transport. Vivid imaginations, those two. Always sticking their noses where they don't belong."

"So, you categorically deny being outside the Fraser home that night?" Bone asked.

"Absolutely. I was home all evening, working."

"Can anyone corroborate your whereabouts? A family member, perhaps?" Bone persisted.

Blackwell's flushed face turned a shade darker. "I live alone, Inspector. Does that make me a serial killer, then?"

"So, no one at all?"

"I just told you," the councillor replied.

Walker produced her iPad. "I'm going to play some video footage recorded on the night of the fire." She loaded up the file and turned the screen so the councillor could see it.

After a moment's viewing, the councillor looked up. "Are you suggesting this is me?"

"Is it you, sir?" Bone asked.

"Of course it isn't. That person is twice my height, and what is that they're wearing? A cloak?"

"A knee-length parka, we believe," Walker said. "Do you own a black or dark-grey parka, sir?"

"No, I bloody do not, and you can search my bloody wardrobe and coat hook by the door if you like. This is insane. I'd like you to leave now."

"You seem quite distressed for someone who assures us he's done nothing wrong, sir," Bone said.

"How the hell would you feel? I'm being accused of this… horrendous crime. Do you know who I am? I am a public servant. I have responsibilities. I am respect…" He started to break down. "It's just very upsetting."

"I'm sorry, sir. If you could possibly put forward the name of anyone who can vouch for your whereabouts, then…"

"Like I told you, I live alone. Not out of choice. My wife, she passed away some time ago. My work and my public duties are…" He inhaled deeply.

"I'm afraid then you leave me no choice but to ask you to come with us to the station for further questioning."

"So, you're arresting me now, on the basis of what? Having no partner? And those sisters are two bats in a belfry. Anything they say should be taken with a hefty pinch of salt. And if you take the word of a couple of batty and bitter old nimbies instead of mine, a respected public figure, then the force is in deep trouble."

"I'm not arresting you. You are well within your rights to refuse, but I may then be forced to arrest you, and that is not a good look, sir."

"I can't believe this."

Bone's phone rang.

"Excuse me a moment." He stepped out. Moments later he returned, ashen-faced. "A word, DI Walker?"

"What's going on?" the councillor asked. "I hope that's your boss on the phone telling you to pull your bloody necks in."

Out in the front garden, Bone stopped.

"Sir?" Walker asked.

"That was Sheila. Transport has found a burnt-out Citroën van at the top of Meikle Hill. They found the missing paramedic on the road, unconscious. He's sustained a serious head injury and third-degree burns to his arms and legs."

"But he's alive?"

"Barely. He's been rushed up to the head injuries unit at Stirling Royal. His wife is up there now."

Bone sighed. "We'll need a couple of officers up there to scene guard the victim."

"She's already done that." Walker nodded. "And ordered them to bag the paramedic's clothes."

"Okay, let's get this one back to the station and stick him in a holding cell for now. I'll grab Mark, and we'll head up to the crime scene for a look."

"What do you want me to do?"

"Could you go to the hospital and speak to the wife? Sounds like the paramedic is not up for a chat."

Walker exhaled. "She'll be distraught."

"Sorry, but it's important."

"Yes, I know, but golden hour and all that."

"We could draw straws if you prefer?"

Walker scoffed. "I'm good, thanks. One crime scene a week is more than sufficient for me, thank you very much. But I'll say this, Sweaty Betty in there didn't seem like a guy who'd just torched a van at the top of the Campsies."

"Maybe, but evil has a nasty way of hiding its ugly face when it needs to," Bone said, and they returned to face the wrath of the councillor.

TWENTY-FOUR

Bone and Mullens drove up to the police cordon. The fire-ruined copse of trees loomed up ahead, a macabre scene of charred branches and blackened earth. The skeletal remains of the once-lush foliage dripped with water from the fire crews' hoses.

Nestled in the heart of this eerie, post-apocalyptic landscape, just off the isolated Meikle Hill Road, the burnt-out chassis of a Citroën Defender smouldered, wisps of smoke still curling from its blackened shell.

"Christ on a bike," Mullens muttered, his face grim.

They flashed their lanyards at the PC, limboed under the tape, and picked their way through the undergrowth, sidestepping the detritus of the fire crews' battle to extinguish the blaze.

A small army of fluorescent-jacketed officers swarmed the area—traffic police, forensics, fire investigators—all buzzing with purposeful activity.

As they neared the van, Cash emerged from the other side of the wreckage, his face even more dour than usual. "I wondered how long it would take you to show up."

Bone grunted. "Not long enough."

Cash gestured to the van's gaping-wide rear doors. "So it would appear King Vestas attempted to incinerate the paramedic in the back of the van. If you come closer, I'll show you. But not too close." He pointed to the detective's scene-suitless attire.

Bone peered inside, the telltale stench of petrol present once again.

"As you can smell, our man's been liberal with the old four star." He knelt by one of the doors. "See the marks on the interior here? Looks like the medic probably kicked his way out before the whole thing went up. The busted roof indicates the extent of the explosion when the accelerant hit the fuel tank." He removed a flashlight from his belt and shone it into the scorched interior. "At the back, there's one of our friend's signature tropes, the steel funnel. Whether he actually tried to use it, only the paramedic might be able to answer that one."

"Jesus wept," Mullens breathed.

Bone's eyes were drawn to a message scratched into the scorched, near-obliterated paintwork on the side of the van. The same chilling words they'd found at the Fraser scene, the first line of the Hippocratic oath: 'First, do no harm.'

"Looks like our nutjob's got a theme going, indeed," Mullens said, his voice tight with anger.

The wail of an approaching siren heralded the arrival of Chief Fire Officer Tennant. He leapt from his Range Rover, his face thunderous as he stormed towards Bone.

"DCI Bone! What the hell is going on here? Another incident, with my officers risking life and limb, and you're still no closer to catching this lunatic! I bloody warned you about him."

Bone bristled, taken aback by the fire chief's verbal onslaught. He squared his shoulders. "We're doing everything we can. My team is working round the clock—"

"Your team?" Tennant spat. "You mean that bunch of oddball misfits you call a rural crime unit? Dithering about while this maniac runs wild?"

Mullens surged forward, his fists clenched. "Now, hold on a fucking minute—"

Bone threw out an arm, blocking his path. "As you were, Mark!" he growled at his colleague, but his eyes never left the chief's face. "I'll handle this."

Tennant sneered. "Handle it? Like you're handling the Fraser case? This psycho needs to be stopped, Bone, before he puts one of my crew in a fucking box. Or maybe next time it'll be one of your lot. How'd you like that, eh?"

Bone's throat tightened. The chief's words hit a little too close to home. He forced himself to take a breath, to keep his voice level. "Unprofessional conduct. Carry on, and I will be taking this further."

"More time-wasting," Tennant retorted.

"We're pursuing every lead, following every scrap of evidence. We will catch this bastard, Chief. I promise you that."

Tennant barked a humourless laugh. "Forgive me if I don't hold my breath. I told you who this is. Why haven't you apprehended him? I tell you why, because you are a bunch of amateur Miss fucking Marples. That psychopath almost cost me my eyesight! If any of my men die at the hands of this maniac, and we came close yesterday, then that is on you." He pointed his finger at Mullens. "And you, hot potato head."

"That's fucking rich, ya over-inflated fart bag," Mullens cursed.

Bone raised his arm again in case Mullens decided to take a swing.

Tennant spun on his heel and stalked away, leaving Bone to simmer in a stew of rage and frustration.

Cash, who had been watching the exchange with a detached sort of interest, piped up. "That was a professional exchange, then."

"Cockwipe," Mullens muttered.

"Anywho." Cash smiled. "Petrol accelerant again, tick, funnel, tick, and deranged message, tick, but no hose down the throat this time."

Bone scowled. "Learning from his schoolboy errors?"

"Or spiralling out of control," Cash said over his shoulder. "So far gone he doesn't know what the fuck he's doing anymore. Hence the paramedic's miraculous escape. I'd call that a fuck-up, big time."

Bone felt a sudden, overwhelming need to be anywhere but there.

He turned to Cash. "Send over the scene photos as soon as you can. Every detail, no matter how small."

Cash nodded. "Probably best out of it for now, Duncan," he whispered so not to be overheard, then went back to the grim task at hand.

As Bone strode away from the smouldering wreckage, Mullens caught up with him.

"Fuck's his fucking problem?"

"I don't know. I suppose frustration, like the rest of us."

"Aye, but there's no call for that bollocks. I wish you'd have let me lamp him one. Fucking arrogant clown."

"Just get in the car, Mark," Bone ordered.

They sat for a moment, both seething in their own skin. Finally, Bone turned. "I heard about your dad."

"Shit, I told the young Jedi to keep that to himself."

"He was worried about you earlier, in the incident room. Are you okay?"

"It came out of nowhere. One minute he was being his usual racist, sexist, happy-go-lucky, offensive self, and the next he'd turned yellow. Doctors said it could be a tumour on his liver or pancreas."

"So sorry, mate. Are they going to operate?"

"Later on today. Then we'll know one way or the other."

"God, you should be over there now, then?"

"Nah. I'd just be stoatin' about, annoying the arse off everyone in the home, no good to nobody." He chuckled. "Even this hellhole and that wanker are easier to deal with than my da."

"How's he doing?"

"Ach, he's no clue. Thinks the home has turned him into a banana."

"Oh dear. Well, that's a blessing, I suppose. Saves him the worry."

"I haven't told my sisters yet. I don't know how to."

"You could wait until they have results."

"Aye, but what if he, you know, pegs it? The doctor said there's a risk at his age."

"Right enough. Then you're probably going to have to."

"Ah, Christ. That's what I was thinking. Six bloody phone calls. Why did my maw and da no' use fucking condoms?"

"And what about Sandra? Does she know?"

"She's her usual practical self. She said he's bloody immortal, so I shouldn't worry."

"It's your dad, though, isn't it?"

"Unfortunately, yes."

"Well, just give me the word and go, okay?"

"I'm all right."

"You could have fooled me. You've had a face like a smacked arse and fists clenched, ready to remove someone's front teeth all morning."

"I'll cool the beans."

"Right, I think we need to put a bomb up those search teams and start doubling down on the persons of interest that are racking up. Let's head back."

"Bombs up arses. You're talking my language, sir."

"Yes, but words, not actual bloody Semtex, Mark."

"Spoilsport." Mullens pulled a face and belted up.

TWENTY-FIVE

Walker approached the reception desk of the head injury unit at Stirling Royal Hospital. The smell of disinfectant and the hushed atmosphere set her nerves on edge.

"I'm looking for Rob McNeil," she said, flashing her ID at the nurse behind the desk.

The nurse nodded, her face grim. "Follow me, please."

"How is he doing?" Walker tried to keep stride with her.

The nurse hesitated. "Not good, I'm afraid." But before she could elaborate, they came to a room marked ICU 1. "He's in here." She pushed the door open.

Walker stepped inside, the steady beep of the life-support machine filling the air. The paramedic lay motionless on the bed, his head heavily bandaged, face battered and bruised, eyes swollen shut. His arms and legs were strapped up, being treated for serious burns. Tubes and wires connected him to various machines.

His distraught wife, Sophie McNeil, sat alongside him, her hand resting gently on her husband's. She looked up at Walker's approach, her eyes red and puffy from crying.

"Sophie? I'm Detective Inspector Rhona Walker," she said softly.

Mrs McNeil nodded, her gaze returning to her husband.

"I'm so sorry to intrude at such a difficult time," Walker continued. "How is he doing?"

Mrs McNeil's voice trembled as she spoke. "The doctors say he has a bleed on the brain. He's in an induced coma. They're waiting on results to determine the extent of the injury." She choked back a sob. "He's in such a terrible way."

Walker pulled up a chair. "I'm truly sorry, but I need to ask you a few questions. Is that okay?"

Mrs McNeil nodded, her eyes never leaving her husband's battered face.

"What time were you expecting him home last night?"

"His shift ended at two, so he's normally..." She swallowed. "He's normally home by two-thirty."

"And what time did you call the station?"

"I knew something was wrong, but I waited until eight-thirty to call. I didn't want to waste police time.

I kept thinking he'd walk through the door any minute."

"Was he often late?"

Mrs McNeil shook her head. "Hardly ever, and never more than an hour. He always texted or called."

"Even in the middle of the night?"

"Yes. He knew I'd worry."

"So, no calls or texts from him last night at all?"

"No, nothing." Mrs McNeil shook her head.

Walker hesitated before asking the next question. "Can you think of anyone who might have wanted to harm Rob? Anyone with a grudge against him?"

Mrs McNeil looked up, her eyes flashing. "It's Robbie. He's called Robbie."

"I'm sorry, Sophie. Anyone who might have wanted to harm Robbie?"

She shook her head vehemently. "No. Everybody loves him. He's dedicated to his job, to helping people…"

"No problem with patients or recent incidents he might have mentioned?"

Mrs McNeil stared at her lap for a moment. "There was that incident a while back, after he attended a road accident."

"What happened?"

"A terrible crash on New Year's morning two years ago. A woman trapped. He was on the scene first and then a doctor who was passing stopped to help, but no one could save her. The boyfriend was furious that she died. Blamed the medics at the scene."

"Including Robbie and the doctor?"

Mrs McNeil nodded. "The doctor who stopped was already responding to an emergency at the hospital. Robbie told him to go. But it wasn't their fault. She was hammered. Should never have been driving. She lost control of the car she was driving. Robbie was really upset about it. But the boyfriend just wouldn't…"

She took a deep breath.

"It's okay, go on," Walker urged.

"A few months later, Robbie was set upon by the deceased woman's boyfriend. It was Easter time, I think. Robbie was on a night out with his colleagues. The boyfriend attacked him in the pub toilet, fractured his cheekbone and broke two ribs. If his colleague hadn't intervened…" Her eyes filled with fresh tears.

"Was the boyfriend arrested?"

"Charged, convicted of assault. Got eight months," Mrs McNeil said, her voice hardening. "Just terrible. Eight miserable months. Did that bastard do this to Robbie?"

"Do you know the boyfriend's name?" Walker pressed.

"Oh yes. Daniel Quillan. Is he responsible?"

"We're investigating all possibilities. Do you remember the name of the doctor who helped at the scene or the name of the woman who died in the crash?"

Mrs McNeil shook her head. "I can't… I can't remember. I want to help, but my brain won't work. I just can't think anymore."

At that moment, a nurse entered the room and moved to check the paramedic's vitals. Sophie's attention snapped back to her husband, her hand tightening on his.

Walker stood. "Thank you, Sophie. You've been a huge help. We'll follow up on what you've told me and keep you updated. We'll do everything in our power to find out what happened to Robbie."

Sophie barely seemed to hear her, her focus entirely on her husband and the nurse attending to him. Walker quietly left the room, the steady beep of the life-support machine following her out into the hallway.

She strode purposefully down the corridor, pulling out her phone to call Baxter.

"Sheila, can you run a check on a Daniel Quillan, convicted of assaulting paramedic Rob McNeil in 2018? Find his latest address. I think we need to pay this guy an urgent visit."

"Will do, ma'am. Oh, and ma'am?"

"Yes?"

"Traffic just informed us that a campervan hired by Scanlon has been sighted in Aberfellan, near Loch Lomond. I've just called the boss to let him know, and Will's gone to nab Mark for support and intercept it.

"ARU?"

"Yes. I've just requested."

"Good, thanks. On my way back now."

She hung up, and her pace quickened, energised by the growing sense that the net might be finally closing in on the scumbag.

TWENTY-SIX

Meeting up on the hard shoulder of the Cumberfield bypass, Mullens climbed out of Bone's Saab.

"And here was me dreaming of a double nugget. Fat bloody chance of that!"

Harper didn't get out of the high performance BMW he'd requisitioned for this task.

"I don't think so, young tricycle rider." Mullens eyeballed him. "I'm driving, shift it."

"I'll go if you prefer, Will," Bone said, leaning out the car window.

"No, for some insane reason, I want him with me," Harper said, reluctantly climbing out and going around to the passenger's side.

"Be careful, okay?" Bone said, but the pool car was already rolling forward.

Mullens hit the gas and screeched back onto the dual carriageway, propelling Harper backwards into his seat. He frantically grappled with his seat belt.

"Now that's how you drive this baby!" Mullens pushed the engine even harder.

It wasn't long before they caught sight of the Armed Response Unit up ahead. Mullens grinned wickedly, pressing down on the accelerator.

"Mark, what are you—" Harper's question morphed into a strangled yelp as they swerved around the ARU, tyres screeching in protest.

"Just giving our friends a proper escort." Mullens chuckled and winked at the wide-eyed officers they'd just passed.

Harper, pale-faced and gripping his seat, muttered, "I'm beginning to regret offering to take this one."

They zoomed ahead. The ARU fell back to follow at a discreet distance, ready to provide backup—or possibly scrape what was left of Harper off the dashboard.

When he had recovered, his thoughts turned back to Scanlon. "Why a campervan, though?"

"Hiding in plain sight, maybe? Just another tourist? Devious, smart bastard."

"Or innocent?" Harper suggested.

"The guy skipped his parole meeting. That doesn't sound like a reformed character to me."

They entered Aberfellan village, and a uniformed officer waved them down. The ARU stopped behind. Mullens rolled down the window and flashed his lanyard.

"We've had a sighting of a blue-and-red Volkswagen campervan an hour ago with a match on the plates. It was parked at the Co-op."

"Did anyone speak to the driver?"

"Aye, staff in the mini market said a guy from the van came in and bought a load of supplies. He then asked about where he could buy fishing tackle."

"And?" Mullens pressed.

"They directed him to a shop in Rowardornoch, you know, on the banks of—"

"Loch Lomond, yes," Mullens interrupted.

He threw the car into gear. The tyres squealed, and they raced out of the village, the ARU struggling to keep pace.

When they reached the lower banks of the loch, the road narrowed and hugged the water's edge. Ben Lomond and the surrounding mountains loomed over them ominously. Approaching Rowardornoch, they screeched to a halt outside a fishing tackle shop. Harper was out of the car before it had fully stopped, Mullens in lumbering pursuit. The shopkeeper, a grizzled man in his sixties, looked up as they burst in.

"Police." Harper flashed his warrant card. "We're looking for this man." He held up his phone with a mugshot of Scanlon on the screen.

The shopkeeper squinted at the handset, then nodded slowly. "Aye, he was here. Bought a few bits and bobs."

"When?"

"An hour or so ago, maybe? Is he a fugitive or something?"

"Did he say where he was going?"

"He said something about him and his brother heading to a popular spot for fishing and camping, just along the loch." He gestured vaguely to the north.

"You spoke to his brother?"

"No, but I could see him in their van."

"Show us where they went," Mullens barked, pointing at the large map hanging behind the man.

Minutes later, they were back on the road, following the shopkeeper's directions.

At the end of a narrow, rutted track that led to a dead end by the loch, Mullens pulled over. The detectives got out and approached the ARU. Two officers jumped down from the cab.

"Keep back for now," Mullens instructed. "We don't want them to shit themselves and do something daft. Me and muggins will go in first, see if we can talk some sense into him. If things go tits up, come in hard and fast. Take the wanker down."

The officers nodded. One went around the back of their vehicle and returned with two stab vests. "You'll need these."

Harper slipped his on and buckled the sides.

Mullens held his up. "Do you have this in a bigger size?"

The officer shook his head.

"To fit an American-style fridge freezer," Harper added.

"All right, Mr Tapeworm," Mullens scoffed.

The officer retreated and moments later was back with another.

"The biggest I could find," he said.

With a huff and a puff, Mullens squeezed into the protective gear.

"Right, let's do this," he ordered.

They set off along the track, the gravel crunching beneath their feet. The loch glistened in the sun to their left, deceptively peaceful.

They rounded a bend, and a flash of colour caught Mullens's eye. He held up a hand, and he and Harper melted into the tree line. A blue-and-red campervan was parked at the water's edge. Two figures sat nearby, oblivious to the detectives' presence. Harper recognised Scott Scanlon instantly. The wiry man sat on a folding chair, a fishing rod in his hands, his gaze fixed on the placid water.

Harper mouthed to Mullens, "That's him."

Beside Scott, in a wheelchair, was his brother, Craig, oxygen tanks strapped to the back of the chair.

Mullens reached for his radio attached to the shoulder of his vest. "Suspect in sight," he murmured. "Hold until I signal."

They crept forward, using the trees as cover. They were almost within earshot when a twig snapped beneath Harper's foot. Scott Scanlon whipped around, his eyes widening. He leapt to his feet, his fishing rod clattering to the ground, fists clenched.

"Police! Stay where you are!" Mullens bellowed.

Scott scanned left and right, looking for an exit, like a cornered rat. He made to run at Mullens.

The armed officers burst from the trees, weapons trained on the brothers.

"I told you to hold it!" Mullens waved his arm at the officers.

In panic, Scott took off along the narrow loch-side beach. His brother let out a strangled cry, his hands scrabbling at his oxygen mask.

"I'll deal with him. You go!" Harper shouted.

"Stand down!" Mullens ordered the ARU officers.

Craig Scanlon slumped forward in his chair, his breath coming in ragged gasps. Harper rushed to his side, his hands steady, adjusting the man's oxygen mask.

"Medical assistance!" Harper called out.

An officer whistled, and a paramedic came running out of the woods.

"Breathe, Craig," Harper murmured. "Nice and slow. You're all right."

Mullens pursued Scott along the beach and across slippery moss-covered rocks towards an outcrop ahead.

"Give it up, Scanlon!" Mullens called after him.

But the fugitive continued on, stumbling over the wet terrain, trying to get past the obstruction. Mullens clambered over a boulder, lost his footing, and landed heavily on his side.

"Fuck's sake, Scanlon. Don't be a dickhead!" He scrambled back to his feet. "Your brother's fucking dying back there."

Scott stopped, turned, and lunged at Mullens, but Mark saw him coming. He countered with a full-force rugby tackle, jettisoning them both into the water.

They thrashed around for a moment, limbs tangled together, until Mullens got the better of him, hauling him upright by his drenched anorak. Scott yelled in pain as Mark extended the man's arm back and up.

"Does that hurt? Oh, I am so sorry, dickwipe!" Mullens glanced back at the beach.

Harper was at the water's edge, sniggering.

"Are you going to help me or what?"

"Or what sounds good," Harper replied, his grin widening. With a sigh, he kicked off his shoes, rolled up his trouser legs, and waded out to assist.

Scanlon swung his free fist. But Mullens swerved and secured his arm behind his back.

"That's enough!" Mullens growled.

Harper cuffed him, and together they dragged their captive back to shore.

"You fuckers better not have killed my brother!"

"I think you were doing a good job of that already, Scanlon," Mullens growled.

Back at the campervan, the paramedic was joined by a second, and they were manoeuvring Craig back to the woods and a waiting ambulance.

"Where are they taking him?"

"Back to the care he needs, shit for brains," Mullens said, wringing out the sleeves of his ruined suit. "Look at the state of this. What a fucking clown you are!"

"This is total fucking harassment," Scanlon snarled. "Armed Response? For missing one parole meeting? You cunts must be fucking bored off your skulls. Is this how you get your fun? Hunting down a free man who's served his time and his brother who has fucking days to live?"

"Scott Scanlon, I'm arresting you for the murder of Dr Andrew Fraser," Harper started.

"Who the fuck is the kid?"

"You do not have to say anything. But it may harm your defence if you do not mention when questioned something which you later rely on in court. Anything you do say may be given in evidence. Do you understand?"

"I understand that you bastards have fucked everything." Scanlon exhaled. "All I wanted to do was say goodbye to my brother. Why don't you just leave us both alone? A few days, that's all I wanted."

Two uniformed officers took Scanlon away.

As they went, he called back, "Please!"

"That went well." Harper's grin returned.

"Shut it, specky." Mullens removed a shoe and emptied the water out.

"I'll have to tell the boss that we have a new wild swimmer in our midst."

"You'll be swimming up your own colon canal shortly, pal." Mullens threatened. "How's the brother doing?"

"Death's door, no thanks to Scanlon."

"Stupid arsehole, taking his brother out of the home like that."

"To be honest, I sort of understand. If it was my brother's last wish to go fishing, I'd probably want to do the same."

"Or if you'd just fried a couple of people, then you might use your brother as cover."

"There's that, too. I suppose when we get him in the interview room, it'll all come out in the wash." Harper chuckled.

"You think you're so fucking hilarious, don't you?"

"My only regret is not taking any photos for the incident board. At least it was a distraction."

"It was until you reminded me, bellend. I can see this is going to be a very long journey back to the station." Mullens pulled at the soaking fabric around his crotch and waddled up the path.

TWENTY-SEVEN

"You're back," Bone said, spotting Rhona by the incident board, sipping a large mug of steaming coffee. "How did you get on? Oh, is there any of that left?"

"Sorry, I pinched the last one. I'll share this one with you, if you like?"

"No, you look like you need it more than I do. Carry on."

"All pretty traumatic, as you would expect, but to be fair to Mrs McNeil, she was very helpful. She reported that two years ago a Daniel Quillan assaulted her husband following the death of Quillan's girlfriend in a car accident. Get this, she told me that a doctor also stopped to help the injured woman, but he had to leave to attend to an emergency at the hospital. The boyfriend blamed McNeil and the doctor for failing to save his girlfriend and lashed out."

"Did Mrs McNeil give you names of the doctor and the accident victim?" Bone asked.

"Sadly not."

"Gotcha!" Baxter yelled from behind her desk.

"God, Sheila. I didn't even see you there."

"Sorry, sir. I've been running checks on Mr Quillan. Two years ago, he served eight months for the aggravated assault of Mr McNeil. I couldn't find an address for him, no council tax records, which suggests he might be in a hostel or B and B. However, he does have a job and is currently employed by Parcels First."

"A delivery driver?" Bone asked.

"Looks like it. Their depot is out at the Cumberfield bypass."

"I've just bloody come from there," Bone complained. "Right, Rhona, let's go. Sheila, can you ping me the exact address?"

"I'll do that now. Oh, and before you distract me again..." She pursed her lips. "Stirling Royal finally got back to me. There was one documented fatality in the neo-natal unit over the New Year period, 2021. A Nathanial Black, mother Sadie Black."

"Father?"

"I know where you're going. But no, Sadie Black was a single mum, no father on the birth register. And sadly, tragically, Sadie Black died of cancer six months ago. So a dead end as far as any potential grieving parents out for revenge are concerned. But... and this is a big but," her eyes widened, "the consultant in charge was none other than Dr Andrew Fraser. Cause of death, respiratory failure."

"Eureka! Great work, Sheila," Bone said.

"I aim to please." She smiled again and rummaged in her bag for her lighter.

"Never a dull moment," Walker said, and put her jacket back on.

***

The Parcels First delivery warehouse was a hive of activity when Bone and Walker arrived. Delivery drivers and loaders buzzed up and down the aisles of the warehouse, shuffling parcels and packages with practiced efficiency. The detectives approached the supervisor's office where a harried-looking man barked orders into a radio.

"Thomas Hanks?" Bone asked, flashing his badge.

The supervisor looked up, his eyes narrowing. "Aye, that's me. What can I do for you, Officers?"

Bone raised an eyebrow. "Any relation to the Hollywood star?"

Hanks sighed. "Not worth it, mate. I've heard them all."

Walker stepped in before Bone could misfire another of his embarrassing jokes.

"We're here about one of your drivers, Danny Quillan."

"What's that wee shite done now?" He stopped, dashed out onto the floor, and bellowed at an employee who'd dropped a parcel on his way to one of the vans. "Any comeback on that one and I'll be on your arse, McCabe."

The packer scowled and returned to the conveyor belt at the other side of the floor.

"Numpties, the lot of them," he complained. "Anyhow, Danny... He's been with us for about seven months now. Not the best employee, if I'm honest. He's got two disciplinary warnings for tardiness and failed deliveries. One more strike and he's out."

Bone nodded thoughtfully. "So not employee of the month, then?"

"He's a sullen, uncooperative loner. Never in the canteen, doesn't talk to the other drivers. Just does his job and leaves with very little to say for himself."

"I like him already," Walker joked, earning a scowl from the supervisor.

"Is he on shift today?" Bone asked.

"Unfortunately for our customers, he is." He sat at his desk, piled high with papers and dog-eared printouts. After a few clicks of the keyboard, he located Quillan's van. "Says here he's out at Shilling Flats, Northfield Heights. Van registration is GS67 OLV."

"Lovely spot. What it lacks in basic human dignity, it makes up for in organised drug dealing," Walker said.

"Aye, our drivers have to keep their wits about them. Vans get broken into all the time. Bloody disgrace."

"Good job Parcel First insurance covers the losses then, isn't it?" Walker said, her dislike for the supervisor growing by the second.

Hanks shook his head. "Drivers have to pay for what they lose. Company policy."

"Of course it is," Bone said. "Well, thanks for your help, Mr Hanks. We'll let you get back to intimidating your staff."

"You try doing this job, see how long you last," the supervisor replied.

They left the depot, and Bone glanced at Walker. "Not fancy it, then?"

"I think even our career choice is marginally better, but it's a close shave."

"Right, Fawlty Towers then?"

Walker rolled her eyes. "I'll try to contain my excitement, sir."

At the car, Walker slipped behind the wheel, ignoring Bone's pained expression as he eyed the passenger seat with trepidation.

"I don't know why I gave in to your demands for a pool car, Rhona." He slid down into the BMW's soft leather upholstery and sighed.

"I was just thinking that very thought." She fired up the engine, and pointed the car in the direction of Shilling Flats.

***

A hair-raising, tyres-screeching ten minutes later, Walker pulled up by a dilapidated seventies tower block. She was out of the car before Bone could prise his white-knuckled fingers from his seat belt. They spotted Danny's van parked haphazardly by the kerb.

Walker squinted up at the building, scanning the balconies.

"There!" She pointed to a distant figure going door-to-door on the sixth floor.

"C'mon, before he makes a run for it." Bone legged it towards the building entrance, Walker hot on his heels.

Six thigh-knackering flights of piss-soaked concrete later, they arrived on the floor, just in time to see the figure disappearing into a flat.

"Police! Open up!" Bone hammered on the door.

A startled cry, then the door cracked open. Bone shouldered his way in to find a terrified postman clutching a handful of letters, chatting to a young woman.

"There he is!" Walker yelled from the balcony, her Hebridean lilt sharpened by adrenaline.

Bone dashed back out just in time to see Danny flick a cigarette high into the air, dash around the side of his van, climb in, and accelerate away.

They raced back down to the car park. Walker vaulted into the driver's seat, Bone scrambling to buckle up as she cranked the engine. The van shot out of the car park and tore off along the street.

"Hold tight," Walker cried.

"Don't worry, I intend to." Bone's knuckles whitened again around his belt.

She stamped the accelerator, and the pool car took off, leaving a plume of burning rubber smoke. She searched under the dash and hit the siren.

Bone's stomach lurched. The car swung out onto the main road, the tyres kissing the kerb with a loud thump.

The two vehicles zipped through the town centre, scattering shoppers and pensioners like skittles. Danny swerved onto Glenbrae Road, almost hitting the number forty-seven bus, then at the bottom of the high street, he took a sharp right and cut across the Coachman Hotel's car park, narrowly missing a cleaner out for a sly smoke.

"Where's this idiot going?" Bone shouted.

Walker drove past the car park entrance.

"He went in there!" Bone thumbed the turn.

"Only one way out on the other side. This way's shorter."

Walker raced on, and the van emerged from the rear exit a few feet in front. She sounded the horn on top of the siren, but the van kept going.

"God's sake," Bone complained.

When they reached the outskirts of Kilwinnoch, Danny's van kicked up gravel; it fishtailed down a country lane. Up ahead, Bone spotted open playing fields. Danny's rear lights flashed red.

"Here we go." Walker hit the brakes, Bone's seat belt saving him from a Glasgow handshake with the windscreen.

Danny leapt out of the van and stumbled across the boggy grass.

Bone thumped the dashboard, his patience unravelling. "Why do they always run? Just once, I'd love one of these muppets to do us a favour and just give it up and save us the pointless puff."

But Walker was already out of the car, sprinting at full pelt and gaining on Danny with every stride. A few feet from the farthest goalposts, she was within grabbing distance. She was about to launch herself at him when Danny stopped dead and spun around, hands raised in submission.

"All right, all right. I'm sorry. Please don't get me sacked."

Bone loped up behind Walker, breathing heavily. "I think you've got a wee bit more than losing your job to worry about."

Walker snapped the cuffs on Danny's wrists, and Bone recited the caution.

"Daniel Quillan, I'm arresting you on suspicion of the attempted murder of Robert McNeil."

Quillan's face crumpled in shock. "The paramedic? Kill him?" he slurred.

"Yup. Word is you had a pretty big axe to grind, what with him not being able to save your girlfriend."

"Oh, come on. I've not been near him."

"Like you weren't near him the night you hospitalised him?"

"Oh, Christ. You think I ran because I killed him?"

"That's how it's looking on the ground right now, Mr Quillan." Bone leaned in, his keen senses picking up the stench of stale booze. "Have you been drinking?"

"I just had a wee snifter this morning to steady my nerves. I wasnae going to drive pished, I swear. Please. I'm no' drunk."

They marched him back to his van, the detectives on either side, propping him up, his legs wobbly. Bone wrenched open the passenger door and picked up a half-empty whisky bottle from the seat.

Danny hung his head, tears and snot mingling on his chin. "That was last night. I forgot to clear it up."

Bone looked skyward in disbelief. "Aye, right. And I'm Shane MacGowan. Wind your neck in and get in the car."

"That's why I belted it one. I've only had a couple. I can't lose my job. I'll be back on the street again." Danny dissolved into snotty sobs, his bravado deserting him. "Why would I kill him now? You think I'm stupid?" he slurred. "I'd be the first person you'd come for."

"And here we are." Walker smiled.

"I did eight months inside for my stupid fucking temper. I've regretted it every fucking day since. Prison was the worst time of my life, which I'm never going to repeat. I cracked up in there, man. You can't send me away again." His sobs intensified. "Please. I learnt my lesson. I swear. I'm a changed man. Changed for good."

Quillan meekly allowed himself to be bundled into the back of the pool car, Walker slamming the door with a bit more force than was strictly necessary.

Bone raised an eyebrow. "Nice driving, by the way. I think my left kidney relocated to my right buttock."

Walker flashed him a cheeky grin. "Just be glad I was behind the wheel, sir. If we'd had to wait for your rust bucket to wheeze her way out of the car park, Danny-boy would be halfway to Venezuela by now."

"Let's get this drunken clown back to the station and see what he's got to say for himself when he sobers up," Bone said wearily.

"Judging by what's left in that bottle and the stench from the human distillery in the back, I think that's going to take a while."

"A while is something we don't have." Pinching his nose, Bone climbed back in the car. "Try not to breathe until we get to the station," he snarled, glaring at his captive.

Danny's head dropped, and he started snoring.

"Oh, dear God." Bone exhaled and wound down his window.

TWENTY-EIGHT

Mullens burst into the incident room, his face a picture of disgust. "Can you believe this?" He gestured at the attire—a lurid purple and yellowish-cream shell suit that looked like it had been rejected by a 1980s aerobics instructor—he'd been forced to change into since his clothes had got soaked in the loch.

"You know what she said?"

"Who?" Harper said, stifling a grin.

"Carol, the equipment manager. She goes, 'It was the only thing in the lost property box big enough to fit a Luton van,'" Mullens said in a high, squeaky voice. "The cheek of her."

Baxter appeared at the door, focused on pushing a pack of cigarettes back into her handbag.

She looked up. "Ah, you're back." Then she spotted Mullens and exploded with laughter.

Mullens scowled. "Aye, laugh it up, three-piece. I'm glad my misfortune amuses you."

Harper continued to battle to contain himself. "To be fair..." He swallowed another laugh. "Carol might be having a wee bit of a laugh at your expense."

"You think?" Mullens thundered, his expression akin to a teenager sulking.

"Can you blame her, though, after everything you've put her through over the years?" Baxter said.

"I'm the model of innocence," Mullens protested.

"You know, I think the shell suit rather suits you. You missed a golden opportunity to be in a boy band back in the day," Harper said.

"Or a drug dealer from the Northlands estate." Baxter chuckled.

Mullens tugged at the jacket, which strained across his broad chest. "Aye, righto." He shook his head. "Let's just get this over with. Where's our firestarter?"

"He's in interview room two. And he's not a happy camper," Baxter said.

"Me and him both," Mullens grumbled.

Mullens and Harper made their way down. Through the newly installed one-way glass, they could see Scott Scanlon, a wiry man with a shock of red hair and a face that looked like it had seen the end of a few fists. He paced the room, his hands clenching and unclenching at his sides, his slight frame vibrating with pent-up anger.

Mullens and Harper entered, the shell suit momentarily throwing Scanlon off his stride.

"Sit down, please, Mr Scanlon."

"How's my brother? Is he okay?" Scanlon asked.

"Now," Mullens ordered, pointing to the chair across the desk.

Scanlon reluctantly complied.

"He's being well looked after," Mullens said after a moment.

"Fucking police brutality, that's what it was. I'll be complaining, believe me."

"You do that. We'll give you the address and number to ring at the end of our wee chat."

Scanlon fell silent.

The detectives sat opposite, Mullens flipping open a file, setting the recorder running and quickly going through the introductory blurb. He sat back.

"Mr Scanlon, before we begin, you have waived your right to a solicitor present, is that correct?"

"I've no' done anything wrong. I just want to get back to my brother before you lot do him in."

"We'd like to ask you a few questions about the fire at the Frasers' house."

Scanlon's eyes flashed with surprise. "What? Oh fuck. I see. Right. I get it now." He shook his head.

"What do you get?" Mullens asked.

"Fucking stitch-up." He smiled and nodded. "Under pressure to solve your investigation, are you? Well, let me tell you right now, for your wee tape." He leaned closer to the recorder. "I had nothing to do with that. I've been with my brother."

Mullens raised an eyebrow. "Aye, about that. You want to tell us why you skipped your parole meeting?"

"Crime of the century, right there. I got a call from my brother's care home. They said…" His face fell. "They said Craig was in his last days. I had to go to him."

Harper cut in. "We understand this is a difficult time, Mr Scanlon."

Mullens shot Will a look.

"But we still need to account for your whereabouts."

"Good cop, bad cop?" Scanlon smirked. He slumped back in his chair and ran his hand over his face. "Craig's all I've got. He looked after me when we were kids, you know? Our parents… They were useless drunks. Craig made sure I had food, clothes, got to school." His eyes welled up. "And now, with his leukaemia, it's my turn to look after him."

Mullens flipped a page in the file. "Says here you were an animal rights activist. Got a bit of a record for targeting health care and pharmaceutical types in the Borders."

Scanlon's head snapped up. "That was years ago. I was… I was in a bad place. Got in with the wrong crowd. They programmed me, exploited me. But I've changed. My stretch in prison, the counselling… It helped me see how wrong I was."

"Programmed you, did they?" Mullens pressed. "What, like the CIA does with their secret army of squirrels? Next thing you'll be telling me they made you wear a tinfoil hat. Very easy to pass the buck, Scott."

Scanlon's face reddened, but he didn't rise to the bait. "I know how it sounds. I take full responsibility for my actions, and I served my time. But I was vulnerable. I am not that person now." He took a shuddering breath. "I blame myself for Craig's illness. The stress I put him through back then… I'll never forgive myself."

Mullens leaned forward. "So where were you on Sunday morning, around two a.m.?"

"I told you, I was with Craig. We were parked in a lay-by off a lane near Loch Lomond. In the campervan I hired."

Harper slid a photo across the table. "For the recording, we are showing Mr Scanlon image 5A, a still shot of a man entering the Frasers' garden on the night of the fire. Is this you, Mr Scanlon?"

Scanlon stared at the photo, his face reddening. "That's not me. I don't know who that is, but it's not me."

Harper produced another photo. "And now a second image, 5B, of a vehicle captured on CCTV."

"Is that your Citroën van crossing Hagg's Hill that night?" Mullens asked.

Scanlon slammed his hand on the table. "Are you deaf? I told you, I was in a hired campervan. I've had it for ten days. That's not my van in that photo. I don't own or drive a Citroën."

Mullens smiled, his tone conciliatory. "Temper, temper, Mr Scanlon. That sort of behaviour can get you into all sorts of trouble, as well you know."

"Piss off." Scanlon folded his arms.

Harper intervened again. "Look, Scott, we can clear this up quickly. Just give us the passcode to your mobile phone. We can check your location data for the night of the fire. If you were where you say you were, you'll be ruled out and you can walk out of here."

Scanlon's face darkened. He shook his head vehemently. "No. No way. You're not going through my phone."

Mullens chuckled. "Come on, Scanlon, don't be a dick. We're not interested in your petrol can porn pics. This is your chance to prove your innocence and get out of here. Though, it sounds to me like you have something to hide after all."

For a moment, it seemed like Scanlon might comply. But then his agitation surged again. "I want a solicitor. You… you'll plant evidence on my phone, twist things so you can bang me up again. I know how you freaks operate."

Mullens stood, looming over Scanlon. "There's only one freak in the room, Mr Scanlon. I think you'd better calm down. Unless you want to add assaulting an officer to your woes."

Scanlon stood, too, his chair clattering to the floor. "I've had enough of this stitch-up. I want to speak to a solicitor. Now."

Mullens glanced at his watch. "Interview paused at eighteen forty-seven." He clicked off the tape recorder. "We'll give you a moment to compose yourself, Mr Scanlon. Then we'll see about that solicitor."

Out in the corridor, Harper turned to Mullens. "What do you think, sir?"

Mullens shook his head. "Hundred and ten percent weirdo."

Harper frowned. "Yes, but his emotions about his brother… They seemed raw and real. And he was pretty adamant about being in that campervan."

"He's a fruit and nut, Will. You saw his file. He ran amok in the Borders, targeting anyone he thought was mistreating animals. He's no' exactly a poster boy for mental stability."

Harper nodded, but he couldn't shake the nagging doubt. "What if someone is setting him up? Copying his crimes to cover their tracks?"

"That might be a bit of a stretch?" Mullens replied.

"Well, it might come down to the phone records, to prove this one way or another. If he's got nothing to hide, why not let us look? It could clear him."

Mullens considered this for a moment, then nodded. "Aye, that's a fair point. Okay, let's get the duty solicitor down here. Scanlon can stew in his own juices for a while." He stopped and checked his watch again. "Until the morning, in fact. That's more than enough for one day. Let's finish up and get the fuck out of here."

TWENTY-NINE

When Bone and Walker returned to the incident room, they were surprised to find Harper's fiancée, Catriona McKenzie, there chatting with the team.

"Well, well, well," Bone said with a grin, "if it isn't the future Mrs Harper. How are the wedding plans coming along?"

Catriona beamed, her excitement palpable. "Oh, it's all falling into place. The Loch Gillan Village Hotel is just perfect."

Bone chuckled, a mischievous glint in his eye. "I've had a word with Andy, the chef. Told him to make sure every course in the wedding breakfast includes mackerel."

Walker's face paled, her eyes widening in horror. "No, no, no," she muttered and shook her head vehemently. "I can't. Not again. The smell, the taste… It was everywhere."

The team erupted in laughter, the tension of the case momentarily forgotten.

Bone, catching sight of Mullens's attire, couldn't resist a comment. "What in God's name are you wearing, Mark?"

Mullens was about to explain his tussle with Scanlon, but Harper interrupted.

"He's starring in a new film about soccer hooligans in the 1980s. It's called 'The Mullet'."

Mullens scowled at Harper. "So hilarious. You should get better writers, mate."

Walker, unable to resist, chimed in, "You'd better not stand too close to an open flame in that outfit. You could go up in seconds." She paused, realizing the insensitivity of her joke. "Sorry, that was inappropriate. Forget I said that."

But the team was already on a roll. And Bone couldn't let it go.

"It's true, though. And stay out of high winds. Once that thing inflates, you could be in the Hook of Holland before you know it."

Baxter nodded. "You'd fit right in there in that get-up."

"So, anyway…" Mullens sighed. "Will, when are you going to confess to Catriona about the er… rash?"

"It's a birthmark!" Harper protested.

"Yes, I secretly swabbed that and sent it off for analysis before I agreed to marry him," Catriona cut in. "He's also shown me his giant wart, and I think we can work around that, though I may need a ladder."

The team erupted in laughter again.

"She's all right, that one." Mullens grinned.

"Oh God, what have I let myself in for? A Mullens at work and now another at home." Harper winked at his bride-to-be.

Baxter grimaced. "Two? Of him? Perish the thought."

Walker changed the topic as it was making her feel queasy. "Are you still running with the *Star Wars* theme for the wedding?"

Mullens's eyes widened. "*Star Wars*? Nobody told me about that. I smell a setup here. I'm not wearing doughnuts on my scone, I'll tell you that much."

"Don't worry, Mark," Will said. "We've got the giant Jabba the Hutt costume all ready for you."

Catriona laughed. "We started with these big, extravagant plans, with all sorts of details from the whole franchise. But then we realised we'd probably be the only ones who would get most of the references, so we've toned it down a bit."

Bone pouted. "Boo. I was so looking forward to wearing a Stormtrooper outfit."

Harper shook his head. "No, sir, we had you down for Obi—"

"Wanker Knobby," Mullens finished.

"The oldest member of the cast, cheers. That has been noted in your record, Will."

"There will still be a few surprises, though," Catriona continued.

Baxter clapped her hands. "Oh, I'm very excited. My husband and I never go out anymore."

Mullens smirked. "Too busy at the loom, weaving all that Harris Tweed?"

Baxter shot him a withering glare, but the twinkle in her eye betrayed her amusement.

As the laughter subsided, the team's focus shifted back to the matter at hand.

"Catriona, I take it you're here not just to laugh at Mark's get-up, but because you've had a look at the latest message scratched into the paintwork of the burnt-out van?" Bone asked, his tone turning serious.

Catriona nodded, her professionalism sliding into place. "Yes, not a comprehensive analysis, but I thought I should call in to give you some initial thoughts."

She gestured to the monitor where Harper had displayed high-resolution images of the scratched message: FIRST DO NO HARM.

"I've conducted an initial analysis. There are some interesting features here."

She pointed to specific letters, her finger tracing the lines on the screen. "You see here, and here, the flatline effect on these two letters? It's common in the handwriting of individuals who tend to scribble and join their lettering, suggesting a person not accustomed to handwriting frequently."

The team leaned in, their eyes following Catriona's explanations.

She continued, "The weight of the scores, the depth of the scratches, indicates someone with significant upper arm strength. But more than that, the inconsistency in the pressure applied suggests a hurried or agitated state. Angry, even. Very angry, I'd say."

Catriona then moved on to a more detailed analysis. She pointed to the 'F' in 'First'.

"Notice the elongated stem, the heavy pressure at the top. This indicates a strong level of determination, almost aggression. The writer was pressing hard, likely due to high emotional arousal."

"Or to get the screwdriver through the paintwork?" Mullens suggested, half sarcastically.

"Yes, there is that, but the nature of the strokes suggest added aggression," Catriona countered.

Moving on to the 'D' in 'do', she traced the letter's shape.

"Here, the curved stroke is interrupted, jagged. Perhaps a sudden change in emotion here, possibly more frustration than anger. It's as if the writer's hand was shaking with the force of their feelings."

The team absorbed Catriona's analysis, their faces grim. She pointed to the 'H' in 'harm'.

"The crossbar of the 'H' is slanted upwards, a sign of optimism, of hope. But look at the final stroke, how it slashes downward, crossing through the other letters. This is perhaps a mark of defiance, of contradiction. It's as if the writer is at war with themselves, their principles clashing with their actions."

Bone frowned. "A conflict between their conscience and a desire for revenge? Justice?"

Catriona nodded. "That's certainly one interpretation. The message itself, 'First do no harm', is of course the core tenet of medical ethics and certainly points to the possibility of revenge for harm-doing, but with clear intent to publicly shame in some way."

Mullens frowned. "So we're looking for an attention-seeking knobhead?"

Catriona smiled patiently. "In a manner of speaking, yes. The writer was likely in a heightened emotional state, and the message was scratched in haste. The depth of the scores, particularly here"—she pointed to a particularly vicious-looking gouge—"is shouting a declaration. It speaks to a level of rage that's quite unsettling."

Bone rubbed his chin thoughtfully. "Rage. Interesting. So we're not just dealing with a calculating arsonist, but one with a serious emotional investment."

Walker nodded. "That tracks with the brutality of the murders. This isn't just about the fires; it's personal. But it could also be an Achilles' heel. A weak spot. Emotion and calculated crimes don't usually mix."

The team fell silent for a moment, each processing the implications of Catriona's analysis.

It was Harper who broke the quiet. "Cat, is there anything else you can tell us? Anything that might help us narrow down our suspect pool?"

Catriona sighed. "Not at this stage. I'll need to do a more in-depth analysis, compare it to any handwriting samples you can provide. But this is a good starting point. I hope it gives you a head start on a psychological profile you can apply to the people of interest."

Bone clapped his hands together. "Right, you heard the lady. Let's start digging deeper into our suspects' backgrounds. Look for any history of violence, anger management issues, mental illness, anything that might fit this profile."

As the team set to work, Bone turned to Catriona. "Thank you very much. This is invaluable. And don't worry, we'll make sure Harper makes it to the altar in one piece."

Catriona grinned. "You'd better. We've got a honeymoon in the Lake District planned, and I'm not going alone."

As she left the incident room, Harper watched her go, a soppy smile on his face.

Mullens sidled up to him. "Ah, two young lovebirds off to the glorious sun-kissed, sparkling paradise waters of… the Lake District? I mean, is that the best you could do?"

"Just between us, I've managed to land tickets to the *Star Wars* Celebration in the Anaheim Convention Centre, California, the biggest in the world. I'm just stringing her along with the lakes thing."

"Well, now you're talking… not." Mullens blew out his cheeks.

"And the package includes meeting Mark Hamill."

"You really are the saddest people I know. And believe me, that's a very low bar."

"Is that part of your best man's speech?"

"Comes just after the sheep joke," Mullens replied.

Harper clocked Mullens's expression and wasn't sure if he meant it or not.

"I suggest you get yourself home and get out of that gear, Mark, before our new look hits the *Chronicle* front page," Bone said.

"At last, some sympathy for my plight. Out of here. See you in the morning, folks." He grabbed his bag and marched to the door.

"Aren't you forgetting something, Mark?" Harper called over.

Mullens pulled a face, then a moment later remembered.

"The Goth gig? Is that tonight?"

"It is indeed."

"Oh great. Just what I need. An evening in a room full of vampire depressos jumping around to death-warmed-up noise."

"On second thoughts, I'm not sure I'll let you go home to change," Bone interrupted.

"Funny haha!"

"I don't know, the boss is right. It's the perfect undercover get-up. You'll fit right in." Walker sniggered.

"Fucking clowns," Mullens cursed. "What time does it start?"

"Seven-thirty," Harper confirmed.

"Okay, see you outside just before they let the bats out."

"Go on. Get out before I really change my mind," Bone ordered.

Mullens zipped up his top, attempted a rap gesture, and left.

THIRTY

Before Bone could sit at the nearest available desk, Baxter's phone rang. She answered, acknowledged the call, and hung up.

"Sir, that was the super. He wants to see you in his office."

"Now?"

"Yup." She pulled a face.

Bone dropped his bag and gave his team a sarcastic wave goodbye.

He entered Superintendent Gallacher's office, surprised to find Kilwinnoch's formidable female provost already seated, her face a mask of barely contained fury. Gallacher, ever the diplomat, was attempting to placate her.

"Provost Rennie, I assure you, we are doing everything in our power to resolve this case as quickly and efficiently as possible."

The provost was having none of it. "And yet, Superintendent, your DCI sees fit to lock up my deputy on baseless accusations. It's an outrage!" Her voice softened slightly, concern creeping in. "Mr Blackwell took some time off after his wife passed, but I don't think it was nearly long enough. He doesn't need this horrific pressure and these falsehoods landing at his door right now."

Bone stepped forward, his jaw set. "With all due respect, the accusations are far from baseless. We have witness statements and footage from a neighbour's security camera that provide compelling evidence of your deputy's involvement."

The provost's eyes flashed with indignation. "Utter tosh! Mr Blackwell is a respected member of this community. He's a good man who has served the people of Kilwinnoch for over a decade with a faultless record and a dedication that inspires my entire team."

She leaned forward, her voice earnest. "He's an accountant, for God's sake. If he comes across as a little odd, overassertive, or even arrogant at times, it's because he's compensating for his recently diagnosed autism. The idea that he could be involved in these fires is so far beyond his capabilities it's laughable."

Bone opened his mouth to respond, but the provost steamrolled on.

"His reputation is in tatters. I wouldn't be surprised if he takes legal action against the force. I certainly would, in his position."

Bone's patience snapped. "Perhaps you should stick to your job and let me get on with mine."

Gallacher, clearly sensing the rapidly deteriorating situation, intervened. "Provost Rennie, I give you my word, if Mr Blackwell is innocent, I will personally make a public statement to that effect. But I'm afraid until we are satisfied that Mr Blackwell is not involved, then we will have to continue to detain him."

"Well, you need to keep an eye on him. He won't be handling any of this at all well, so see to it that you find the evidence you need and release the poor man." She stormed out of the office, her anger still palpable.

Bone watched her go, his own frustration simmering just below the surface.

As the door closed, Gallacher rounded on Bone. "Duncan, what the hell are you playing at? You've got three people in custody. Surely they can't all be responsible for these murders?"

Bone stood his ground. "Sir, the evidence against each of them is compelling. We have an arsonist with a history of targeting medical professionals, a man who served time for assaulting the critically ill paramedic, and now a councillor in a vulnerable state of grief with an eyewitness and possible video placing him at the scene at the time of the fire."

Gallacher shook his head. "Come on, Duncan. Even you must see how this looks. It's chaos."

"You know me too well by now to be swayed by appearances. I'm interested in catching the bastard responsible for these crimes."

"And what about Katherine Fraser?" Gallacher demanded. "You may be hell-bent on catching this lunatic, but you're still no closer to finding her. The press is having a field day."

Bone sighed. "With respect sir, there's a nationwide search ongoing and my team is working literally round the clock, as we always do. We're doing everything we can and we'll get there."

"You'd better. And as for Mr Blackwell, either charge him or release him. We can't keep him in limbo."

"Just give me one more interview. I think I'm close to cracking him."

Gallacher snorted. "Cracking up, more like." But he relented. "Fine. One more interview, but don't let him stew any longer. If the provost is right, he's vulnerable."

"They always are, sir." Bone shrugged.

"If you don't have anything concrete, release him immediately, and I'll start grovelling to the powers that be to avoid a lawsuit." He fixed Bone with a hard stare. "Your scattergun approach is starting to remind me of how you were before. I need to know you're in control."

Bone met his gaze unflinchingly. "I assure you, my actions are guided by evidence, not instability. It is the nature of this particular crime, not the state of my mind. We're close. You have to trust me."

"I have so many times before, and you see where that got me."

"With a track record of solved crimes," Bone retorted.

"Just bear in mind, Duncan, the fact that the provost is putting her own reputation on the line to support her colleague indicates that she trusts him implicitly. She truly believes he's incapable of these crimes. That's a risky move for a politician. Doesn't that tell you something?"

Bone paused at the door. "With respect… Reputation, respect, and trust have provided some of the best cover for the headbangers we've locked up over the years. A cloak of goodness to cover the truth. And let's not forget, we have a hostage situation and a national manhunt. I'm prepared to lock up as many suspects as it takes if it means we find Katherine Fraser alive and get the maniac off the streets and behind bars."

Gallacher's face reddened. "You don't need to remind me of the gravity of the situation. I'm in the middle of preparing yet another public statement and fielding increasingly aggressive phone calls from my boss in Edinburgh."

Bone scoffed. "Those office clerks at St Andrew's House have completely lost touch with on-the-ground policing."

"That may be," Gallacher countered, "but they hold the gun to our heads—to my head—and I'm at the stage now where I'm beginning to wish they'd just pull the fucking trigger."

A heavy silence fell between them.

Finally, Gallacher spoke. "Just find Katherine Fraser. Find her, and find the bastard responsible for all this. Before it's too late for all of us."

Bone nodded, then left the office, the weight of the case pressing down on him with renewed force.

THIRTY-ONE

As Gallacher ordered, Bone's last job of the day was to reinterview the deputy councillor. He apologised to Walker for extending her day even more, but she was happy and willing, as always, to support him.

Bone and Walker entered the interview room, the councillor visibly distressed and anxious, sitting hunched at the table, his hands fidgeting restlessly.

Bone took a seat opposite him "Mr Blackwell, before we begin, I want to make sure you're still comfortable proceeding without legal representation."

The councillor nodded vigorously. "I'm innocent. The fewer people who know about this misunderstanding, the better."

Walker's intuition prickled. There was something in the councillor's demeanour, a hint of embarrassment or secrecy, that suggested he might be hiding something.

Bone continued, his face grim. "We appreciate your cooperation, but we need to ask you a few more questions."

The councillor's eyes darted between the detectives, his breathing shallow. "I've been in that cell for hours. It's humiliating. I... I can't cope with enclosed spaces. I'm claustrophobic."

Walker's expression softened. "We understand this is difficult for you. If you need a break at any point, just let us know."

The councillor nodded, swallowing hard. "I've been diagnosed with autism. I find all of this too much."

Bone leaned forward, his elbows on the table. "I must remind you that there is hard evidence stacked against you. We have video footage of a man in the Frasers' next-door neighbour's garden around the time a witness identified you crossing the street. This was just before the fire was reported."

The councillor's face crumpled. "Okay, I was in the wrong place at the wrong time."

"What do you mean?"

The councillor exhaled, and his gaze dropped to the floor.

"Councillor Blackwell. Unless you can prove you were elsewhere, we'll have no choice but to charge you."

At this, Blackwell became extremely upset. Tears welled in his eyes, his voice cracking. "My career, my standing in the community, it'll all be tarnished forever."

Bone's tone was matter of fact. "That'll be the least of your worries if you go down for murder."

The room fell silent, save for the councillor's shaky breaths.

Finally, after a long moment of internal struggle, he spoke. "I've been so lonely since my wife died," he confessed, his voice barely above a whisper. "It's so hard to go back to an empty house, an empty bed, after so many years of marriage." Tears spilled down his cheeks. "I miss her so much. Please, don't judge me."

Bone and Walker exchanged a glance.

Bone pressed on. "If you have information that can clear your name, now is the time to share it."

The councillor hesitated, his mouth opening and closing as he grappled with his words. "I… I was on a date that night. Not exactly a romantic date."

Walker's eyebrows rose. "You mean Tinder?"

The councillor nodded reluctantly. "Yes."

Bone leaned back in his chair. "We'll need the name and contact details of your date."

The councillor's eyes widened in alarm. "Is that really necessary? I mean, can't it be kept confidential?"

Bone pressed on. "If you want to clear your name, we need to verify your alibi."

"Please," the councillor pleaded, "if I give you the name, can you assure me it won't be made public?"

Walker stepped in, her voice reassuring. "If your alibi checks out, that'll be the end of it. Your personal life is none of our business."

The councillor seemed to consider this for a moment, then nodded slowly. "The contact is on my phone. Her name is Joyce. She'll be able to confirm how long I was with her and when I left."

"And what about the sighting of you on Horsbrugh Close?"

"Yes, I was on my way home, but the person on your recording is not me. I wouldn't dream of going through the Finniestons' garden. Your witness probably saw me cutting across the close, heading for the pathway at the end that runs through to my road. Crazy." He shook his head and took a long, deep breath, his chest shaking with his exhale. "But it was the first and last time I'll be using a site like that. It just made me feel even lonelier."

Bone stood. "Okay, interview suspended at six oh three p.m. We'll retrieve your mobile from evidence. Sit tight, Mr Blackwell."

The detectives left the room, the door clicking shut behind them. In the corridor, Walker turned to Bone.

"I feel for him," she said. "Losing a spouse, the loneliness… It can't be easy."

Bone nodded. "Let's hope this alibi pans out. If it does, he's off the hook."

Walker agreed. "He seems genuinely upset. And does he really look like a guy who could lug forty-litre jerry cans along with a kidnapped wife to and from a van?"

"We'll know soon enough," Bone said.

They made their way to the evidence store.

He paused for a moment, then added, "I didn't want to say before we went in, but Gallacher had a visitor earlier."

"Not head office?"

"Possibly worse. Our lady provost, Rennie. She was beside herself with fury that we'd picked him up in the first place. Threatening all sorts."

"What? That's ridiculous, and potentially prejudicial to our investigation."

"The super, of course, was pressing me to either charge or release the councillor."

"Ah, that explains the urgency. Jesus Christ, does the provost realise the gravity of the case? There's still a missing woman out there."

Bone shook his head. "She seemed more concerned about us mistreating her friend. But if he's innocent, we're probably in the shit yet again."

Walker sighed. "We're damned if we do, damned if we don't."

"That should be our motto," Bone replied.

But Walker could see he wasn't joking.

THIRTY-TWO

Harper checked his watch. Seven thirty-five. "Where the hell is he?" he muttered.

The queue of Goths, metalheads, and assorted horror extras outside the student union building was slowly dwindling, and the doorman, a hulking pitbull-faced sumo-giant of a man, kept eyeballing Harper with suspicion. He checked his watch again, sighed, and was about to join the back of the queue when Mullens arrived.

"I can't believe I'm missing tatties and mince night at the Fells for this," Mullens grumbled. He turned to eyeball Harper's outfit. "My turn this time. What the hell are you wearing?"

Harper tugged nervously at his too-tight black t-shirt. "I'm just trying to blend in."

Mullens snorted. "Aye, well, you look about as undercover as a Technicolour duvet, son." He shrugged. "Well, are we going in or what?"

"I was waiting for you before I joined the queue."

"Queue? Fuck that." He marched straight to the front of the line, Harper trailing sheepishly in his wake.

The doorman stepped in front of them, blocking their path.

"Oi, lads, back of the queue like everyone else," he growled.

Mullens puffed out his chest, ready to flash his warrant card, but Harper grabbed his arm, shaking his head frantically. The last thing they needed was to blow their cover before they even got inside.

With a muttered curse, Mullens allowed Harper to lead him to the end of the line, ignoring the slow clap and jeers from the assembled Goths.

After what felt like an eternity, they finally reached the front again. The doorman greeted them with the same incredulous frown. "Tickets?"

Harper patted his pockets, feigning surprise. "Ah, shite, I think we forgot them, eh, Mark?"

Mullens grinned, leaning in conspiratorially. "Listen, pal, we're on official business, if you get my drift." He flashed his warrant card discreetly, but the doorman barely glanced at it.

"I don't care if you're Miss fucking Marple, mate. No ticket, no entry."

Mullens's face turned an alarming shade of puce, but Harper quickly stepped in, fishing out his wallet.

"Two tickets, please," he said, handing over a crumpled twenty.

As the doorman grudgingly stamped their hands, Mullens leaned in, his voice a low growl. "I'll be having a word with your boss about this, ya besuited breeze block."

"Aye you do that," the doorman snarled and reluctantly let them pass.

***

Inside, the Student Union Building was a seething mass of black lace, leather, and facial piercings.

Harper grabbed the arm of a passing Goth and hollered over the din, "Who's that playing now, mate?"

The Goth, his pupils the size of dinner plates, grinned dopily. "It's B-Moth, man! They're fucking brilliant!"

Mullens, towering over most of the crowd, carved a path through the throng, his bulk parting the sea of Goth princesses and metalhead warriors like Moses through the Red Sea. Harper ducked in behind him.

On stage, the band lurched into their final number, a discordant mess of growled vocals, chugging guitars, and blast beats. The singer, a lanky lad with a face full of metal and a complexion that suggested he'd never seen daylight in his lifetime, hunched over the mic, his hair hanging in a greasy curtain.

They pushed to the front, and a flailing elbow caught Mullens square in the face.

"Right, that's fucking it," he roared and grabbed the offending Goth by the scruff of the neck. "You're coming with me, you little shite."

Harper intervened just in time, pulling Mullens away before he could start a full-scale riot. "Leave it, Mark!"

The audience response to B-Moth's set was lukewarm at best, a smattering of applause and a few half-hearted whoops.

"Christ, that was painful," Mullens grumbled, rubbing at his ears. "I've heard cats in a food mixer sound better than that shower of shite."

Harper dragged him towards the bar, where the members of B-Moth held court.

As they approached, the singer eyed them warily.

"Nice set, lads," Mullens said, all jovial bonhomie. "Real, eh, unique sound you've got there."

The bassist, another beanpole with hair dyed the colour of an oil slick, perked up.

"Wait, are you guys from a record company or something?"

Mullens grinned, playing along. "Aye, that's right. We're from, eh, Shitehole Records, based out of Glasgow. Always on the lookout for fresh talent, you know?"

Harper choked on a laugh but managed to turn it into a passable cough.

The band exchanged excited glances, but the singer's eyes narrowed. "Hold on a fucking minute," he rasped, his voice like sandpaper on rusty metal. "You two are fucking polis, aren't you?"

Mullens held up his hands in mock surrender. "Guilty as charged, pal. Was it the fact that I don't look like one of Frankenstein's solder-scars that gave it away?"

The band tensed, suddenly on edge.

"What do you want with us?" the guitarist asked, nervously fingering his ripped Cannibal Corpse t-shirt.

Harper stepped in, trying to defuse the tension. "We're looking for Josh Fraser. Heard he used to drum for you lot."

The bassist shrugged. "Used to, aye. But he fucked off to Australia ages ago. Haven't seen him since."

Mullens leaned in, his smile turning predatory. "Funny, that. Because we've got it on good authority that Josh is still kicking about Kilwinnoch."

Harper glanced over, surprised but approving of Mullens's bluff.

The band shifted uneasily, avoiding eye contact.

"Of course," Mullens continued, his tone conversational, "I could always put a quick call in to the drug squad. I'm sure they'd be very interested in the contents of most of these punters' pockets. And then there's your homes. The DS dogs will have a field day sniffing around in there, I'm sure."

The singer caved. "All right, fuck's sake. I might have seen Josh a couple of weeks back, coming out of that old farmhouse on the edge of Campsie Village. But I wouldn't swear to it."

"What farmhouse?" Harper asked.

"You know? The squat up there."

"Not that roach-infested dump overrun with drunks and druggies?"

"You may disapprove, but the law sees it differently," the singer said smugly. "They have squatters' rights. All property is theft, man."

"Aye, right, if that's so, then I fancy trying my hand at your guitarist's damn fine-looking Fender Strat. I'm having that."

"You are welcome to it. It's a crap copy, and the piece of shit doesn't tune properly," the guitarist piped up.

"Ah, that explains it. And here was me thinking it was the music that was making the entire audience hate that cacophonous shite you were pumping out."

The singer shrugged, pretending not to care.

Harper redirected the conversation. "Why'd he leave the band anyway?"

The bassist sniffed. "Because he was a fucking liability, man. Always wasted, starting fights, missing rehearsals. He couldn't even keep time by the end, he was so out of it."

"Aye, a real piece of work, was our Josh," the guitarist chimed in. "I mean, we're not exactly choirboys, but that cunt was on another level."

"Right, well, it was emotional. We'll be in touch if we need anything else."

Mullens turned to leave, Harper falling into step beside him.

"Oh, and by the way," Mullens called over his shoulder, "I'd think about changing that fucking name. B-Moth? Sounds like an insect porn movie."

As they pushed through the crowd towards the exit, Harper leaned in. "So, what now?"

Mullens grinned, a feral flash of teeth. "Now, my wee Goth-loving friend, we take a trip out to Campsie Village. See if we can't flush young Master Fraser out of his hidey-hole."

"If he's there then maybe his mum too? Should we request ARU support."

"Let's just go see what's going on first. We still don't know if the clown's in the country. But maybe take a couple of uniforms to help us."

"What car? We arrived separately, remember?"

"If you think we're going in your mum's Astra, then think again, sunshine. I'll drop you back for it later."

Harper sighed and followed Mullens to the pool car.

THIRTY-THREE

Mullens veered the car onto the verge of the narrow lane leading up to the derelict house, just visible beyond the trees. The detectives climbed out. Harper fished in the boot and retrieved two stab vests. Mullens tugged at the straps, grumbling under his breath.

"Not this again. Too bloody small, as usual," he moaned.

Harper smirked. "Aye, that's right, Mark. It's not you, it's the entire world that's too small."

Mullens shot him a withering look, but before he could retort, a squad car drew up behind them. Two uniformed officers stepped out, nodding at the detectives.

"Right, lads," Mullens said, his tone serious now. "We're headed into a notorious squat. Place is a haven for the town's disaffected disasters—drug users, musicians, dropouts, and general waste-of-space bumholes. Some of these squatters might be trouble, with a history of violence against coppers, so stay alert. We're after a guy called Josh Fraser."

"Is he related to the doc that fried in the fire?" one of the PCs interrupted.

"Not appropriate, Constable," Mullens pulled him up.

Harper's eyes widened at the flagrant irony.

"Sorry, sir. We're on a late one."

"You don't have to bloody remind me," Mullens snapped back. "There is also a possibility that Katherine Fraser might be in there as well, maybe being held against her will. So we'll need to search room to room." He gestured to the crumbling house. "Watch the entrances, but…" He eyed the empty window frames and a side wall that had partially collapsed. "Well, considering the state of the place, do your best."

The uniforms nodded.

"And be careful," Mullens added, his voice grim. "Remember, there are off-their-face nutbags in there. And Mrs Fraser, if she's in there, could be injured."

With that, the detectives set off, navigating the narrow, pothole-ridden track that led to their destination.

At the gateless gap in a disintegrating wall, Mullens gestured for the two officers to go around either side of the building. They picked their way through the garden, stepping over mounds of split rubbish bags, rotting, rancid food waste, and empty booze cans and bottles.

When they reached the entrance, the door was swinging back and forth, hanging precariously from only one hinge. With a quick look at one another, they continued on.

Inside, the air was thick with the sickly sweet stench of marijuana and the acrid tang of unwashed bodies. A group of youths lazed on moth-eaten sofas pushed up against graffitied walls. They barely acknowledged the detectives' presence, most too wasted to notice. Music thrummed from somewhere deeper in the house, a discordant mix of thrash metal and psychedelic rock.

"Dr Andrew Fraser's son, Josh," Mullens announced, holding up a photo. "Seen him?"

A few heads turned, glazed eyes struggling to focus.

"Try the back," a girl with a purple mohawk mumbled, before slumping back into her drug-induced haze.

Mullens and Harper exchanged a glance and pressed on, winding their way through the labyrinthine house. They passed a makeshift recording studio, where a group of musicians in ripped jeans and leather jackets argued over a riff, and a room filled with abstract art canvases, the paint-spattered artist herself sprawled unconscious in the corner, still clutching her brush.

"Fuck's sake," Mullens mouthed.

At the very back of the house, they found a door barricaded with a broken sofa.

"Give me a hand," Mullens grunted.

Together, they wrestled the obstacle out of the way, the effort leaving them breathless.

The stench hit them like a physical blow as they forced the door open. Vomit, sweat, and the unmistakable odour of heroin. There, on a stained mattress in the corner, lay Josh Fraser. His skin had a greyish tinge, his lips blue, his body covered in his own sick. A used syringe rested on the floor beside him.

"Shit," Harper breathed. "Is he…?"

Mullens was already moving, his fingers searching for a pulse. "He's alive. Barely. Call an ambulance, now!"

Harper fumbled for his radio. Mullens rolled the young man into the recovery position, clearing his airway as best he could. Vomit smeared his hands, his clothes.

"They're on their way," Harper said, his face pale. "But in this traffic…"

Mullens looked up, his expression grim. "He might not have that long."

Harper nodded, understanding. He dashed out of the room, back into the main living area where the squatters lounged in various states of intoxication.

"Naloxone!" Harper shouted, his voice cracking with desperation. "Anyone got Naloxone? The lad is overdosing!"

The semi-comatose residents stared at him blankly, some giggling, others too far gone to react. Harper wanted to shake them, make them understand the urgency, but there was no time.

"Oi, mate," slurred a skinny youth with a mohawk. He stumbled towards Harper with a half-empty bottle of Buckfast in his hand. "Calm down, mate. Ye want some o' this? That'll sort ye right out."

Harper brushed past him, barely resisting the urge to slap the bottle out of his hand.

And then, from the corner, a figure stirred. It was an old man, his grey hair hanging in matted dreadlocks, his weathered face etched with the lines of a hard life. He wore a tattered army surplus jacket adorned with peace symbols and anti-war slogans.

"Did you say you need Naloxone, son?" His voice was rough, but his eyes were clear and sharp.

"Aye," Harper gasped. "Please, if you have any, quickly…"

The old hippie nodded, already rummaging in his battered rucksack. "Always carry it, ever since my own boy…" He shook his head. "Ye never know when someone might need it."

He pulled out a small green pouch and handed it to Harper. Inside was a nasal spray, the lifesaving drug that could reverse an opioid overdose.

"Thank you," Harper said breathlessly, clutching the spray like a talisman.

The old man waved him off. "Go on, son."

Harper hesitated, his mind racing back to the barricaded door. He rounded on the hippie, his eyes blazing.

"The door was blocked with a sofa," he snarled, right in the man's face. "Why? What the hell were you playing at, locking him in there?"

The hippie held up his hands, taking a step back. "Easy, man," he said, his voice calm but firm. "The kid was causing trouble, all right? He was out of his head, waving a knife around, threatening folks. He needed time in the cooler, you know? Before someone got hurt."

Harper's jaw clenched. "So you just barricaded him in and left him? Even though you knew he'd taken something?"

The old man shrugged, glancing away. "Thought he'd sleep it off. Didn't realise he'd gone and OD'd in there, did I? Not until you lot showed up."

Harper wanted to argue, to vent his fury and frustration, but there was no time. With a last, disgusted look at the hippie, he turned and sprinted back to the room.

Mullens was still crouched over the lad, his face grim. "He's barely breathing," he said, his voice tight with strain. "Tell me you found something."

Harper held up the Naloxone spray. "Got it. Let's just pray it works." He inserted the nozzle into the boy's nostril and pressed the plunger.

For a heartbeat, nothing happened. Then, with a shuddering gasp, the boy's eyes flew open. He retched, his body convulsing, but Mullens held him steady, while trying to avoid any more puke splatter. Just then, two paramedics burst through the door and took over.

Mullens stepped back. "Suspected heroin overdose. We've just administered Naloxone, and the idiot, I mean boy, has just come back from unconsciousness."

As the paramedics worked on stabilising Josh, Mullens and Harper retreated to the overgrown garden, the fresh air a welcome respite from the stench inside.

Mullens looked down at his clothes, grimacing at the vomit stains. "Oh, for God's sake. I'm now officially out of clean clothes."

"You could always slip back into your shell suit."

"I'll be slipping something sharp and deadly into your gut in a minute."

Harper didn't smile. His mind still reeled from what the old hippie had told him. "That'll make two of you."

"How do you mean?" Mullens asked, puzzled.

"The old guy in there, the one who gave me the Naloxone. He said Josh Fraser was threatening the squatters with a knife. That's why they'd barricaded him in that room."

Mullens frowned, his eyes sharp. "So he was even more unhinged than we thought."

"Aye. And if he's capable of that, in the state he was in… maybe he's capable of more. Maybe even harming his own parents."

Mullens blew out a breath. He was about to straighten his hair when he cautiously sniffed his palm, grimaced, and changed his plan. "But would someone so doolally be up to planning and executing such a complicated set of murders?"

Mullens's question was interrupted by the paramedics who emerged from the house with the Frasers' son strapped securely to a stretcher. They loaded him into the waiting ambulance, the doors slamming shut behind them. The vehicle pulled away, sirens blaring. One of the support PCs approached.

"No sign of Katherine Fraser on the premises or rear garden, sir. Would you like us to widen our search?"

"I think we're on a hiding to nothing. But we'd better inform the head of search teams to send more officers over for a thorough scan. And sadly, before we can go home, we're going to have to go back into that shithole and attempt to skew statements out of the half-dead dopeheads in there."

With collective weary sighs, they all shuffled slowly back to the house, Mullens's loud yawn echoing out across the Campsie valley.

THIRTY-FOUR

The old farmhouse stood quiet and still. Bone pulled into the driveway. He glanced at his watch and sighed. It was late, and he knew Alice and Michael would have already eaten dinner. The weight of the day hung heavy on his shoulders, and he trudged up the path and let himself in.

The warmth of the kitchen enveloped him as he stepped inside.

Alice glanced up from the sink, her hands submerged in soapy water. "You're late," she said, a hint of irritation in her voice.

"Sorry. You know how it is. Oh, and sorry about last night."

Bone sank into the old sofa chair pushed into the corner, his body melting into the cushions. Kicking off his shoes, he massaged his weary feet.

"How is it looking now?" Alice asked. "The roof, your cabin. You said it was still leaking."

"Oh, aye." Bone remembered his white lie. "Junior, of all people, fixed it. So all good now."

From upstairs, the sounds of laughter and shouting filtered down. Michael, his ten-year-old son, was playing Xbox with his best mate, Clark. Their hollers and whoops of excitement sent a ripple of joy through Bone's chest.

"I should go up and say hello," Bone said, making a move to stand.

Alice shook her head. "Best leave them to it. You know how Michael gets when he's with his friends."

Bone settled back into the chair, aching in every limb.

Alice, seeing the weariness etched on his face, softened. She dried her hands and walked over, enveloping him in a hug.

"I'm worried about you," she whispered.

Bone leaned into her embrace, drawing strength from her warmth. "I'm okay," he said, but even he could hear the uncertainty in his voice.

Alice pulled back, searching his face. "And your PTSD? How's that been? You're not hiding anything from me, are you?"

Bone sighed. "Of course not. I'd never do that again. I'm keeping a close eye on it. I'm aware it could potentially be escalating again. I had a swim last night, and that helped."

Fear flickered in Alice's eyes, the unspoken worry that had haunted their marriage for so long.

"I've also booked a group therapy session for Saturday morning," he reassured her. "And I've been in touch with my counsellor."

Alice nodded, visibly relieved. "Good. That's good. Just as long as you keep talking to me, Duncan."

Their moment was interrupted by the thudding of feet on the stairs. Michael appeared in the doorway with a distracted look on his face.

"Any more crisps?" Michael asked, his tone sullen.

Bone frowned at his son. "Hello to you too."

Alice shook her head. "You've had enough."

The tween huffed, his attitude palpable.

Bone, his patience wearing thin, snapped. "Hey, be nice to your mum."

Michael glared at his father, then turned on his heel and stormed back upstairs. The sound of his bedroom door slamming echoed through the house.

"The shape of things to come, eh?" Alice said, a wry smile on her lips. "He's always like that now when he has mates round. I'm afraid to say it but we're moving into the 'ashamed to be seen dead with us' phase." She walked over to the fridge and pulled out a bottle of ale, the condensation glistening on the bottle. "Thought you might need this."

Bone eyed the beer but shook his head. "I could use something stronger. A whisky, maybe?"

Alice nodded, then paused. "I forgot to get Irn Bru. We could use some of Michael's Coke?"

Bone balked at the idea. "Mixing a perfect Macallan with Coke? Sacrilege."

Alice chuckled. "Says the man who doesn't know the meaning of irony."

She disappeared into the living room and returned clutching a bottle of twelve-year-old. Pouring a generous double, she added a splash of water and handed it to Bone.

He took a sip, the amber liquid warming his throat. He sighed, stretching out his legs, letting the tension of the day ebb away.

"I can heat up some of the pasta," Alice offered, gesturing to the leftovers on the stove.

Bone shook his head. "I'm too tired to eat."

Alice frowned. "You need to eat, Duncan. It helps keep the anxiety and PTSD at bay, you know that."

Bone knew she was right. He watched her spoon some pasta into a bowl and pop it into the microwave. The hum of the appliance filled the kitchen as she set a place at the table.

"Sit," she ordered, and pointed to the chair.

Bone complied, too weary to argue. While he waited, he looked up at Alice, her face lined with concern.

"Are we okay?" he asked, his voice quiet.

Alice met his gaze. "Of course. It's just this relapse in your PTSD…"

"Relapse is a bit strong. It's more—"

The microwave pinged, interrupting him.

She removed the warm dish and placed it in front of him. Before he could continue, she glanced at the clock.

"Shit, it's getting late. I'd better tell Clark it's time to head home."

Bone stared at the steaming bowl for a moment, picked up a fork, and stabbed at the fusilli.

A soft breath by his ear whispered, "Eye for an eye."

"What?" He turned. "I thought you'd gone." But Alice wasn't there, and the room was empty.

He got up, and at the kitchen window, he saw Alice helping Michael and his friend into the back of the Land Rover. They drove off, revealing the red-haired boy standing by the fence, illuminated from behind by some unseen flickering red light. He raised his small hand and, with his index finger, touched his right eye and smiled.

Bone quickly drew the curtains shut. He stood for a moment, trying to make sense of the boy's actions. Then, rushing through to the hall, he fished his laptop out of his rucksack and returned to the kitchen.

Pushing the bowl of pasta to one side, he set the laptop down on the table, flipped the lid open, and typed *Jedburgh Arson Attack* in the search bar. He sat, took a couple of swigs of whisky, and hit return.

THIRTY-FIVE

The next morning, the team gathered in the incident room, weary but champing at the bit for round three.

"Okay, folks, here we go again," Bone said when he arrived. He glanced around the room. "Where's Mark?"

"He'll be in shortly," Harper said. "He's called into his dad's care home to make sure everything's okay for this morning."

"What's happening?" Baxter asked.

"His dad's going in for an operation. Mark's worried he'll kick off, so he's helping referee."

"Is George okay?" Walker asked.

"Exploratory operation. Mark'll find out later this afternoon. He doesn't want anyone making a fuss."

"Got you." Walker nodded.

"Did you get the message I left you about Josh Fraser?" Harper asked Bone.

"Yes, good work on that, and well done tracking him down."

"He was in a bad way, though, and they took him up to the hospital." He turned to the team. "Mark and I found him last night, overdosing in a squat up near Campsie Village."

"So he's not in Australia, then?" Baxter said.

"Scamming his parents out of year abroad money to fuel a drug habit, I think," Harper replied. "We just managed to keep him alive until the paramedics arrived."

"So he's still with us?" Bone asked.

"Yes. I just called the unit, and they confirmed he's alive but in severe withdrawal."

Bone nodded. "Good." He put his bag down on the nearest desk and went over to the board.

The room fell silent.

Walker approached. "You okay, sir?"

Bone continued to eyeball the wall.

"Sir?" Walker nudged his elbow.

"It's like an itch I can't quite scratch, you know?" Bone said finally.

"I am tempted to do a Mark on that comment, but I'll resist," Walker said. "What do you mean?"

"I can't help thinking it's staring us right in the face and we're just not seeing it."

"What?"

"The killer."

"Isn't that always the case, though?"

"I know, but I keep thinking about this car crash girl." He tapped the photo. He rubbed at the scar on his temple and scanned the myriad of notes and images once more. He spun around. "Okay, so we have two POIs in custody and the son in hospital. I suggest we split this up between us. Will, can you head up to the Infirmary and interview the son? Though it sounds like he might be in no fit state to talk."

"Or commit the crimes?" Harper suggested. "He was skin and bone, barely able to lift an arm, never mind a couple of heavy petrol canisters."

"Just see what he has to say for himself. Rhona, can you reinterview Scanlon and see if we can get any more out of him? And I'll put the bozo boyfriend with a hangover from hell through the wringer, see what comes out the other side, hopefully not vomit." He clapped his hands. "Up and at 'em, people."

They all shot him the same collective stare.

"What? I've always wanted to say that."

"And indeed, you have now," Walker said with a smile.

"What about me?" Baxter asked.

"Keep rooting around in our three POIs' pasts. Whatever it is we're missing, it's in there somewhere."

THIRTY-SIX

Bone found Daniel Quillan slumped at the interview desk, his body a crumpled, shaking mess of alcoholic withdrawal. Bone sat opposite and waited until Daniel finally looked up.

"Good morning, Mr Quillan. I'm Detective Chief Inspector Bone."

"A bit fucking heavy for a drink driving all this, isn't it? For fuck's sake, just charge me and let me go. I need to get out of here," Daniel croaked. He ran the back of his hand across his dry lips.

"Would you like a glass of water?"

"Have you got something stronger?"

"By all accounts, you had more than enough yesterday, while in charge of your work vehicle."

"That's what I'm on about. Stop the game-playing and just get the fuck on with it."

Bone started the recorder, and while he ran through his introductory spiel, Quillan squirmed as though there were snakes slithering around under his clothes.

"Do you remember why my colleague and I arrested you yesterday?" Bone asked.

"I was pished," Quillan replied through tight lips. "And I apologise for that. I'd had a very tough…"

"Two days ago, Robert McNeil was found unconscious with severe head injuries, lying next to a burnt-out stolen van," Bone interrupted.

Quillan sat up. "What? You mean…?" He stopped. "Who do I mean?"

"I don't know." Quillan feigned ignorance.

"Let me remind you. The same paramedic you violently assaulted two years ago."

"Oh no. Hold on a minute." Quillan raised his arms in defence. "I served my time for that. I fucking regretted lamping him the second after I did it. You can't… You don't think I did that to him. Jesus Christ!" He took two or three rapid breaths and tried to control his legs that bounced up and down under the table.

"Are you an alcoholic, Mr Quillan?"

"Naw, I've got fucking Parkinson's. What do you think? I was doing so well, off the sauce for almost a year, but a couple of months ago everything just got too much for me again. And now I've probably lost my job thanks to you lot."

"That's entirely your own doing, Daniel. You were eight times over the legal limit. You were so drunk you could hardly see."

"I'm sorry. I need help." Quillan's head fell into his hands.

"Where were you on Sunday morning between twelve and three a.m.?"

"I didn't fucking do this. It's bullshit."

"Where, Mr Quillan?"

"I don't fucking remember. I've been hitting it hard lately, so by that time I'm usually out of it, sleeping it off until the next fucking day and the circus starts again."

"Where were you sleeping it off?"

"I've a room in a house on the Glasgow Road."

"You have housemates?"

"Housemates. You think it's like fucking *Friends* or something? It's a fucking doss-house."

"Would any of the tenants be able to verify you were there between those times?"

"No clue. Don't know any of them. It's like the night of the living fucking dead in there." He stopped. "Hold on. Sunday… I worked Saturday."

"Until when?"

"Not too late. I went for a fish supper after at Sandinos. That's right. I remember now. Then the Fells. But after that, no clue."

"Does your hostel have security cameras on the door?"

"Aye, but no idea if they work. There are fights in the hallway all the fucking time, and nobody comes to break it up." He started breathing hard. "Come on, Inspector. Is there any way you could spot me a can or a snifter of something? I'm fucking dying here."

Bone changed tack. "Did you start drinking when your girlfriend died? That's Kelly Dobson, isn't it?"

"My ex-girlfriend. We split a couple of months before she died."

"Why was that?"

"I let her down."

"In what way?"

He paused, his lips tightening. "My drinking. She couldn't handle it. I couldn't either. I was devastated. She was my life, but I totally understood. I mean, someone like Kell didn't deserve a total fuck-up like me, especially after everything that she'd been through."

"What do you mean?"

"When I met her six years ago, she'd just moved up from Jedburgh."

"She lived in Jedburgh?" Bone interrupted.

"Aye, grew up there. At the time, she was trying to get away from her bastard, abusive father who was causing her and her mum loads of grief. And it just got worse when Kell's mum died."

"What was he doing?"

"Total fucking twenty-four-seven harassment. She said it got unbearable, and it didn't seem to matter how many fucking non-harassment orders he got. He just kept coming at her."

"So she fled to Kilwinnoch?"

"That's the sum of it, aye. But it didn't stop there. She told me she thought he'd followed her, and her nightmare just kept going."

"What was her father's name?"

"I asked her over and over, but she never told me. I think she thought I'd do something stupid. And she was right. I was a total hothead back then. That's why I lamped that paramedic. When I saw him in the pub that night, all laughing and joking with his pals and living his life, I lost it. The rage got the better of me."

"How did you know it was him who attended to your ex?"

"The day after the accident, the local did a story on drink driving, and he was on talking about the crash and warning people not to do it." He exhaled. "But I swear I knew instantly what a fucked-up, terrible thing I'd done, and to this day I regret it. I understand now the guy was only doing his job to the best of his ability. Kell was off her face that night. She never should have got behind the wheel."

"Like you shouldn't have yesterday."

"Aye, well. She was a better person than me. She deserved to live. I don't. I whacked the poor sod because I felt guilty and ashamed and angry she'd dumped me. It was all about me, not her, as usual." He swallowed as if the pain was still raw in his throat.

"Why do you think the father harassed her so much?"

"Oh, Christ. She said it was always the same. He would send her messages grovelling for forgiveness for the way he'd treated them both when she was growing up. All the abuse and violence."

"He was physical?"

"Oh, aye. He hospitalised Kell's mum a couple of times. God knows what he did to Kell. She never told me the half of it."

"And this carried on?"

"Aye, so he'd start all sweetness and light, then he'd get angry again and threaten her. Call her a stuck-up bitch like her mother. She used to tell me and she'd crack up. She'd even tried to take her own life before I met her. It was that bad. He was making her life a misery. He was behind all the rows we had."

"Did you row a lot, then?"

"Only about him, or it would come back to him. He was trying to destroy her. Fucking creature." He shook his head. "You know he even harasses her now, even when she's dead?"

"How do you mean?"

"The sick fucker keeps leaving a single red rose on her grave."

"How do you know it's him?"

"There's always a note attached. 'Sorry' or 'I miss you' or 'forgive me', stuff like that. Makes my skin crawl. If I go up, I bin them as soon as, but I've been finding it too upsetting. I don't want to remember her dead." He tapped his forehead with shaking hands. "In here, she's with me, alive, giving me that kind smile she kept for me."

"Where's her grave?"

"Up in the town's cemetery. She's by the oak tree at the back boundary gate. She loved trees." His eyes welled with tears. "Please, Inspector, I didn't attack the ambulance guy. I'm too lost for all that shit anymore. I just want a drink." He sobbed.

"I'll need to check your whereabouts with the hostel. I'm afraid while I do that, I'm going to have to hold you a little longer."

"Oh, Christ. I beg you. I can't take much more of this."

"I'll call the addictions team and see if they can sort you out with some support and medication."

"The only medication I need is forty proof."

"Interview terminated at nine-fourteen a.m." Bone stopped the recorder. "Wait here, and I'll get a PC to escort you back to your cell."

Quillan held his head in his hands, his shoulders rising and falling with despair.

Bone quickly exited and went to find help.

THIRTY-SEVEN

Approaching the room where the Frasers' son was being treated, Harper was stopped by a uniformed officer.

"Sorry, sir, this is a restricted area," the PC said, his hand hovering by his radio.

Harper held up his lanyard. "DC Harper, RCU. I'm here to question the patient."

The officer nodded, stepping aside. "Of course, sir. Sorry. I thought you were a reporter."

"Anything but a detective, it seems," Harper muttered.

"What was that?"

"Nothing. Has the patient had any visitors?"

The PC shook his head. "Apart from a stream of doctors and nurses, no. You're the first."

As Harper reached for the door handle, a doctor emerged from the room, his expression a mix of concern and irritation.

"DC Harper. Here to see Josh Fraser."

"Detective, is this really necessary?" The doctor gestured towards the uniformed officer. "I'm pretty certain the boy isn't going to do a runner in the state he's in."

"I'm afraid he is a person of interest in our investigation of Dr Fraser's murder."

The doctor's eyes widened in shock. "Murder? I hadn't heard…" He shook his head. "I must say, I'm surprised that the son of the Frasers could possibly be involved, given his physical and mental state. The number of syringe holes in his body suggests long-term heroin addiction."

Harper's brow furrowed. "How is he now?"

The doctor sighed heavily. "He's going through severe withdrawal. Nausea, vomiting, muscle spasms, anxiety, insomnia… it's a horrific process. His body is essentially revolting against the lack of the drug." He paused, then added, "You know, whoever gave him that adrenaline shot last night before the paramedics arrived certainly saved his life."

Harper shifted uncomfortably, not wanting to take credit. "Is that so?"

The doctor nodded. "Absolutely. Without that quick thinking, he might not have made it to the hospital."

Harper cleared his throat. "I understand, Doctor. But I must ask you to let me speak with him. I'll be brief, I promise."

The doctor hesitated, then with a last, concerned look through the gap in the door at his patient, he nodded. "Very well. But please, be gentle. He's in a fragile state."

"I understand. I won't be long."

The doctor stepped aside, allowing Harper to enter the room.

The boy was in a bad way, his skin clammy, his eyes sunken. The withdrawal was hitting him hard.

Harper pulled up a chair, Josh flinching at the scrape of its legs on the floor.

"Well, I have to say you don't look any better than you did last night," Harper said, his voice low and steady. "We need to talk."

Josh's eyes flickered open, bloodshot and unfocused. "If this is about the drugs, I'm not saying anything."

Harper leaned forward. "It's about your parents. I'm really sorry to have to tell you, but your father is dead, and your mother has possibly been kidnapped."

Josh's face remained impassive, a flicker of something cold in his eyes. "Is this some sort of joke?" he mumbled. "They're probably off on one of their fancy five-star holidays."

Harper shook his head. "Sorry, Josh. I'm not joking. There was a fire at your house. Your father was murdered, and your mother is missing. We need your help."

Josh stared at Harper for a long moment, searching for any hint of deception. Slowly, the reality began to sink in. "Dead to me anyway." He sniffed.

Harper's anger surged. "But you were happy enough to climb down off your high horse and take their money when it suited you, eh? I'd say that sounds more like a spoilt wealthy brat than a rebellious Marxist son rejecting his decadent, bourgeois background."

Josh scoffed. "Means to an end. Money they don't need anyway."

Harper's eyes narrowed. "Your manner suggests you'd be happy for them to be dead. Eager to claim that inheritance, are we?"

Josh's face twisted, a flicker of pain breaking through the cold facade. "I didn't... I don't..." He shook his head as if trying to clear it. "My dad's really dead? And Mum... She's missing?"

Harper could see the devastating impact of the news starting to hit. Josh's feigned indifference was melting away, replaced by a dawning horror.

"I thought you were here about the drugs. I didn't know... Oh God." Josh's voice broke, tears welling in his eyes. "I've been so out of it. I had no idea."

As Josh's armour crumbled, Harper's tone softened slightly. "I know this is a lot to take in. But I need you to help me if you can. Anything you can tell us could help find your mother."

Josh nodded, wiping at his eyes with shaking hands. "I don't know nothing. I swear. I was holed up, out of it."

"We know you threatened people with a knife."

Josh shook his head. "I can't remember. I was totally shitarsed. That's how I ended up barricaded in the room. I wanted to get clean, but I found some smack and the temptation was too much. But something wasn't right with it."

Harper pulled out a photo, holding it up for Josh to see. "Do you recognise this baby photo?"

At first, Josh squinted at the image, no flicker of recognition in his eyes. He shrugged. But then, slowly, a memory seemed to surface.

"Wait… yeah, I remember now. One night I got back late and Dad was still up in his office. I tried to sneak past, but he called me in. I thought he was going to give me another of his fucking holier-than-thou sermons, but he was hammered. He'd been on the hard stuff. And he was upset, I mean really upset, actually kind of bawling like a wean. I'd never seen him like that before. He was holding that." He pointed to the photo, his hand shaking slightly. "Waving it about, going on about how the baby died because he stopped to help some stupid drunk woman who'd gone off the road."

"Did he mention anything else about this drunk woman?" Harper asked.

Josh shook his head. "No, just that the accident stopped him getting to the hospital in time to save the baby. He just kept saying 'that stupid drunk woman' over and over."

"Did he ever talk about it again after that night?"

"Never. The next day, he was business as usual with us. I'm not sure he even remembered talking to me." His voice cracked, tears spilling down his cheeks. "But dead... Man, that's fucking heavy." He looked up at Harper, his eyes pleading. "And where's my mum? For fuck's sake, why haven't you found her?"

Harper shifted the conversation. "What about your father's relationship with his boss, Professor Baird, the medical director?"

Josh's face twisted in disgust. "He's the cunt you should be arresting. He's the one who slept with my mum."

Harper's surprise was clear. "They had an affair? Did your dad know about it?"

Josh let out a bitter laugh. "I have no clue. But that's my dad, isn't it? He'd only see what he wanted to see."

Harper pressed further. "Do you think Professor Baird might be capable of killing your father, kidnapping your mother, and then attempting to murder a paramedic?"

Josh threw up his hands in frustration. "I don't fucking know, do I? Maybe the ambulance guy was blackmailing him or something. That's your job to figure out. But I'm telling you, the rich smarmy creep was probably obsessed. It was so obvious they were at it. It was disgusting the way they flirted when he was round at the house."

"Do you have any actual evidence that they were having an affair?"

"My eyes. That's all I needed." He frowned.

"When did you last see them together, flirting like that?" Harper enquired.

"A few years back, when I was still at school. Made my fucking skin crawl. But Dad didn't even notice. Thought it was all just a bit of a joke. But you'd have to be totally fucking blind not to see what was going on. Probably been at it all this time. He's the guy you need to arrest for this. He's the one."

Suddenly, Josh's body convulsed. He coughed and choked, his eyes rolling back. Harper jumped up and called for help. A nurse and the doctor rushed in They worked on the boy quickly, administering medication and oxygen. After a few tense moments, Josh's fit subsided. He lay back on the bed, pale and exhausted.

The doctor turned to Harper, his expression stern. "That's enough, Detective. He needs to rest now."

Harper nodded and backed out of the room.

Out in the corridor, he dug out his phone and dialled Bone's number. It rang and rang, but there was no answer.

"Shit."

He dialled again and left him a message, then hurried back through the warren of corridors to the exit, his mind racing with this new lead.

THIRTY-EIGHT

Bone squinted through the relentless sheets of rain pummelling Kilwinnoch's graveyard, his brogues squelching on the sodden earth. He'd picked a hell of a day to examine the resting place of Kelly Dobson.

The godforsaken place was a bleak affair at the best of times, but under the onslaught of the heavens, it took on a particularly sinister air. Crumbling headstones jutted from the ground like rotten teeth, and the twisted branches of ancient yews clawed at the imposing grey sky.

Bone trudged towards the farthest boundary wall, his old coat less than useless at keeping out the damp.

And there it was. Kelly Dobson's modest grave, the simple headstone bearing only her name and the stark dates of her too-short life. The plot was slightly overgrown, a tangle of weeds threatening to reclaim the stone.

Propped against the weathered granite was a single rose, its crimson petals defiantly bright in the gloom. Bone knelt to inspect them, ignoring the freezing rainwater seeping through his trousers.

A plain white card was nestled behind the bloom. Bone plucked it out and read the words inscribed in large, bold capital letters: *Soon, my love, soon.*

A sudden caw pierced the air, and Bone snapped his head up. A fat crow eyed him up from atop a nearby monument, but then he spied a figure heading at pace out of the side gate.

"Oi!" Bone called out. He pushed the card into his pocket and leapt to his feet.

The figure broke into a run, and Bone gave chase through the gate, vaulting over a low wall and pelting across the adjacent playing field. The rain had turned the grass into a treacherous bog, and Bone lost his footing more than once, his arms flailing as he fought to stay upright.

The figure had a lead on him, darting onto the main road without a glance at the oncoming traffic. Bone followed, narrowly avoiding a white van that blasted its horn, swerving around him.

Somehow, Bone made it to the other side intact, just in time to see his quarry vanish into the rabbit warren of a council estate. He raced on into the maze of low-slung tenements, his heart hammering and his lungs burning.

The figure ducked into one of the closes, and Bone followed, emerging into a dank back green. He caught a glimpse of movement on the far side and sprinted towards it, weaving through a gauntlet of drooping laundry lines.

He brushed past one of the lines, and it snapped. Bone found himself momentarily entangled in a web of damp sheets and XXL-sized undergarments.

On the other side of the green, a group of teenage neds huddled beneath a dripping awning, their hoodies pulled tight against the deluge. Bone scanned the surrounding streets, but there was no sign of his mystery man.

Panting, he jogged over to the gang. "Any of you boys seen a bloke come tearing through here?"

The boys turned their sullen, pimple-pocked faces towards him. "Get tae fuck, paedo," one of them sneered. "We ain't seen shite."

"Aye, mebbe he's aff tae buy yer Werther's Originals, ya auld perv," another one jeered.

Bone snatched out his lanyard. "Beat it!"

At the sight of his credentials, the boys legged it.

Defeated, he trudged back to the graveyard, his clothes plastered to his skin and his shoes making obscene squelching noises with each step. At the entrance, he spotted a large compost bin squatting amidst the overgrown shrubs. On a hunch, he lifted the lid and peered inside.

Grimacing, Bone plunged his hands into the sodden, reeking mass of decaying vegetation. He rooted around, cursing at cold, slimy gunge coating his skin and working its way under his fingernails.

He was about to give up, but his fingers brushed against something solid. He grasped it and pulled, revealing a clump of wilted, rotting flowers. Clinging to the stems were the remains of a white card, the ink all but obliterated by the damp. He could just make out the words: *One more, my love.*

Bone extracted himself from the bin.

A gruff Glaswegian voice behind him said, "Haw, pal, whit ye think yer daein' in ma compost?"

Bone whirled around to find a grizzled old gravedigger glaring at him, a spade clutched in his gnarled hands.

"Ah hope yer no' pinchin' they flooers, mate. That's bawbag behaviour, that is."

Bone flashed his warrant card. "DCI Bone, Kilwinnoch CID. I'm investigating a case."

The gravedigger squinted at the ID, then grinned, revealing a mouthful of crooked teeth. "Saints alive, a real polis! Ah thought ye wis just some sad basturt oan the pull."

Bone held up the wilted rose and the mouldy card. "I'm interested in these, and the ones on that grave over there by the back gate. You seen anyone leaving flowers and cards like this there recently?"

The old man scratched his head. "Wish ah could help ye, Inspector, but ah huvnae seen hee-haw. I know there's aye flooers on her grave and they get replaced regular. Every two weeks, like clockwork."

"How long has that been going on?"

"Long as ah've been here, and that's gaun oan three year noo."

"And you've never seen who leaves them?"

The gravedigger shook his head. "Naw. Wan minute there's nowt there, the next, a fresh wan appears. It's like they ken ma schedule, when ah take ma tea breaks and that."

Bone frowned. "You notice anything else unusual? Any strange characters hanging around?"

"No' really, naw. But like ah says, folk are in and oot ay here aw the time, payin' their respects. Easy tae miss something, especially me. Withoot ma glasses, I'm blind as a bloody bat in a bell tower."

Bone thanked the gravedigger and walked back to the grave, the rose still there, leaning crooked on the stone, while the wind did its best to blow it over. He plucked it up and glanced back at Kelly's name etched into the marble. Then a bomb went off in his head. He dashed back to the gravedigger, who was now busy turning the compost with a fork.

"What did you say just now?" he asked.

"God, now yer askin'. When?"

"Just there. The last thing?"

"What, about me needin' ma glasses?"

"That's it. Thanks."

Bone raced out of the cemetery, still clutching the rose, some of the petals tumbling onto the path in his wake. He jumped into the Saab and drove as fast as he could back to the station.

THIRTY-NINE

In the incident room, Harper set upon Bone with his news. "Did you get my message, sir? I think—"

"Hold on, Will." Bone moved to the middle of the room. "Listen up, people. I have some critical information from my interview with Daniel Quillan."

He paused, ensuring he had everyone's full attention.

"Quillan told me his girlfriend, Kelly Dobson grew up in Jedburgh."

"I knew it!" Mullens jumped in. "There's our link to that arsonist bastard, Scanlon."

"No, Mark," Bone interrupted.

The team looked puzzled.

"Kelly was relentlessly stalked and harassed by her estranged father, a man with a history of abuse. It got so bad that she had to take out multiple court orders against him." Bone paced the room. "And when Kelly's mother died, things got even worse. She was so terrified that she fled to Kilwinnoch, hoping to escape her father's torment."

"Sounds like a piece of work, this father," Walker said.

Bone nodded grimly. "A dangerous one, too. Quillan painted a picture of a man obsessed, unwilling to let his daughter live her life in peace."

Mullens chimed in, "You think this bastard followed her to Kilwinnoch?"

"Quillan said Kelly was convinced her father had pursued her here," Bone replied. "And that he was following her around, maybe watching her?"

Walker's eyes widened. "Was the abuse physical?"

Bone nodded. "The boyfriend confirmed the father was physically and mentally abusive to both her and her mother. He was relentless in his torment."

The room fell silent for a moment, each detective processing this new, disturbing information.

Bone continued. "Today, I went to Kelly's grave. The boyfriend told me her father had been leaving flowers and notes there since her death, which is true. There was both a red rose and a note that read, 'Soon, my love, soon.' When I was by the girl's grave, a man started through the gate. He legged it as soon as he saw me, and I lost him."

Harper ventured, "Could 'soon' be revenge?"

Bone nodded. "Or justice." He turned to Baxter. "Sheila, did you find out any more about the Fire

Chief's former post in Jedburgh and any details of his injuries?"

Baxter looked at Bone, surprised by his request, but consulted her notes. "No, just that the fire chief was injured while saving a security guard during a warehouse fire in Jedburgh eight years ago. He received a medal for bravery."

Walker intervened. "Where are you going with this, sir?"

Bone held up a hand. "Bear with me. Harper, put the night-cam footage up on the monitor, the still shot of the hooded figure with only the eyes exposed."

Harper complied, and the grainy image filled the screen. DS Mullens winced at the sight of the glowing, cat-like eyes staring out from beneath the hood.

Bone approached the monitor, studying the image intently. "It hit me this morning. We've been staring at this image for days, but the killer is right there."

Walker shook her head. "I'm not following."

Bone pointed at the figure's eyes. "Notice how the suspect's left eye is brighter than the other? Why would that be?"

Harper piped up. "Maybe the night flash caught the angle of the retina weird?"

Bone nodded. "Or?"

Realisation dawned on Walker's face. "The attacker has only one eye. The right one is fake."

Bone turned back to Baxter. "Sheila, what was the nature of the fire chief's injury in Jedburgh?"

Baxter consulted her notes again. "Head wound from falling debris."

"Specifics?" Bone pressed.

Baxter shrugged. "Sorry, sir. That's all I have."

Bone leaned forward. "Last night, I had another dig around. I found an old news article buried in the archives. It revealed that the fire chief was blinded by the debris in that warehouse fire. The doctors managed to save his left eye, but his right was beyond repair. He's had a glass one ever since."

Walker interjected. "I thought you said this all came to you this morning."

Bone shrugged. "Call it an organic epiphany."

Mullens's eyes widened. "So the other eye was a goner?"

Harper cut in. "Doh!"

Walker nodded. "He has a glass eye. That explains the intense stare!"

"A glass right eye, to be precise," Bone clarified. He tapped the monitor. "We have our man."

Walker held up her hands. "Hold on. I know the guy is a prick, but is he really behind all this?"

Bone nodded. "It makes sense, though, doesn't it? He's found out that Scanlon is out and skipped parole. Now he has the perfect cover for his crimes."

Walker frowned. "How would he know that?"

"Maybe a former colleague told him, warned him?" Harper suggested.

Bone pointed at Will. "Exactly. The amateurish attempts to ignite Fraser with the hose helped with the finger-pointing."

Baxter nodded. "Yes. And the hose itself was made of the same material used in fire extinguishers."

"Aye, that day at the paramedic's crime scene the ball sack totally lost it because we hadn't nailed Scanlon yet."

"It didn't make any sense at the time," Bone cut in. "But do you remember, Mark, in the midst of his rant he said, and I quote, 'The psychopath almost cost me my eyesight.'"

"He did!" Mullens agreed.

"Sorry, I know I've said this before but why go to all that trouble of waiting to frame Scanlon, and then blow it with the email and graffiti, completely wide of the arsonist's MO?" Walker persisted.

"To me it looks like he didn't expect her to be there and his plan took a more desperate dive bomb. Anyway, all these contradictions in behaviour point to an individual who has completely lost any sense of reason or reality, and as a result even more dangerous than when he planned all this mayhem."

Mullens whistled low. "Hiding in plain sight."

"He is definitely our man. My head and gut are one on this."

The gravity of the situation settled over the room.

Bone's tone hardened. "Okay, we need to move fast and smart to nail this lunatic and prevent more bloodshed, but remember we are dealing with a probable hostage situation, so due care is also required." He glared at Mullens.

"Sir." Mullens nodded.

"Sheila, we need two ARUs. Will and Mark, you'll go to the fire station. Rhona and I will go to his house."

The team burst into action, grabbing coats and keys.

The hunt was on.

FORTY

Mullens ordered the ARU officers to park in the street adjacent to the fire station and await his orders. He pulled the BMW into the station forecourt and stopped.

"Ready?" he asked.

Harper nodded and climbed out of the car.

They strode across the expansive forecourt, the building's imposing brick walls and giant red double doors looming over them.

Approaching the entrance, they spotted an officer going through equipment laid out on the forecourt in front of a gleaming red fire engine. The detectives introduced themselves, flashing their warrant cards.

"Morning," the officer greeted them. "What can I do for you?"

"We're looking for your chief," Mullens said. "Is he in?"

The officer shook his head. "Haven't seen him yet. His office is upstairs." He pointed to two poles at the rear of the forecourt.

Mullens grimaced. "We'll have to climb up those?"

The officer laughed. "No, there are stairs."

The chief's office was locked, so the detectives headed to the kitchen area where the rest of the crew was gathered. The room was scruffy, with dirty plates and cups piled up, battered sofas, yellowing walls, a pool table, a dartboard, and a calendar featuring a sports car with a girl in a bikini draped across the bonnet.

Harper shook his head.

As they entered, the loud conversations and laughter stopped.

Mullens broke the awkward silence. "DS Mullens and DC Harper from Kilwinnoch. Has anyone seen Chief Tennant?"

The room remained quiet, until one officer finally spoke up. "No, we haven't seen him. Has he been caught speeding in the fire engine again?"

The team laughed, but there was an edge to it. A female officer sat alone in the corner, not joining in.

"We want to speak to him about the Fraser arson."

"Well, you've come to the right place," the officer joked again.

More guffaws.

Another chimed in. "Aye, that pyromaniac from Jedburgh's on the loose again. The chief is doing his nut in about it."

"We need to ask him a few more questions about that," Mullens said, choosing his words carefully.

"Why the Cagney and Lacey routine?" the fireman asked suspiciously.

Harper pressed on. "We just need to cross-check some vital information."

The joker in the group cut back in. "We've told you he's not here."

A collective grumble rattled round the room, but Harper noticed the female officer wincing and twisting uncomfortably in her seat.

Mullens pressed again, "Does anyone know where he is?"

"Not until you tell us the real reason you are looking for him," the joker responded again.

"Thanks for your help," Mullens snarled.

As they headed out, one of the officers called out, "Why don't you take the pole?" The place erupted in laughter again.

On their way back to the car, Harper stopped and glanced up at the kitchen windows. One of the group was watching them leave.

"They think it's all a bloody joke," he said.

"And I thought we were bad." Mullens exhaled.

Their conversation was interrupted by the female officer, who had followed them out.

"I'm so sorry about what happened in there just now. The guys let their banter get the better of them sometimes." She tried a smile, but her cheek twitched.

"That was more than banter," Mullens replied.

"Is there something you want to tell us?" Harper asked, picking up her anxious demeanour.

The officer sighed. "I don't want…" She glanced nervously up at the window. "My job has become very difficult since the chief got the job."

"How?" Harper quizzed.

"He's turned this station into a lads' party."

Harper nodded. "Like that inappropriate calendar."

She threw up her hands. "Exactly! But what's the point of complaining? It just goes up the chain and nothing changes."

"Have you complained or spoken to anyone about this?"

"I just keep quiet and let them get on with it, hoping they've got my back in a fire. And after Helen fell through the ceiling at the Frasers' house , I'm not so sure anymore."

Mullens shook his head. "Jesus, that's horrible."

"And the chief is part of this, too?" Harper continued.

"It's so hard, you know? I feel quite vulnerable. Even here, now, with you. They're probably watching me. But yeah. He's at the centre of it, in my opinion. He's a sexist bully. I can't stand him. He puts on this front. That he cares about his men, his people, but it's all bollocks. He's totally out for himself. He's gunning for more and more power, and if he gets it, God help the fire service. That's all I can say. He's not what he seems."

"Do you know where he is?"

"If he's not at home, he often goes up to his run-down bothy he's been doing up for years, near Clachan Pass. Calls it his breathing space. He invited me up there once. I got almost to the door, but I just felt…"

"What?" Harper prompted.

"Scared, if I'm honest. It was so isolated. I didn't really know why I agreed, but I think he just bullied me, and I didn't want to say no to him."

"Do you have an address?"

"I don't think it'll have one. It's the only building for miles at the end of a farmer's track off the pass road. It should show up on Google Maps. Do you think the chief could be behind the attacks?" she asked.

"At this stage we can't…" Harper started.

But Mullens nodded a confirmation.

She stepped back, her jaw falling open. "That's horrific. Even for a scumbag like him, that's pretty fucked-up. Why? Jesus. If he's behind all this then…"

"You shouldn't have to put up with those arseholes in there," Mullens said, changing the subject. "It's totally unacceptable. Couldn't you approach your union or something?"

"Pointless. The men in power close ranks and deny. People like that psycho." She shook her head and set off across the forecourt.

"Are you sure you want to go back in there?"

"I'm on shift. I don't have a choice," she shouted, clearly no longer caring if the men above could hear her.

"Someone needs to help her," Harper said.

"Agreed. But first, we have to catch the cock who's created this shite."

They got into the pool car, and Harper pulled out his phone. "I'll ring Bone."

FORTY-ONE

The fire chief's house stood in darkness when Bone and Walker pulled up outside, every curtain drawn tight. The ARU officers, clad in their black tactical gear, emerged from their vehicle and took up positions on either side of the front door, their movements precise and practiced. The detectives joined them, warrant in hand, hearts pounding with anticipation.

"Fire Chief Gregor Tennant, this is the police!" Bone called out, his voice cutting through the quiet neighbourhood, echoing off the surrounding houses. "We have a warrant to search the premises. Open up!"

No response. The house was still, as if holding its breath, waiting for Bone's next move.

Bone nodded to the ARU officers, a silent command. "Go."

With a splintering crack, the door burst inwards, the lock no match for the battering ram's brutal force. The officers surged inside, weapons at the ready, Bone and Walker close behind, adrenaline pumping.

The acrid stench of petrol assaulted Bone's nostrils, so strong it made his eyes water and his throat burn. Walker pulled a face, her hand instinctively reaching for the radio on her stab vest.

"Jesus, it reeks in here," she muttered.

Bone flicked on his torch, the beam slicing through the dimly lit interior, casting eerie shadows on the walls. "Tennant! Police! Show yourself!"

Silence.

They moved cautiously into the living room, every step a calculated risk. Bone's torchlight swept across the space, revealing a scene in disarray. Furniture overturned, papers scattered, the signs of a mind in chaos. On the back of the door, a soot-covered black coat hung, its sleeves and shoulders singed. Bone pointed to the stairs.

In the bedroom, the torch beam fell upon a photograph on the bedside table. A young woman smiled up at him, her face hauntingly familiar. A chill ran down Bone's spine. It was the innocent face of Kelly Dobson caught forever inside a cheap wooden frame.

A crash from the wardrobe had them jumping. Walker wrenched open the door. A shoebox tumbled to the floor, spilling its secrets. More photographs of Kelly cascaded out, along with a pair of tiny baby mittens and two plastic unicorn toys.

Walker met Bone's stare. A silent understanding passing between them, the pieces finally falling into place, painting a picture of obsession and grief, of a man controlled by his demons.

A sudden cry from the garden snapped them back to the present. They sprinted downstairs, bursting outside just in time to see the fire chief knock an ARU officer to the ground with a vicious elbow to the face, the sickening crunch of bone on bone.

"Tennant!" Bone roared, launching himself at the chief, rage and determination propelling him forward.

They hit the ground hard, grappling and swearing, a tangle of limbs and fury. Tennant lashed out, his fist connecting with Bone's jaw. Pain exploded through Bone's skull, but he held on, his fingers clawing at Tennant's jacket, refusing to let go.

With a growl of strained effort, the chief broke free, staggering to his feet, desperation etched on his face. Before Bone could react, he vaulted over the garden wall and disappeared around the corner.

The roar of an engine shattered the air. Walker, already halfway up the wall, called out that she'd caught a glimpse of taillights speeding out from a gap in the trees behind the house.

"He's getting away!" she yelled and dropped back down beside Bone.

Bone hauled himself upright, jaw throbbing, determination burning in his eyes. "The car!"

They sprinted around the side of the house, Walker already on the radio, barking orders, the situation escalating by the second. The pool car and the ARU vehicle sat at the kerb, engines running, ready for the pursuit.

"Go, go, go!" Bone shouted, throwing himself into the passenger seat.

Walker slid behind the wheel. The ARU team piled into their van, sirens screaming to life, piercing the air.

Tyres squealed as Walker floored the accelerator, the sudden momentum slamming Bone back into his seat, the world blurring past the windows.

He pressed the ball of his hand against his jaw and moaned. "Bastard!"

They tore off down the road, chasing the rapidly receding taillights.

"Suspect vehicle, black Audi, reg F64 GUU, heading north on the A81," Walker relayed into the radio. "Request an FIM to authorise a stinger deployment at the Blairgoyne crossroads."

Bone braced himself. Walker took a sharp bend, the pool car's suspension groaning in protest, the vehicle pushed to its limits. Tennant's car was a distant blur now, weaving recklessly through the light traffic.

The gap slowly narrowed. Bone held on for dear life. Walker kept her foot to the floor, knuckles white on the wheel, her focus unwavering.

Suddenly, the chief's car veered off the main road, tyres screeching. It careened onto Campsie Fells Road, a treacherously windy pass into the heart of the mountains.

"He's heading for the hills!" Walker yelled. She wrenched the wheel to follow, the pool car fishtailing, fighting for traction on the uneven surface.

Ahead, Tennant's taillights dwindled.

"Shit, I'm losing him," Walker complained. She wrenched the wheel around another tight bend, tyres skirting the edge of a sheer drop on the passenger side.

"Oh, Christ!" Bone closed his eyes.

They raced on, the road narrowing further. Walker coaxed every ounce of power from the straining engine, the speedometer needle quivering in the red, the car pushed to its breaking point. But it wasn't enough. They came to the top of a blind summit, and the fire chief's car had vanished.

Walker slammed on the brakes, the pool car skidding to a halt, gravel spraying from beneath the tyres. She threw the car into reverse, tyres spinning, and backed up.

"Maybe we missed a turn?" she said in desperation.

But the narrow track offered no reprieve, no alternative path. The car lurched and shuddered, the wheels sinking into the soft mud, the undercarriage scraping against rocks and debris.

For a heart-stopping moment, they were stuck, the engine revving futilely, the wheels spinning in the mire. But Walker refused to give up. She rocked the car back and forth until finally, with a shuddering groan, the car broke free and stuttered back onto the road, mud spraying in its wake.

Bone's phone buzzed, the sound harsh in the tense silence. It was Harper.

"Boss, one of the fire officers just told us Tennant owns a tumbledown bothy. It's in the middle of nowhere, at the end of a track, near Clachan Pass at the top of the Campsies. It's the only building for miles, so easy to find."

Bone's pulse raced. "Good work, Harper. Meet us there. We're on our way."

"Already on it, sir," Harper replied, his voice crackling with urgency. "And we've got the cavalry with us."

Bone turned to Walker, a grim smile on his face. "Clachan Pass. Let's go."

Walker nodded, throwing the car into gear, the engine roaring. They sped off into the gloom.

FORTY-TWO

Harper gripped the door handle, Mullens fighting to keep the pool car on the narrow muddy track, the vehicle bouncing and skidding over the uneven terrain.

"Jesus Christ, Mark!" Harper shouted. They careened through the mud. "Are you sure this is the right way?"

"I'm following your fucking directions, numbknob!" Mullens snapped back. "It's not like there's a bloody signpost for 'Psycho's Hideout'!"

Suddenly, the track ended, and Mullens hit the brakes. The path ahead was impassable, blocked by dense undergrowth and fallen trees.

Harper checked his phone. "There's a building marked on the map, just on the other side of that burn and through the trees."

Mullens peered down at the fast-flowing stream at the bottom of a small ravine. "Oh, fantastic."

He scanned the area for any sign of Bone, Walker, or the Armed Response Unit, but they were nowhere to be seen.

Harper frowned at his mobile. "I've lost the signal."

With a resigned sigh, they climbed out. Harper fished two stab vests out of the boot, and they set off on foot. Mullens attempted the slope but instantly lost his footing and slid down the bank, landing at the bottom in the icy water.

"Fuck's sake, not another fucking suit!" he cursed.

Harper, with nimble grace, successfully hopped across a line of boulders to the other side.

"Smart arse," Mullens complained.

They scrambled up the opposite bank, fighting their way through the thick underbrush. Branches snatched at their clothes and scratched their faces, but they pressed on.

In a clearing in the middle of the wood, Harper spotted the bothy—a wreck of a building with tarp partially covering attached outhouses. They took cover behind a fallen tree to observe. The fire chief's work Land Rover was parked next to it.

"So, there must be another way in," Mullens grumbled. He wrung out his sodden trouser leg. "And you made me drown myself crossing the fucking Amazon."

They neared the bothy, and the stench of petrol grew stronger. Harper gestured for Mullens to go one way, while he went the other, edging closer to get a better look.

Harper crept along the side of the bothy, his heart pounding. He reached the corner of the building, and his foot suddenly slipped. He teetered on the edge of a narrow trench that seemed to appear out of nowhere.

"Fuck!" he hissed, windmilling his arms and regaining his balance.

Kneeling, he examined the trench more closely. It was dug into the soil, running left and right, across the front of the building. The walls were lined with black plastic tarp, and to his horror, he realised it was filled to the brim with petrol. The fumes were overwhelming, his head spinning.

"Jesus Christ," he muttered, the pieces falling into place. This was no mere hideout—it was a fucking deathtrap.

With a newfound sense of urgency, he carefully stepped over the trench and continued along the wall, every sense on high alert. There was no telling what other surprises the deranged fire chief had in store.

At a window, he ducked down under the sill and edged up to peer inside. Katherine Fraser was in the centre of a bare, stone-walled room, arms and legs tied to a chair, mouth covered with packing tape. She was in a terrible state, her clothes torn and dirty, her hair matted and greasy from days in captivity. Empty food containers and water bottles were scattered around the room. She was very distressed, rocking back and forth, her muffled sobs audible even through the wall.

Harper carried on to the wooden front door. It was slightly ajar.

An invitation?

He squinted around the frame. The narrow hallway was dark and gloomy, but still no sign of the fire chief. He crept inside, edging closer to the door leading to Fraser. But as he passed the threshold, the front door slammed shut behind him with a bone-chilling finality. Heart all but in his throat, he tried the handle, but it was locked. He was trapped.

With no other choice, he dashed through to help her.

Inside, a battery lamp stuttered, casting eerie shadows that danced across the bare stone walls.

Harper approached. The gagged woman moaned and nodded frantically towards the door, her eyes wide with terror. But Harper was focused on freeing her. With shaking hands, he fumbled with the knots. But he froze at a voice behind him.

"What are you doing?"

Harper spun around.

Tennant stood in the doorway, a menacing silhouette against the flickering light.

"Please don't do that. I need her," the chief continued, taking a step forward, his hand tightening around a lighter.

Harper lunged at him, desperation fuelling his attack, but Tennant was too quick. With a swift, brutal motion, he knocked Harper to the floor, the taste of blood filling Will's mouth.

"Don't be a stupid wee prick, son," Tennant sneered and loomed over him. "You see, I can't let you take her. She's my ticket to end this. When I have justice for my daughter, then you can have her."

Harper moaned in pain. "The ARU are all over you. You're done. This is over," he mumbled through the blood.

Tennant let out a loud, near-pantomime laugh. "It doesn't look over to me."

With a cruel smile, he held up the lighter. Harper's eyes widened in horror; the chief's thumb hovered over the spark wheel.

"You see…" The chief flicked the wheel, a tiny flame appearing. "I know a thing or two about fuel. And I know it will take less than two minutes to engulf this building, especially when we're all soaked in the magic stuff."

"No!" Harper cried out.

The doctor moaned in terror as Tennant knelt. And with a wide, deranged grin, he tipped the flame to a thin trail of petrol that snaked under the door.

Moments later, the trench outside ignited in a fireball that raced around the bothy in either direction. The inferno was intense, flames over eight feet high shooting into the air, the light blinding, the heat searing Harper's skin even from inside.

But the chief wasn't done. He reached over and grabbed a bucket hidden in the shadows. He wrenched it up and threw the contents all over Harper, some splashing on Fraser. The distraught woman let out a muffled, hysterical scream, coughing and spluttering through her gag, the liquid soaking her.

Tennant raised the lighter again, the flame dancing in his crazed eye. "I demand justice for my Kelly, and if you're here to stop me, then I must stop you."

Harper, wiping the liquid frantically from his hair and eyes, tried to reason with the madman. "What good is killing Katherine Fraser? The armed officers will just shoot you, and your precious Kelly will be forever remembered as the poor, abused victim of her father who was a psychopathic killer."

Tennant's face contorted with fury.

Harper jumped to his feet and lunged at him again, desperation powering his attack. They grappled, but the chief overpowered him again, wrapping his hands around Harper's neck, throttling him.

Harper lashed out with the last ounce of strength he had left, but Tennant tightened his grip, a manic gleam in his eyes.

"Die, you weedy little shit," he snarled, spittle flying from his lips.

The door flew open with a deafening crack, wood splinters spraying in every direction. Two ARU officers, clad in full protective gear, set upon the chief. They fought, a furious melee of fists and kicks, and finally managed to subdue him, wrenching him away from Harper.

They dragged him out of the door, the high wall of flames closing in by the second.

Outside, the chief fought free, staggered through the firestorm, and tumbled into the ditch. His clothes ignited, and with an insane howl, he clambered out and careened directly towards Mullens, his arms waving in crazed defiance.

Mullens stumbled back, but before the human torch could lunge, the flames finally overwhelmed him and he toppled to the ground, a fiery plume of smoke and sparks rising on impact.

Two ARU officers rushed forward, braving the flames. They rolled the chief over the ground, trying to stem the fire and save him.

Inside the bothy, Harper clutched at his throat, gasping and spluttering, thick acrid smoke filling his lungs. An ARU officer grabbed his vest and yanked him to his feet, then went to untie Fraser. But she fought him, screaming and throwing fists.

"Leave me!" She broke free from his protective arms and stumbled to the back of the room.

Harper staggered over to help. "We're police officers, Dr Fraser. We have to go, now!"

"It's petrol!" She cried out, rubbing at her drenched blouse.

The ARU officer shot a look at Harper, then buried his face in Harper's soaked vest.

"It's water! Come on!"

The fire was getting closer by the second, the heat unbearable, searing their skin, singeing their hair. Harper could barely breathe through the thick smoke, each inhalation a struggle, his lungs burning.

"Please, you have to trust us!" Harper pleaded. "We'll get you out of here, but we have to go now!"

Finally, something seemed to break through Dr Fraser's panic. With a sob, she nodded, letting the officer guide her up.

The officer removed his protective jacket and placed it over Dr Fraser's head.

"After three, jump through the fire, okay?"

Dr Fraser clutched the jacket tight around her face.

"One. Two. Three."

The officer threw open what remained of the door, and the furnace billowed into the room.

"Go!"

Dr Fraser stepped back for a second, then made a leap for it. The officer slammed the door shut again, blocking some of the surging flames.

"You next," the ARU officer said to Harper, urgency increasing in his voice.

Harper hesitated, looking down again at his vest, the pungent stench of petrol filling his nostrils. "Are you sure this is water?" he asked, his voice shaking.

The officer nodded firmly. "Positive. The bastard's playing mind games with you. Now come on, we need to move!"

Trusting the officer, Harper stepped closer to the door. The officer opened it, grabbed Harper's arm, and together they burst out into the inferno. They hit the ground hard, rolling in the grass, smothering the flames that clung to them.

Choking for breath, Harper looked up to see Katherine Fraser being led away by another officer, shaking and sobbing, but alive. He coughed violently, clutching at his throat where Tennant had tried to strangle him, each breath a painful rasp.

Mullens approached, concern etched on his soot-stained face.

"Are you okay?" he asked, helping Harper to his feet.

Harper nodded, still coughing, his voice a hoarse whisper. "Where the fuck were…?"

"Don't speak." Mark called for help, and a paramedic ran over.

Harper tried to wave him away. "I'm—" He coughed again.

"You need oxygen, mate," the paramedic said. "Let's get you to somewhere a bit safer." Mullens helped Harper to his feet. "And that jaw's going to need some attention, too, by the looks of things."

"Broken?" Mullens asked.

"Possibly, yes."

"Oh, shite. You might be wired up for your wedding. Though, it will give you a wee taster of how it's going to be once the honeymoon's over."

Harper attempted to swear at him, but the movement sent fresh waves of pain across his face.

Bone and Walker came running over from a path on the perimeter of the chaos. An ARU officer stepped in front of them, but Bone pushed him aside. Walker held up her lanyard. They dashed over to the pair, who were now slumped on the ground a safe distance from the smoke and fire.

"Jesus. What utter devastation." Bone surveyed the carnage.

"The fuckwipe set a booby trap. Will went in to save Dr Fraser. They were lucky to get out alive."

"Are you okay, Will?" Walker knelt to check on him.

Mullens stopped his colleague attempting to speak again. "He's fine. Just showing me up, as usual, with his hero tactics."

"He's suffering from smoke inhalation, possible lung damage and a broken jaw," the paramedic said, preventing Harper from trying to stand.

"And Katherine Fraser?" Walker asked, concerned.

"Alive, but scarred for fucking life, thanks to burnt toast over there." Mullens jerked his thumb towards the chief's body, a smouldering black mass of melted cloth and skin.

One of the medics attending to Tennant stood, then approached the detectives.

"Will he make it?" Bone asked.

"He's gone, I'm afraid," she said. "The injuries were too severe. There was nothing we could do."

Bone nodded. "That's the guy who attacked your colleague."

She looked down at the smouldering corpse, her eyes filled with a mix of sorrow and anger. "The tragedy just keeps piling up. What a sorry mess this is."

As the ARU officers brought the blaze under control, the detectives surveyed the scene. The bothy was reduced to a smoking ruin, the trees around it blackened and charred.

"Stroke of genius you had with the eyeball thing, sir," Walker said.

"Aye, I'm not usually one for solving crimes. I let you lot do that and I take all the credit."

"To be fair, it's usually more flack than credit, which is why we're happy to let you." Walker smiled.

Bone put his hand to his face. "I think it's time we got the hell out of here. The stench coming off that evil bastard is making me feel sick."

"So, in the end, it was an eye for an eye, eh, sir?" Mullens chuckled.

"Aye!" Bone smirked.

They helped Will past the chaos to an ambulance parked up on a lane behind the bothy.

"Look at that. A proper road in as well. You tool!" Mullens nudged his shuffling colleague, Harper, who winced in pain, his teeth buzzing with an unintelligible expletive.

FORTY-THREE

The community centre's fluorescent lights buzzed overhead. Bone walked into a once familiar room, the scent of stale coffee and anxiety hanging in the air. He nodded to the regulars, fellow officers who, like him, had seen too much and had suffered too deeply in the line of duty.

There was Jackie, who hadn't been able to set foot in a burning building since that factory fire went south. And Mike, still jumping at backfiring cars after that drug bust turned into a shootout. They were a motley crew, bound by trauma and a shared dedication to the job that had nearly broken them.

Bone scanned the room, looking for McKinnon, but the journalist was nowhere to be seen. A flicker of disappointment crossed his face. Maybe it was too much to hope for, that he'd actually show up.

"Well, look who it is," Jackie called out.

Bone took his seat.

"The walking dead himself," she said. "How's the zombie life treating you, Duncan?"

"Oh, you know," Bone replied, his tone dry as a desert, "just another day in paradise. Living the dream, one sleepless night at a time."

The group chuckled, the dark humour a familiar coping mechanism.

Just as Sarah, their counsellor, was about to start, a sheepish figure appeared in the doorway. Colin McKinnon, looking like he'd rather be anywhere else, hovered uncertainly at the threshold.

A ripple of tension went through the room, the officers recognising the infamous journalist.

"Who the fuck invited that slug?" one of them spat, his voice laced with venom.

Bone stood, meeting the accusatory stares head-on. "I did."

McKinnon, his face flushed with embarrassment and anxiety, seemed like he was about to bolt. But Sarah stepped in smoothly.

"Everyone is welcome here," she said, her voice calm but firm. "Why don't you come in and take a seat?"

McKinnon wavered, clearly torn between flight and the tentative promise of support. After a long moment, he stepped into the room, ignoring the grumbles and hostile stares.

Bone caught his eye, offering a small smile and a nod of encouragement. McKinnon returned it, a flicker of gratitude in his haunted eyes. He settled into a chair.

Sarah addressed the group. "I want to remind everyone that what is said in this room, stays in this room. This is a safe space, where we can share our struggles and support each other without fear of judgment or repercussion. Okay?"

One of the officers scoffed, his derision palpable. But Bone cut him off before he could voice his objection.

"Give the guy a break," he said, his tone brooking no argument. "He's going through it, just like the rest of us."

An uneasy truce settled over the room, and the meeting began in earnest.

Malcolm, the quiet ambulance driver, raised his hand. "My sense of smell has gone to shit."

Sarah leaned forward, her brow furrowed. "Can you elaborate on that?"

Jackie cut in, a mischievous glint in her eye. "What, you mean you stink even more than you used to?"

Malcolm shook his head. "No, everything smells like Chanel No. 5."

Jackie laughed. "Lucky you. The last time my husband bought me that, it was some knockoff from Thailand, and it was calamine lotion I was wearing instead."

Sarah gently steered the conversation back to Malcolm. "Please, continue."

Malcolm's face grew sombre. "It was what the girl was wearing, the one we pulled from the wreckage.

It's like she's back in the room, in my clothes and bed sheets. Even my fucking beer smells of it."

A murmur of sympathy rippled through the group, each of them intimately familiar with the way trauma could linger, seeping into every corner of one's life.

Sarah offered Malcolm a compassionate smile. "That's a very common experience. Our senses, especially smell, are closely tied to memory. It's your brain's way of processing the trauma."

As the session continued, Sarah turned to Bone. "Duncan, would you like to share anything with the group?"

Bone hesitated, his gaze flickering to McKinnon. The thought of sharing his fears in front of the journalist made his stomach clench. But as he looked closer, he saw the wreck of a man McKinnon had become, the haunted look in his eyes all too familiar.

Taking a deep breath, Bone began, "The nightmares, the hallucinations... they're still there. But different now."

"Different how?" Sarah prompted.

"It used to be Peekaboo, the bastard who blew me up. I'd see him everywhere, hear his voice. But now... Now it's a kid. A wee red-haired boy, can't be more than ten."

"Is it him as a kid?" Malcolm ventured.

"No, but he might be a relative. Who knows? It's all just PTSD madness, isn't it?"

"Well, it's not madness, Duncan," the counsellor cut in. "It's processing and recovery. It's good that you're manifesting your trauma differently."

"Is it?" Bone replied sceptically. "It doesn't feel like that sometimes."

A heavy silence settled over the room, the weight of unspoken horrors pressing down on them all.

"Of course I know the hallucinations aren't real," Bone continued, his voice strained. "But the frequency is increasing, and that's a concern. I know how that can play out."

McKinnon looked up from staring at the floor, a flicker of recognition in his eyes. The same fear, the same dread, etched on his face.

"Aye, well, no one ever said our demons played fair, did they?" Bone tried for levity, but it fell flat.

Jackie tutted. "Where's the fun in that? Got to keep things interesting, haven't we?"

The group chuckled, the moment of levity a much-needed break from the heaviness.

"I know that you told us before about the fragment moving in your brain," the counsellor chipped in. "And your consultant telling you that your PTSD may change as a result, but it's as though your mind is working hard and working well to process these tiny alterations, and you're now in a much better place to maintain your equilibrium and continue with recovery. We believe in you, Duncan."

The group clapped spontaneously.

Bone mouthed his thanks and smiled.

When the session approached the end, Sarah turned to McKinnon. "Would you like to share anything with the group? It's okay if you're not ready, but please know that you're among people who understand what you're going through."

McKinnon shifted uncomfortably, his gaze darting around the room. "I... I don't think I'm ready. Not yet."

Sarah nodded, her expression one of gentle understanding. "That's perfectly all right. Whenever or never, both are fine. We'll be here to listen. We're all fellow sufferers in this room, myself included. We feel your pain, and we want to help in any way we can."

The hostile officer from before looked like he was about to interject, but Sarah silenced him with a glare.

"Thanks," McKinnon mumbled, his voice barely audible. "My name's Colin."

Sarah smiled warmly. "Well, Colin, this is a brave first step, and we're proud of you for taking it."

The meeting wrapped up, and the attendees started leaving. Sarah caught Bone's still anxious eye, her expression one of grim solidarity.

She leaned in. "Keep at it, Duncan," she said, her voice low but firm. "You've got this. And when you don't, you've got us."

Bone met her gaze. The group was never a promise of a miracle cure, a magic wand to wave and make it all better. But it was something real, something solid. A lifeline, a hand to clasp in the darkness. His fears had been addressed, and that was the most important step to take. Always. He smiled his thanks.

Noticing McKinnon had left, he grabbed his coat and chased after him.

He caught up with him in the corridor and placed a hand on his shoulder.

"Hey," he said, his voice uncharacteristically gentle. "Sarah was right. What you did in there, that was incredibly courageous."

McKinnon stared at him, a mix of emotions playing across his face. Before he could respond, Sarah approached them.

"Colin, would you like to grab a coffee?" she offered. "Sometimes it's easier to talk one-on-one."

McKinnon hesitated, then shook his head. "Maybe next time, eh?"

Sarah nodded, understanding. "Of course. Whenever you're ready."

McKinnon walked away.

Sarah turned to Bone. "How about you? Care for a caffeine fix?"

Bone chuckled, the tension of the meeting slowly easing from his shoulders. "Aye, that would be grand. I think I need a strong one after that."

Sarah smiled, a knowing glint in her eye. "It's never easy, confronting our demons, especially new ones. But it's the only way to start and continue the healing. You're doing the work, Duncan. Don't forget that."

"I hope I never do," Bone said.

EPILOGUE

The Loch Gillan Village Hotel had never seen anything like it. The Highland inn was transformed into a geeky wonderland for Harper and his new bride, Catriona's, wedding reception. The cosy dining room was festooned with *Star Wars*-inspired decor, from the starry night sky projected on the ceiling to Death Star balloons dangling from pillars and lightsaber lamp centrepieces on each table.

As the happy couple made their entrance to the *Star Wars* theme song, the crowd of colleagues, friends, and family cheered, none louder than the Rural Crime Unit team gathered at the front table. Mullens, resplendent in a kilt, grinned from ear to ear in his terrifying role as best man.

Bone scanned the room, taking in the familiar faces. He spotted Baxter, dressed in her best tweeds, accompanied by her husband in full Highland regalia. He nudged Alice. "Going well, so far. Speeches next though." He pulled a face.

Alice nodded. "Such a shame, though, about Will's broken jaw. Talk about bad timing."

"I suppose it's a blessing for Catriona—she won't have to listen to him ramble about computer code on their wedding night." Bone sniggered.

Alice snorted, trying to stifle her laughter. "Be nice, Duncan. Though I must admit, it's the first time I've seen a groom nod his vows in Morse code."

"Aye." Bone chuckled. "And every time he smiles, it looks like he's eaten half the silver service. I just hope he doesn't set off any metal detectors on their honeymoon." He pointed to the bar. "Drink?"

"G and T," Alice said, licking her lips.

"Michael?"

"Vodka," Michael half joked. "Coke, ta."

On his way over to the bar, Bone spotted Mullens who'd now shifted closer to the kitchen door where he furtively attempted to sneak a peek at food preparations.

"You're under arrest!" Bone said, and stuck his fingers in Mullens's side.

"Holy shite!" Mullens hollered involuntarily, his voice bellowing round the hall, stopping a few guests in mid chat.

"God, it's you, sir. Gonnae no dae that." He laughed.

"Great news about your dad, Mark."

"Is it? I mean, they have him on these new drugs that have literally given him a new lease of life, and a new lease of life in my da's world is not a pretty sight, believe me."

"All clear, though."

"Aye, to think he put us all through the wringer—again!—for a non-malignant cyst. I mean, nothing more than a giant pluke, for God's sake. So typical of him."

"I know you're pleased, though. You can't hide it from me."

Mullens smiled. "The man is immortal. It'll be him, Keith Richards, and a couple of cockroaches left."

"Let me buy you and Sandra a drink," Bone offered. He looked round the hall. "Where is she?"

"She's gone down with the flu. Well I hope that's what it is otherwise she's off with the milkman to the Seychelles as she was looking at brochures last night."

"Sorry she's missed it."

"I'm not. While the cat's away." He grinned and pointed to the bar.

"Well let me get you one then."

"Happy days for you, boss."

"How so?"

"One less moth you have to let out of that wallet of yours."

They went over to the bar where Gordon, the landlord, wrestled with one of the temporary beer pumps.

"How's it hangin', big man?"

"Duncan! Mark!" Gordon leaned over the counter and shook their hands. "What do you reckon? Quite the shindig, eh?" He gestured to the animated room.

"Aye, it's a far cry from our usual murder mayhem, though it's still early days." Bone chuckled. "I must say, the place looks fantastic. You've outdone yourself, Gordon."

"Well, when young Will came to me with his ideas, I couldn't say no. Such a nice lad, and Catriona's a lucky lass, though Luke Skywalker in NHS glasses is not the best of looks, if I'm honest." Gordon beamed. "Oh, and wait until you try the wedding breakfast! Ross has whipped up a feast fit for a Jedi master."

"I hope it doesn't involve any mackerel," Walker said, joining the three of them.

"Ah, no. He told me in no uncertain terms that nobody wanted to be reminded of our snowbound nightmare."

Bone winced. "I was on the brink of sacrificing Mark just to avoid having to eat another one."

"Aye, there's enough on him to last a whole year," Gordon joked.

Mullens pinched a couple of inches of his girth and winced.

Just then, Walker spotted her partner, Maddie, and their two-year-old daughter, Erin, approaching. Maddie looked elegant but tired, Erin squirming in her arms.

"So there you are," Maddie called out, relief evident in her voice. "Thank goodness. My arms are about to drop off. This one's been a handful all day."

Walker took Erin from Maddie's arms, giving her a quick kiss. "Has she now? And how's my wee troublemaker?" She tickled the toddler who giggled helplessly.

Bone smiled at the little girl. "Hello there, Princess Leia. Fancy a dance with an old Jedi?"

Erin reached out for Bone. He scooped her up.

Maddie sighed, leaning against Walker. "I swear, I haven't had a full night's sleep in two years. How do you two manage to look so… functional?"

Mullens snorted. "We're coppers. Expert liars."

As Bone bounced Erin on his hip, making silly faces, she suddenly turned on Mullens and blurted out, "Fuck sake!"

There was a moment of shocked silence before the adults burst into laughter.

"Oh no." Maddie groaned, covering her face. "Not again! She's already sworn at the registrar."

"She took the words right out of my mouth." Walker giggled.

"More women hassling me," Mullens complained.

"Well, at least she's expanding her vocabulary," Bone said through stifled laughs.

"Best not to make a fuss or she'll keep doing it," Walker whispered.

Bone handed the giggling child back to Maddie. "I'd say she's got a promising future in law enforcement."

"Where's that drink you promised me?" Alice interrupted, with Michael dragging his heels sullenly behind.

"Sorry, love. This wee one here distracted me," Bone replied.

"Wow. Look at you, Erin!" Alice exclaimed.

"Great to see you again, Alice," Walker said. "And you back there." She frowned affectionately at Michael, whose face turned crimson.

"He's sulking because I wouldn't let him wear his Nirvana t-shirt."

"You like Nirvana?" Walker said. "I love, love, love Nirvana."

Michael braved a tentative smile.

Just then, a commotion at the entrance caught their attention. In walked Junior, the village legend, wearing a flowing, shimmery silver gown and a lopsided tiara. He sashayed into the room, drawing stares and chuckles from the guests.

"Well, that's quite something," Walker muttered.

"Junior! What are you wearing, man?" Gordon called out.

"It's a Jedi cloak, I'll have you know!" Junior slurred, striking a pose. "I'm here to bless the happy couple with the Force." He produced a golf club from under his gown, bedecked in Christmas glitter décor.

Bone and Walker exchanged amused glances.

"Well, at least he's embracing the theme." Bone shrugged.

"Aye, if *Star Wars* had been directed by Wes Craven," Walker joked.

Suddenly, a voice cried out from across the room. "Oi, Junior. That's my bloody dress." A middle-aged woman in extraordinarily high heels stormed over to the drag Jedi. "You bloody nicked that from my line. Get it off."

Junior attempted to deny the theft, but the enraged woman yanked at the hem as though trying to undress him in the middle of the dance floor. Her husband came over, and after a few moments of negotiation, the husband took the woman's arm and escorted her back to their table. Junior gave the pair a drunken curtsey, found a seat at an empty table, and poured himself a glass of champagne from another guest's open bottle.

As the laughter subsided, Bone's eye caught a flash of vibrant red hair at the back of the hall. He blinked, then adjusted his position, craning his neck to try and get a better look. Alice noticed his sudden movement. "What's up?" she asked, concern in her voice.

"Nothing," Bone muttered, still trying to locate the figure. But when he looked back, whoever it was had vanished. A chill ran down his spine as he wondered if his PTSD was playing tricks on him again. "Not today, please..." he thought to himself, a mix of frustration and worry washing over him. He shook his head, trying to clear the unsettling feeling, and turned his attention back to the festivities.

At the wedding meal, Bone and his family were seated next to Gallacher and his wife, along with Walker, Maddie, and little Erin. They were all delighted to see Gallacher's wife looking so fit and well.

"Remission has given me a new lease of life," she said with a radiant smile. "Poor Roy is finding it hard to keep up with me." She winked suggestively at her husband.

He rolled his eyes in mock dismay. As the others chatted amongst themselves, Gallacher leaned in for a quiet word with Bone.

The superintendent's face grew serious. "About time we had some happy news after that nasty business last month," he said, shaking his head. "How a headcase like that made it to Fire Chief, I'll never know."

Bone grimaced, the tragic image of the murdered doctor and the smiling photo of the chief's poor daughter still fresh in his mind. "Just goes to show, evil can hide in plain sight. Small relief we stopped him before he killed Katherine Fraser, but horrific all the same."

"And not to mention Jaws up there." Gallacher cocked a thumb at Harper. "But serious respect to the female firefighter who formally complained about the behaviour of her male colleagues. That couldn't have been easy."

"She's an absolute hero. And her bravery has opened the door for other female officers to come forward, and not just in Kilwinnoch but from right across the whole service."

Gallacher nodded. "And I reckon a root and branch public enquiry now looks highly likely. But what about the paramedic? How is he doing now?"

"No change as of this morning. Still in a coma. The doctors are cautiously optimistic, but…" Bone trailed off, leaving the grim possibilities unspoken.

"Christ," Gallacher muttered.

"The doctor's son is in drug rehabilitation though, and Dr Fraser's returned to work."

"That's quick isn't it?" Gallacher grimaced.

"She told Rhona that she's determined not to let that bastard's actions crush her."

"Good for her. Well, keep me posted on the paramedic. All we can do is hope."

"And trust our wonderful NHS."

Gallacher glanced over at his now radiant wife. "Aye, indeed." He smiled. "But enough of that for now. This is supposed to be a bloody celebration, after all."

Their conversation was interrupted by the loud clink of a glass, and Mullens lumbered to his feet.

"Oh, oh, here we go. Best man speech incoming." Bone turned to view the spectacle.

Harper and Catriona anxiously bowed their heads, anticipating the impending doom.

Mullens shuffled around anxiously for a moment, took a large gulp of Guinness, cleared his throat, and began.

"When Will asked me to be his best man, I was so moved, I almost shed a tear," Mullens said. "But then I realised, aside from me, all his other friends are imaginary, so I was his first, last, and only option!"

The guests roared with laughter as Will buried his face in his hands.

"Now, we all know our young Will isn't exactly well-versed in the ways of women," Mullens continued. "In fact, I reckon before he met Catriona, the only date he'd ever had was with his Jedi Knight hand puppet!"

Will's face turned crimson.

Mullens carried on his relentless roast. "And I hate to break it to you, Catriona, but we're not even sure if they've actually dropped yet, so you might be in for a night of box set bingeing rather than boisterous bonking."

The room erupted again. Bone glanced over at Catriona's parents and winced.

"But seriously…"

"Oh God, there's more," Bone whispered to Alice.

"We always thought Will's ideal partner would be some kind of AI Fembot fashioned on Princess Leia. And let's face it, our Will's DNA is probably eighty percent robot anyway, so who are we to judge."

More uncomfortable sniggering.

"So imagine our shock when he lands himself a living, breathing, beautiful human being like Catriona! I guess he's the living proof that even supergeeks can have all the luck!" He looked over at the pair and smiled. "And just before I shut up, much to everyone's relief, especially Will and Catriona's, I'm sure… I pondered long and hard about an appropriate wedding present for you both."

Harper mouthed another, "Oh God."

"After much searching and internet trawling, that almost cost me my job and my marriage, I hasten to add, I finally found the perfect geek-appropriate his and hers gift. In fact, I loved them so much, I bought one for myself."

With gasps and screams of horror, he grabbed the hem of his kilt, whisking it up above his waist to reveal a pair of oversized white boxers adorned on the front with a screen print of Darth Vader, his helmet strategically placed. Then he spun round, bent over, and flashed a second image of an exploding Death Star emblazoned on the back.

He waited a moment for the laughter to subside and then raised his glass. "To Will and Catriona, may your love be as strong as a Wookiee's body odour! And may your adventures in the bedroom not be a disastrous flop like some of those bloody awful sequels in the franchise."

The room toasted the happy couple. And Mullens finally sat back down.

The party got into full swing. Catriona dragged a bashful Harper onto the dance floor. The guests gathered round as the newlyweds took their positions. The room fell into a hushed silence. They looked at each other nervously, and for a moment, it seemed like they might stumble through an awkward slow dance. But then, the opening notes of 'Human' by The Killers filled the room, and everything changed.

Harper and Catriona suddenly broke into a perfectly choreographed routine that had everyone's jaws dropping. They started with robotic movements, mimicking droids from *Star Wars*, before launching into a series of bizarre moves. Will moonwalked across the floor while Catriona pretended to use the Force to push him back. They then linked arms and spun rapidly, their feet barely touching the floor, whirling like twin tornados.

The crowd erupted in laughter and cheers. The couple continued their performance. At one point, Will dropped to the floor and started doing the worm. Catriona leapt over him, narrowly avoiding his flailing legs. They finished with a dramatic pose, Will on one knee, pretending to propose with a lightsaber, Catriona on tiptoe, arms raised triumphantly to the ceiling. When the song ended, the room exploded with applause and wolf whistles. Will and Catriona, red-faced and breathless, took a bow before collapsing into each other's arms, giggling uncontrollably.

The night wore on, and the booze flowed freely. Baxter, tipsy on too much free champers, dragged her hapless husband onto the dance floor and flailed about to 'I'm Too Sexy'. Walker twirled by, jiving expertly with her partner, Maddie, their toddler, Erin, bouncing gleefully between them. And somehow, Mullens and Junior ended up dancing together, locked in some kind of semi-combative waltz, their moves threatening to take out dancers who ventured too close.

Walker retreated outside and found Bone in the car park, admiring Harper's elderly neighbour's beautifully restored burgundy 1960s Saab. The old man was enthusiastically explaining the technical details to an awestruck Bone.

"And you see here," the old man said, "I've replaced the original carburettor with a custom-built fuel injection system. This has improved the fuel efficiency by fifteen percent without altering any of the original spec!"

Bone nodded, eyes wide. "Incredible! And the body work is immaculate. How did you manage to get that shine?"

Walker rolled her eyes. "Oh, dear God, there's actually two of them."

"Mr Burroughs, this is my colleague, Rhona. She's a heathen and doesn't understand the spiritual importance of our wonderful moving temples," Bone retorted, running his hand reverently along the Saab's bonnet.

The old man chuckled. "Nice to meet you, Rhona."

"I have to say, at least yours looks like it could actually move."

"She's a beauty, all right. Took me five years to restore her, but she purrs like a kitten now."

"Unlike Duncan's rust bucket," Walker quipped. "It coughs like a sixty-a-day kipper-lunged granny."

Bone shot her a glare. "My Saab has character, I'll have you know."

"Is that what we're calling tuberculosis these days?"

Ignoring her jibes, Bone turned back to Mr Burroughs. "I'd show you her…" he started, but Sergeant Brody called over from the entrance and approached.

"There you are! I've been looking all over for you two."

Walker raised an eyebrow. "Everything all right, Brody?"

"Oh aye, yes, aye. Great news. I just got a message from the station. Rob McNeil, the paramedic? He's woken up from his coma!"

Bone and Walker exchanged surprised looks.

"That's fantastic news," Bone said. "How's he doing?"

"Better than expected," Brody replied. "The bleed on the brain wasn't as bad as the doctors expected. "They said he'll make a full recovery."

Walker let out a relieved sigh. "That's brilliant. After everything that happened, it's good to have some good news about this horrific case."

Just then, Gordon called from the hotel entrance, "Oi, you lot! Will and Catriona are about to leave. Get your arses back in here!"

"Oh. That's my cue," Bone said mysteriously, and disappeared round the side of the hotel.

The newlyweds prepared to depart for their honeymoon at the *Star Wars* Celebration. Will and Catriona made their rounds to say goodbye. A slightly sozzled Will threw his arms around Bone and Walker, tears in his eyes. He attempted to speak, but his incomprehensible words of affection hissed through his wired teeth like a broken lawnmower.

Walker gently pried him off. "Yes, yes, we love you, too, Will. Now go on, before you pass out from that half a shandy you've been sipping all day."

Unbeknownst to the rest of the team, Bone had one last surprise up his sleeve. He'd secretly decorated his ancient, bottle-green Saab '96 with ribbons, tin cans, and a 'Just Married' sign. As Will and Catriona emerged from the hotel, Bone ushered them into the car, Sergeant Brody in the driving seat, ready to chauffeur the happy couple to the airport in style.

"I can't believe you did this, Duncan!" Catriona exclaimed, grinning from ear to ear.

"Consider it my wedding gift," Bone replied with a wink.

"Or grounds for divorce, depending how the journey goes," Mullens added from the side."

The newlyweds climbed into the car.

Walker leaned in with a smirk. "Don't worry, the boss is in the AA." She spun round. "Please tell me you're in the AA, aren't you?"

"Yes he is, Rhona, but possibly not the one you're thinking of," Mullens joked.

Bone raised his hand, signalling Brody to start her up.

True to form, the Saab coughed, spluttered, and with all-round cheers of relief, she finally wheezed to life.

The gear box crunched into first, and Brody rolled out of the car park, the tin cans clanking merrily behind and guests showering the car in confetti.

The Saab rattled off down the Highland road, and the guests returned to the reception. Bone grabbed Alice at the entrance.

"Where's Michael?" he said.

"He's at the table on his phone to his mate. I can't be bothered telling him off. Not today."

"Right. Let's have a wee walk, shall we?"

"Sounds ominous."

They walked in silence out along the harbour, the tension growing between them with each step. The wooden planks creaked underfoot, and they made their way to the end of the pier. The loch stretched out before them, the afternoon mist settling just above the water's surface, creating a beautifully tranquil scene. Finally, at the pier's edge, Bone spoke.

"Alice, I need to tell you something."

"What?"

"I'm going to stay at the cabin for a while. I'm not handling being in Kilwinnoch well at the moment."

"Is it... is it me? Are you not handling being with me?"

"No, no. It's not that. I just don't want to risk putting you through any more of my PTSD nonsense. I'm not quite right, and I am dealing with it, but I just need to be here to help heal my head again."

"But, Duncan, I'm here for you. You know that. We can work through this together. That's what we do now."

"I know, and I appreciate that. But I need to be here right now by this cold water and in amongst these mountains. They helped me before, and I'm sure they will again."

Alice's eyes glistened with unshed tears. "How long are you talking about? What about Michael?"

Bone sighed, running his finger along the scar on his temple. "It won't be for long. Just a short time until I work out what's going on with my head. I need to get myself sorted before I can be the partner you deserve, the father Michael needs. But you can both come up any time," he offered, knowing it sounded weak even as he said it.

"Oh gee, thanks." Alice's anger was rising, her voice taking on a bitter edge. "That's exactly why we need to talk it out, support each other! You can't just push us away like this."

"I'm not pushing you away, I'm trying to protect you," Bone insisted, frustration creeping into his voice. "I never want to put you and Michael through any of my shit again. That's why I need this time."

Alice shook her head, tears now falling freely. "Duncan, that's not how relationships work. We're supposed to face these things together."

Bone opened his mouth to respond, to try and make her understand, but something caught his eye. Back at the hotel entrance, the figure with striking red hair, a middle-aged man in a beige suit lingered, seeming out of place among the dispersing wedding guests. There was something strangely familiar about him that made Bone's instincts kick into high gear.

"Wait here," he said to Alice, his tone suddenly urgent.

Before she could reply, Bone was already moving. He ran back along the pier, his dress shoes clacking against the wooden planks. As he approached the hotel, the red-haired man seemed to sense his presence. Their eyes met for a brief moment, and recognition flashed across the stranger's face.

The man turned and bolted, disappearing around the side of the hotel. Bone quickened his pace, pushing through the crowd of guests who were saying their goodbyes. He rounded the corner just in time to see the man fumbling with car keys.

"Hey! Stop!" Bone shouted, but it was too late.

The stranger jumped into an Astra and accelerated out of the car park, tyres squealing on the gravel. Bone sprinted across the car park but he was too late, and staggered to a halt, staring at the retreating taillights as the vehicle sped down the winding Highland road.

Panting, Bone bent over, hands on his knees. His mind raced. Who was that man? Why did he run? And why did he seem so familiar?

Alice caught up to him, concern etched on her face. "Duncan, what the hell's going on? Who was that?"

"You saw him?" Bone asked. His question throwing her for a second.

"Of course. What do you mean?"

Bone straightened up, his brow furrowed in concentration. "Someone who didn't want to speak to me. But I've seen them somewhere before. I'm sure of it."

As the sounds of the wedding party faded behind them, Bone stood there, staring down the now-empty road. The mist from the loch was creeping in, shrouding the landscape in an ethereal haze, like a blanket of cool, temporary comfort. But in that moment, caught between the pain of his past and an uncertain future, he couldn't ignore the nagging feeling that this was the beginning of something much bigger and perhaps more dangerous than anything he'd faced before.

The End

TG REID

DCI BONE RETURNS IN…

A Devil's Share

A DCI Bone Scottish Crime Thriller (Book 8)

TG Reid

JOIN MY DCI BONE VIP CLUB

AND RECEIVE YOUR *FREE* DCI BONE NOVEL

WHAT HIDES BENEATH

Secrets Always Surface

Scotland's hottest summer on record is already too much for DCI Duncan Bone. As if the water shortage wasn't enough, a body turning up at the bottom of Kilwinnoch's dried up reservoir sends Bone to boiling point.
With three suspects on the loose and time running out, the Rural Crime Unit needs to find the smoking gun and nail the killer before another victim is slain.

Visit tgreid.com to sign up and download for *FREE*.

Your monthly newsletter also includes updates, exclusives, sneak peeks, giveaways and more…

TG REID

THE DCI BONE SCOTTISH CRIME SERIES

Dark is the Grave

Blood Water Falls

Dead Man's Stone

The Killing Parade

Isle of the Dead

Night Comes Falling

Burn it all Down

A Devil's Share

More thrillers by TG Reid

Agency 'O'

TG Reid

DCI BONE COUNTRY

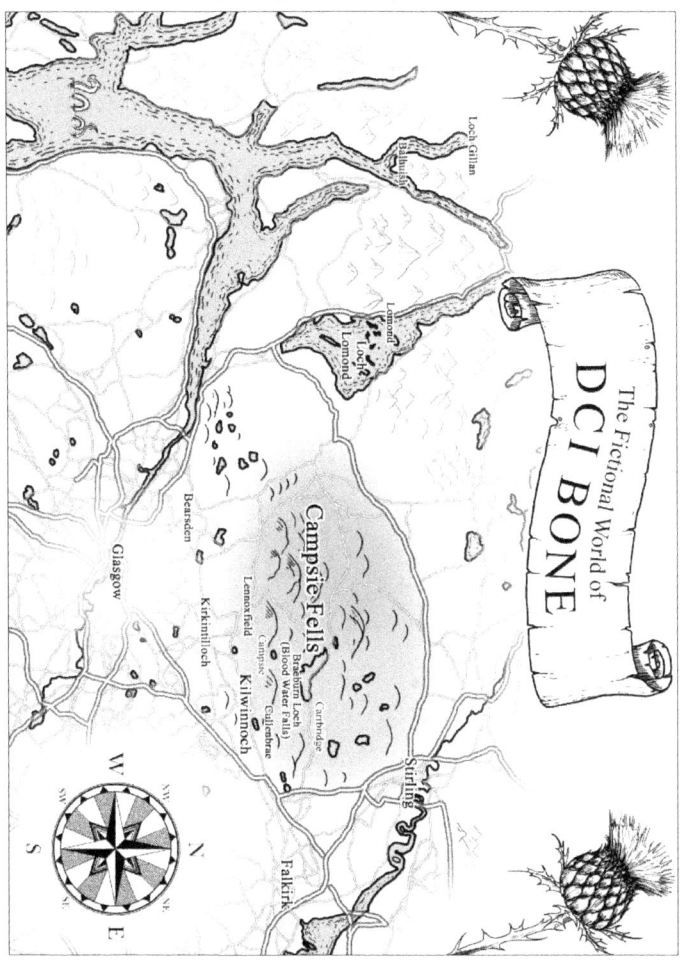